The Facebook Killer

DON WESTON

Copyright

ISBN: 978-0-9968647-0-1

\#

DEDICATION

Thanks God. Without a motivating force to guide me, I would never have written and finished this book.

Author's Note

This story is pure fiction. It came to me when I observed so many people posting about their lives on Facebook. So many personal things, many of which I enjoy reading. But I cringe whenever I see someone posting about going on vacation, or posting pictures when they are on vacation. This means their home is likely unattended and ripe for theft. As I researched this book, I was appalled to see how many people don't use their privacy features. I also learned that if I am a *friend* of one person, I can see all of that person's *friends*, and *friends of their friends*, and what they are doing and where they are going to be—unless they have their privacy features turned on.

All of the events in this book never happened, but could they happen? Yes, and it already has happened. In 2013 a man in Bangor Maine lured a teenage girl to a meeting using a phony Facebook profile, killed her, and left her body in Old Town there. Scores of Facebook-related burglaries have been reported in the media, including one in Beaverton, a suburb of my home in Portland, Oregon.

Other social apps are also at risk. If you check in on one of many mobile apps to tell people you are at the airport, or out on the town, guess what? You are a target because people know you aren't home. The best advice: use common sense, privacy settings, and wait until you get home to tell us about your vacation.

Chapter 1

"Time to go Facebook phishing," Trixie said to himself. "Three new *friends*, that's nice." Women loved his cute frog avatar and seemed to feel more comfortable responding to his *Trixie* pseudonym rather than a man's name.

His choice of *Trixie* was ironic. It reminded him of *the Trickster*, the mythical god, which could change into an anthropomorphic animal, with great intellect and secret knowledge he used to play tricks on his victims.

Trixie carefully read the profiles of his new *friends*. Mary Johansen, blonde, age 32, active hiker, loves to read, works at Murder by the Book bookstore. Nice of her to let me know where I can find her, Trixie thought. Her picture reminded him of another woman in his life-his own mother. Trixie liked them attractive and a little buff. He might risk being seen in that bookstore to meet Mary.

Onto the next one. Connie Martin, age 35, strawberry-blonde. Nice. Not married, no kids, a runner. This one had possibilities. By her profile picture, he knew she was a fitness nut. Score. More pictures of her in her Running Album clad in skimpy running gear showing off her long legs and muscles-can you believe it-look at those biceps and quads. She must lift weights to have a bod like that. She'd probably put up a fight too. That would make things interesting.

His last potential new *friend* didn't quite look like his type at first. She was 33-years-old and wore her blonde hair in a short Pageboy style. Her skin was milky white and he had never seen bluer eyes. She had a cute nose, full lips, a smooth, symmetrical face, and she looked like she worked out.

But her picture also portrayed her to be confident and determined, as if she'd had to fight for everything she got, and he preferred the princess or daddy's girl. He liked to watch them suffer when real adversity came upon them, probably for the first time in their lives. And Trixie was an expert at bringing adversity.

Still, this last one had possibilities. The right looks and figure from what he could see of her profile picture, and maybe even a true blonde. She might be too much of a challenge, he thought. She was a P.I. and a former cop with the Portland Police Bureau. This excited him and made him anxious at the same time. He expected the others to fall for his cute frog avatar, but a former cop would be wary. So why did she accept his invitation?

"I think I'll put Miss Billie Bly on the back burner for now," he muttered. "Connie it is. Are you waiting for me, Connie?"

Just for fun he hit the poke button on Connie's Facebook page. Those guys at Facebook think of everything. He could let her know he was thinking of her and still remain completely anonymous, hiding behind his frog avatar.

"Sweet dreams, Connie. I'll see you soon."

Eric Switzer watched Jimmer in front of the computer. He couldn't tell whether his friend actually saw the screen, or if he was just high. Jimmer smoked crack all morning, and Eric knew his addiction was out of hand.

They had been friends since third grade and for some mystical reason Eric put his college plans on hold to support his friend's habit. There were times when he wished he could walk away from his friendship with Jim Bodette. But Jimmer had saved his life by him pushing out of the path of a speeding car when he was twelve, and that event seemed to cement their dependent relationship.

"Snagged one," Jimmer said. "This dude's in Maui and his wife is posting about some hairpin curves, whatever they are."

"It's a road called the Hana Highway," Eric said. "It can take up to four hours to drive fifty-two miles because it has over six hundred winding curves in the road."

Jimmer turned to face Eric. "Sweet. I was afraid some broad was doin' up her hair like that Medusa chick we learned about in high school."

Eric wondered how long Jimmer could continue to abuse himself with drugs. He'd lost forty pounds, sported black bags under his red-streaked, dilated eyes, and coughed like a chain smoker. He didn't seem to be able to get through the day without multiple hits.

"Hey man, her husband's a retired cop. This will be poetic justice."

Eric sighed. "Where do they live?"

"On the west side," Jimmer said. "We could be there in ten minutes."

"This has to stop," Eric said. "We can't go on breaking into houses to support your habit."

"I know," Jimmer said. "I'm going to stop. I just need a little time to steady myself, man. I need one or two more little jobs to keep me going."

Eric walked over and read the post. "Jeez, you'd think these people on Facebook would have half a brain."

"You'd think so," Jimmer said. "But, even high, I still have more brains than they do. As long as they want to brag about not being home, I think we have an obligation to teach them the error of their ways, don't you?"

Eric laughed at his friend's warped sense of humor. He might be right. These people *did* need to learn a lesson. Eric didn't want to break into any more houses, but he knew if he didn't help Jimmer, his buddy would go ahead and do it anyway. He also knew Jimmer would get caught, because in his frame of mind he didn't think straight. He sometimes wondered if he *should* let his friend get busted. Maybe a judge would sentence him to rehab.

There was another reason Eric didn't want to do any more robberies. The last one netted him a personal prize. It was a schematic plan for a revolutionary new computer system. He found the design on a computer they had freed from its previous owner. That's what Jimmer called it: *Setting the stolen items free.*

The schematic represented a lot of effort and Eric could see, even with his abbreviated college work in computer engineering, whoever designed this apparatus showed a lot of creativity. But the creator had taken a wrong turn and Eric had a few ideas about how to fix the design. He wished he could work on it in collaboration with the inventor, but to do so, he would have to explain how he got the schematics. It was ironic how his thievery opened this door for him and also shut it tight.

"Let's do a drive-by tomorrow and see if they have house sitters or alarms," Eric said.

"The only thing I'm worried about is dogs." Jimmer shivered. "I don't like getting bit. I know you can disconnect any alarm system alive with your hacking skills."

"We'll watch for dogs too," Eric said.

Portland, Oregon's reputation as a rainy city is misleading. The clouds may drift through the sky for huge stretches of the day without dropping moisture. But it can rain into early summer and although April was dry and sunny and May had both sunshine and the drizzly stuff, it was a rainy, blustery June night when I was babysitting Meg Simpson.

My name is Billie Bly and I'm a P.I. I've been referred to as a pretty little thing, a blonde bimbo, and a tough bitch, not necessarily in that order. When being blonde and attractive doesn't get me what I want, the tough bitch part comes in handy.

But I wasn't feeling attractive or tough tonight. I fingered my stringy wet hair as rain pellets played a rat-a-tat symphony on the canvas convertible top of my small M.G. Triumph. The night was black and soulless, the moon hiding behind thunder clouds, and huge tree limbs swaying menacingly above my car. A faint light flickered from the window across the street in Meg Simpson's house.

I couldn't see through the windows of my little M.G. -- not because of the darkness or rain -- it was my own tears that blurred my vision. I wiped them away with a tissue and tried to stifle a sob.

Billie Bly, the tough P.I. If my clients could see me now they would shake their heads. It had only been two years since I quit the Portland Police Bureau and set up my own business, and I was a wreck.

I wasn't crying because of my separation from the police bureau. I like being a private investigator. I get to help people, and I don't have to follow a bunch of rules and policies like I did when I was on the job.

I don't have a lot of rules, except I try not to take divorce cases because I don't like following cheating spouses. It makes me feel cheap. But I will take a case involving an *ex* threatening his wife or girlfriend. That's why I was sitting by myself in front of Meg Simpson's house on a gloomy June evening.

Meg came to me because she was afraid her ex-boyfriend, Jeremy, might hurt her or her four-year-old daughter. After she had broken it off with him, he had started leaving harassing notes inside her house while she was at work. Sweet tidbits, like *"I'll never let you go"* and *"Till death do you part."*

The messages had been enough to get a restraining order and it stopped him for a while. But one day Meg spotted him following her on the way home from work. She saw him in the grocery store and at the gas station. He became bolder and bolder. He entered her house and rearranged furniture, putting the kitchen table in the middle of the living room.

He phoned her and hung up without speaking. Then, during the past week, he started with the threats again over the phone. The police couldn't do anything and she came to me, figuring a woman might be more understanding. My job was to collect evidence of his unwanted attention she could take to a judge.

Meg's ex-boyfriend had passed her house eight times in three days since I began watching. I slept during the day while Meg worked and followed her to and from her job.

I'd been camping outside her house overnight as sort of a bodyguard. My little red MG, I affectionately named Myrtle after my favorite aunt, was littered with bits of potato chips, peanuts, and food containers. I had my camera, my gun, and my guilt to keep me company.

It was nine o'clock and Meg's little girl, Amy, would be tucked into bed under nice warm covers. I wanted to be tucked under nice warm covers, in front of a crackling fireplace, instead of shivering as the wind buffeted my car.

I squinted through the windshield trying to catch a glimpse of Meg through her home's front window. Light flickered from the television and offered scant glimpses of the front porch and a few small bushes outside.

I sighed and flashed back to the day my younger brother, Darrin, stepped in front of a bullet meant for me. It happened six months ago, and I was still experiencing severe pangs of grief and guilt. If I could stop feeling guilty, maybe I could survive.

My cell phone rang and I fumbled in the darkness to find it. "Yes?" I tried to sound normal, but my voice cracked. I dabbed at my eyes with a tissue and cleared my throat.

"Have you been crying?" It was my assistant. Angel is a five-foot-two firecracker of a woman, who carries three guns on her person at any one time, changes her hair color monthly, and tries to set fashion trends in a city where hipster crazes run amok. She quit smoking a few years back and inadvertently hoists two fingers and a phantom cigarette to her mouth in times of stress.

I clicked on the wipers for a second to clear the stream of water and pine needles from my windshield. "I'm okay. Just too much time on my hands."

"Well, I'm working on a way to get more business," she said. "I've set up a Facebook page for you."

"Why in the world would you do that?" I'm not an online type of woman. I prefer to be out meeting people in person. I never got why someone would spend so much time posting about their lives, and I haven't got much patience for the whole damn thing. Of course, that may be because my life is a soap opera I wouldn't want anyone to watch.

"You said you want to keep busy," Angel said. "This is a way we can drum up more business."

"Yeah, but Facebook?" There was a silence on the line and I could almost hear Angel taking a drag of a cigarette that wasn't there.

"We've got to do something," she said. "Since Darrin's death, we haven't done much business. People tend to stay away during a person's grieving period. We need to let them know you're back in business."

I narrowed my eyes through the windshield toward a fleck of movement near the side of Meg's house. The rain started to taper off and some light from the TV lit up the yard. I thought I saw a shadow lurking at the side of her home. It could have been my imagination, but . . .

"Okay, do whatever you think is necessary," I told Angel. "I've got to go." I wriggled into my blue jacket and zipped it up tight, tucking my .38 revolver into the side pocket.

Raindrops stung my face as I ran across the street toward Meg's house. I slid up to the front window and peeked in. The living room was empty with the exception of Amy's toys scattered on the floor. I circled around the back and opened a chain-link fence gate just as the kitchen window light flicked on.

I heard a man's voice. He was swearing and it echoed into the night. I put my hand in my pocket to feel the reassurance of my gun. The back door leading to a sun porch was ajar, so I flattened myself to an exterior wall next to it.

"You're not ever going to leave me," the voice boomed. It was Jeremy. "I'll kill you first."

"Please don't yell," Meg said. "You'll wake Amy."

I heard a crisp smack and guessed it was his fist connecting with Meg. I scooted through the door onto the sun porch. The door to the kitchen stood open, but I couldn't see Jeremy or Meg.

"You belong to me," Jeremy said. "Amy belongs to me. I want you to drop the restraining order. If you don't . . ."

I heard a dull fleshy thud, and Meg crying, so I stepped into the house. On the other side of a kitchen island, Jeremy stood defiantly. I assumed Meg was on the floor behind the cabinet.

"Maybe you need another lesson." Jeremy was big and muscular, with a square jaw, and unruly brown hair cascaded down the side of his face.

"Maybe you should pick on somebody your own size," I said.

He turned, and his eyes widened. "Who the fuck are you?"

"I'm a friend of Meg's. Do you get off on beating women?"

His dull brown eyes gave me the once over. Slowly, a wicked smile grew on his chiseled face.

"Yeah. I guess I do. You must want to be next." He started to move around the kitchen island toward me.

"Not tonight." I raised my .38. "Maybe another time."

"That's not very nice." He cocked his head and laughed. "You talk all tough, but then you pull a gun?"

"I need to make sure Meg and Amy are safe."

"Billie," Meg cried. "I'm okay."

I backed around the other side of the kitchen island and saw her on the linoleum. There was a red welt on her cheek and blood on her lip. When I looked back to make a crack about Jeremy's cowardice, a frying pan struck my hand, knocking my .38 to the floor.

Jeremy closed the distance quickly and slugged me in the face before I could react. I backed into a corner and brushed my cheek with the back of my hand.

"Your turn to learn a lesson," he said.

"Maybe not," I said.

He came at me again and missed with a wild swing. As he twisted in the follow-through I hit him in the kidney with my fist. He winced and slowly straightened his contorted body.

"You'll pay for that." He came at me with both hands headed toward my throat.

I moved aside and struck him with a karate chop across the back of the neck. He turned and scowled at me. *Shit*, I thought. *It's going to take a sledge hammer to put this guy down.*

"I'm going to kill you slowly," he said.

"Is that the best you can come up with?" I said. "Slowly?"

"Jeremy, stop." Meg stood up holding my gun. He ignored her and came at me again. She squeezed the trigger and an exploding bullet whizzed between us.

"Meg, put the gun down before you kill someone," I said. Jeremy took advantage of my distraction to launch me across the room with an uppercut, and I bounced against a wall and crumpled to the ground. He stood over me, snarling, with both fists clenched.

"I'm warning you, Jeremy." Meg's voice trembled. "Leave now."

He turned and knocked the gun from her hands. "I'm the one who gives the orders." Jeremy slapped Meg with the back of his hand and she reeled onto the linoleum again. He picked up the gun and stood over her.

I grabbed the heavy cast-iron skillet he'd used to knock the gun from my hands, and struggled to my feet. Jeremy was aiming the pistol at Meg. She cowered and put her hands in front of her for protection.

"Jeremy!"

He turned toward me and I hit him square in the face with the ten-pound fry pan. He winced and looked at me with a blank expression. I kicked him in the gut and slugged him on the chin when he bent over. He still wouldn't go down.

My knuckles hurt from the blow and I realized I still had the iron skillet in my other hand so I hit him with it again. He snarled and grabbed me by the throat. I dropped the pan and whipped my arms inside his to break his hold. Then I tweaked him in the eyes with two fingers and launched a solid fist on his nose. I slugged him in the gut. He keeled over, and I karate-chopped him on the back of the neck again, this time with both hands.

He tried to stand up straight, so I pushed him backward, and he started to topple. It was like watching a tall tree falling in slow-motion. He hit the floor with a thud and I swear the kitchen shook like an earthquake had hit it.

I kicked him in the side. "Slug me, will you?" I kicked him again. "Try to kill Meg, huh?" I booted him again for good measure.

"Billie, that's enough." Meg reached toward me from the floor for help up. "You'll kill him."

"You're right. I guess I got a little carried away" I looked at her hands, reaching toward me for help, peered back at the woman-beater, and kicked him again.

"Just wanted to make sure he knows he was in a fight with a woman and she kicked his ass."

Chapter 2

"You're going to be lucky if you don't have a shiner." Angel stood over me pressing a bag of ice against my cheek.

"Nothing a little makeup won't fix." I sat in an oak chair next to her desk and tried to take a sip of my morning coffee as she fussed.

"What happened to Meg's ex-boyfriend?" She put my free hand on the ice bag for me to hold in place and walked around to sit behind her computer.

"He's in jail for now," I said. "Meg says nobody will bail him out. Apparently he's burned too many bridges with his family and friends."

"I hope he rots there." She tapped at a few keys on her computer and glanced up at me. "What will Meg do?"

"Now that Jeremy's out of the picture she has some time to plan her way out. She's packing and I think she'll wind up staying with a cousin Jeremy doesn't know."

"What about her job?"

"The insurance company she works for will let her transfer to Eugene." I thought about Meg packing up all of her belongings, uprooting little Amy, and moving her to a new world. Kids are resilient, aren't they? Something inside told me they would be moving the rest of their lives to stay a step ahead of Jeremy.

Angel switched her attention to the computer so I scooted my chair toward her. "What are you doing?"

"I spent the last week sending *friend* requests to your friends and clients. I went through your high school yearbook and found about forty classmates on Facebook and sent out requests to them to join your page. It's called *friending.* Next I'll invite people to attend our events, talk about our business once in a while, and ask them to refer clients to us."

I leaned over her shoulder. "Okay . . . what are these events you're talking about?"

"Each month we'll schedule a seminar. I've already planned a self-defense workshop. You can either charge a minimal amount and make some money or offer the classes for free and encourage people to tell their friends about your services."

I moved the ice bag away from my cheek. "Seems like a lot of work. What if no one shows up?"

"I'll do all the organizing, and if they don't show up, so what? I'll tell your *friends* that the workshop was a great success."

"I can't see how this could help," I said. "We need something now and this could take a year or longer before it brings any customers. If it works at all."

Angel moved my hand with the ice bag back to my cheek and tapped at the keyboard again, ignoring my comment. I've learned not to underestimate her. On her desk, lie four books about Facebook. As usual, she'd done her homework and, as usual, she planned to launch this endeavor no matter what I said.

"Look here," she said. "We got a new friend request last night."

"That's nice." I angled over Angel's shoulder for a closer look. "Who is it?"

"I don't know," Angel said. "The avatar is a picture of a frog. Cute little thing named Trixie." She clicked on the frog and a profile appeared: *I am a little tree frog, but someday I hope to become a toad and be kissed by a . . . then I would become a . . . Would you kiss me?*

"Great! My potential client is a frog," I said. "It doesn't say if Trixie is a boy frog or a girl frog."

She clicked the accept friend button. "Trixie is a mystery and we deal with mysteries," Angel said. "I think it's an omen."

A few days later, Angel strolled into my office with a grin and winked at me. "I've added another hundred friends on your Facebook page.

"That's nice." I sat at my desk going over a stack of past-due bills. "Has it generated any *real* business?"

She grinned and I knew my sarcasm had steered me into a trap.

"As a matter of fact, we have a client coming in this morning for a preliminary interview."

"Is this one of my *friends*?" I was trying to save face by applying some of my new Facebook terminology.

"Yes, it's Martha Roy from your high school."

"Who?"

"Her maiden name was Martha Swinford. She married a guy named Robert Roy."

"I remember Martha. She stole my boyfriend in my junior year. I planned on never seeing her again as long as I live."

"She's a paying customer," Angel said. "Maybe you should consider forgiving her. It's been at least fifteen years."

"More like ten, I think."

Angel rolled her eyes. "Yeah, in that case, I'm still a virgin."

Had it been that long since high school? I was a bit of a tomboy back then, but I still had plenty of guys interested in me. College and nine years as a police officer helped me mature, but maybe hadn't softened me much as a woman.

As a cop and a P.I., it's been difficult to meet many guys who aren't looking at jail time. I've been dating Steve Thomas, my former partner and a Lieutenant on the Portland Police Bureau. But there's no real intimacy between us, only sex.

I'd like to be more ladylike. My mother died when I was a teenager and it was hard to be feminine when growing up with four brothers. I don't know how to show my soft-side, or even if I have one.

My therapist thinks I need to get in touch with my feelings, but I think getting in touch with my femininity is what I need. I've decided I'm going to let my hair grow long enough to rest on my shoulders and maybe buy a few more dresses. Maybe I should schedule a makeover.

"Someone's coming up the stairs," Angel said. "If it's your friend, Martha, you two can reminisce about what it's like to be twenty-seven."

My home is a few blocks from Legacy Good Samaritan Hospital on Northwest Lovejoy Street. My neighborhood is one of those magnet communities with upscale shopping and scads of restaurants for foodies.

My best guess is foodies are people who don't own a spatula or frying pan and prefer eating out, often preferring vegan or gluten free-meals, or whatever the current food fad.

I rushed into my inner office where I could watch through my glass door as Martha walked into the outer office. Normally when a new client enters, Angel taps at her computer to appear busy and I scatter old files onto my desk and pore through them.

This time, however, I elected to look Martha up on Facebook. I found her on my *friends* list and clicked onto her profile while Angel gave her some paperwork to fill out.

Martha's profile picture showed her with long blonde hair, center-parted. A wry smile and evasive eyes made her appear part model, part nymph. I couldn't believe she hired a professional photographer for her Facebook profile photo.

I gazed through my door's window at her. She wore a different hairstyle today. It was kind of auburn with blond streaks combed in a near shoulder-length graduated bob. She never looked that good in high school. Her thin frame was also an improvement from her Rubenesque figure in high school, when my cheating boyfriend dug her curves and her demure brown eyes.

I forced my attention back to her profile: Married. Husband, Robert, a software engineer at Intel in Beaverton. No kids. Hobbies: art collecting, traveling, reading, gourmet cooking, wine tasting.

I clicked around her page and found some recent postings. Most of them were about things she'd bought for her home, fancy restaurants she ate at, and other pompous scrawling of grandeur.

Angel opened the door to my office and Martha strolled in. She wore a stylish green dress, pearls around her neck and a rock on her ring finger which must have weighed half a pound.

"Billieee," she said in a sugary tone. "Long time no see."

I rose and shook her hand. "Hello, Martha, how are you doing?" Her musk and rose perfume overpowered me, and I leaned back to escape the kill zone.

"Call me Mar," she said. "Haven't gone by Martha since the good old days."

"Mar?" Good grief, I thought. This woman has totally reinvented herself. Maybe there's hope for me.

"Yes. Mar rolls off the lips. Martha always sounded to me like people were chewing something when they enunciated it."

I offered her a chair and sat in mine. "Always reminded me of marshmallows," I said.

She winced. Then she went into a catch-up session, telling me about the wonderful husband she married; his wonderful paycheck, bonuses and stock options; and her wonderful fairy-tale life. I tried not to gag. Okay, maybe I was a tad bit envious. I didn't have a husband, or the money to buy nice clothes, and I didn't look half as feminine as Mar. She had that perfect 'cat eye' thing going on that looks like jigsaw puzzle pieces on my eyelids when I try to use eyeliner.

"You're still a policeman, I see." Her eyes meandered around the room, taking in cheap prints of long-stem pink tulips and a bloomed red rose against a gray wall, my wobbly oak desk, the worn hardwood floor, and two antique filing cabinets. She shifted her weight on my stiff oak chair and managed a polite smile

"I'm afraid I live in the real world where people actually work to make a living," I said.

"Well, I'm sure you are doing the best you can." She looked at her watch. "I don't have much time. I have a hair appointment in an hour."

"What can I do for you?" I asked.

"We were burgled. I still have a hard time believing it could happen. Robert installed all of those high-tech security devices and someone managed to circumvent them. My hubby is very upset. He's trying to get a refund from the security company."

"When did this happen?"

"A few weeks ago, while we were in Paris," she said. "The insurance will take care of the monetary value, of course, but there is the emotional attachment you just can't put a price on."

"Such as?"

"Oh, you know, some antique jewelry passed down from my great-grandmother, a case of one-of-a-kind bottles of Chateau Latour 2005, a French Bordeaux, worth maybe two thousand dollars a bottle. Here's a copy of the list I gave to the insurance company."

My jaw dropped. "Did they back a U-Haul up to the door?" The list was two pages, typewritten and single spaced.

"Actually, they were very selective," she said. "It was as if they knew what they were looking for. They stole nearly all the things that were nearest and dearest to me. Except for some high tech computer gadgets of Robert's."

I looked over the catalog and found scads of jewelry, watches, paintings, twenty South African Gold Krugerrands, two laptops, a computer server, three cell phones, a computer tablet, networking gear and miscellaneous cables and jacks. One item piqued my interest.

"What's a Hologram Quarter Conceptual Computer?"

Mar made a sour face. "It's some computer design Rob was working on at home. He said it would make us rich and it would be the first major technological advance of the 21st century."

"How does it work?" I asked.

"It's a computer the size of a quarter. You touch the quarter and an interactive hologram screen projects in front of your eyes. Rob says you can touch pictures in the hologram and they run computer programs. He says people could have their computer on their watch or maybe even on an earring. The hardware is all in the clouds, he says. I don't know what he's talking about."

I did. Angel told me the cloud is where information is stored on computer servers using the Internet. I guessed that Mar probably didn't do much more than hunt and peck on her computer. She was likely too busy spending her husband's money.

"Was Robert very upset about his designs being stolen?" I asked.

"He's still going on about it two weeks later," Mar said. "The thieves stole his backup something or other and he says he lost everything."

"Couldn't he back it up on the cloud?"

"He doesn't trust the clouds for his baby," she said. "He gets all paranoid that someone might steal it."

"Was this a work project?"

"No. He only worked on it at home. He didn't want the executives at Intel to come after him claiming, ownership, if he was successful."

"Sounds like quite a loss," I said.

"I told him he should just sit down and start over and he screamed at me." She made a pouty face. "He said it took him five years to get as far as he did."

"So you'd like me to track down the thieves and recover his designs?"

Her brown eyes lit up. "Could you do that? I just wanted my great-grandmother's antique jewelry and my wine back. But if you could find Robert's computer thingies, maybe he'd quit yelling at me."

"I'll see what I can do." I gave her a small notebook and pen. "Can you jot down the dates you left and returned from Paris? Also, where you stayed and who you told."

She nodded and began writing. "I told a lot of people."

"Concentrate on people who aren't close friends. Acquaintances, people who do your hair, deliver your paper, the guy you flirt with at the grocers . . ."

"I don't . . . oh," she said, and jotted down some more names. When she finished, I ushered her to Angel, who collected a hefty retainer. I rubbed my aching forehead and sneezed as Mar pranced out the door, leaving behind, perhaps forever, the awful smell of her perfume.

"Do we have any aspirin?" I asked Angel.

Something Mar said struck me. I went back to her Facebook page posts and there it was. Her last entry said she was going to get her hair done. I remembered seeing it while she cooled her heels in the outer office.

She must write about everything she does, I thought. There was no mention of seeing a private investigator, but she wouldn't be the type of person who shared her problems online.

I scrolled down and read her itinerary from the day before and continued back another two weeks on her Timeline thingy and learned where she went, what she did, and what she bought.

"Angel," I cried. "Come in here quick!"

"What's up?" Angel entered my office and sat beside my desk with a notepad.

"I'm reading Mar's posts on her webpage and look at this."

"You're on her Timeline, good for you," she said.

"This lady puts her entire calendar on Facebook. She's bragging about where she's going and what she's doing."

"Everybody does it," Angel said. "It's a way people can stay connected with their friends when they don't have time to see them."

I scrolled further down. "Does everyone tell the world when they go on vacation?"

"Oh," Angel said. "Some people do, I guess."

"Mar not only did, but she gave a day-by-day account of their trip. Ten days' worth."

"So?" Angel was hesitant, unsure what I was getting at.

"Who can see her page?" I asked.

"Just her *friends*," Angel said.

I looked over to a sidebar. "All two hundred and twelve of them?"

"Uh, I think I see what you're getting at. You're saying one of her *friends* or a *friend of a friend* might have seen her postings about being out of town and . . ."

I scrolled down Mars' Timeline. "What do you mean *friend of a friend*?"

"Oh, simple." Angel put her notepad down on my desk. "The default on Facebook is to let a *friend* see all of your *friends* and your *friends' friends*. You know, peek at their postings and photos and stuff."

"How many people would that be?"

Angel scratched her head. "I don't think I can count that high."

I clicked one of Martha's *friends* and saw all of her *friends* and clicked one of their profiles. "Unbelievable." I clicked on *friends of friends of friends* and kept going, viewing all of their personal data, events, and pictures-some of which should be censored in my opinion. The list was endless and although some women's pictures couldn't be seen, many others were open to the world.

"What's wrong with these people?" I figured Mar probably neglected to tell me about her Facebook postings because she knew her bragging probably led to the break-in. Now I knew why Robert screamed at her.

"You think someone read her Facebook page and burgled her house?" Angel asked.

"She might as well have put a sign on her front door saying 'Help Yourself, No One's Home.'"

Chapter 3

Trixie ran through the tall pines in Portland's Forest Park dirt trail at a moderate pace. He didn't like nature much and preferred to run on the streets. And he didn't usually rise so early to run, but this was a special occasion.

He'd started his new regimen about a week before and stuck with the same trail. He wore high end Adidas running shoes and an Under Armor outfit, consisting of compression tights and a body hugging T-shirt, to show off his sculpted body. Trixie hoped by running regularly here, the other female runners would notice his professional attire and be less weary of his presence. He took the precaution of wearing a runner's visor to shield his face from future potential witnesses.

It was a three-mile trek and at the halfway point he would catch up with Connie after giving her a head-start. He noticed she ran with something in her hand and guessed it was pepper spray or a warning whistle. The first two days he stayed respectfully behind her, not attempting to catch up.

The third day he found her running with a female friend. He feared the other runner might identify him if things went wrong, so he pulled his visor over his eyes and darted past them.

The next day she'd been alone again and actually slowed down to let him pass. This was good, he reasoned. She was becoming comfortable with him. He nodded and kept running, not stopping to chat, or otherwise make a pass at her like he figured she expected him to do. He was almost ready now. He had scouted her routes and knew she varied them some days. He guessed her taking the shorter trails had to do with her work schedule. He had located a spot where he could park his car along one of the routes for a quick snatch and getaway.

But on the fifth day Connie was a no-show. He arrived early and sat in his blue Toyota Prius for thirty minutes past her usual start time. He looked around the parking lot again for her forest green Subaru Forester when he finished his run, but it was nowhere to be seen.

He sighed as he climbed into the Prius and watched attentively as other runners finished the course. Some of them were really attractive, but they didn't have Connie's regal cadence. Or maybe he had too much invested in her at this point.

Today there was another glitch. He couldn't catch up to her. Either she ran a faster stride or she went off on a side trail. He wasn't happy about her change in routine. Unexpected occurrences increased the likelihood he might get caught and that wasn't part of his game.

As he walked toward his car, he spotted Connie sitting on the tail end of her Subaru, the hatchback up. She had removed her running tights so he could see her long white legs and noticed her rubbing her left calf.

"Cramp," she said, smiling at him as he paced toward his car.

His heart raced so loud he thought she might hear it beating. She had started a conversation with him. What should he do? He hadn't foreseen his plan working this well. He had hoped she would relax a bit and drop her guard so he could grab her in some desolate spot along the trail.

But there were people around. He couldn't risk anything now. He stopped, gave her a sideways glance, and did something against his master plan. He lifted his visor so she could see his face and smiled.

"Probably dehydrated. Do you have some bottled water?"

"I forgot it," she said.

"I have some in my car." He went to his Prius and found the bottle he'd brought for himself. "Try this." He admired her shapely legs as she took a few swigs.

"I've seen you before," she said. "Have you been running here long?"

"I just heard about it a week ago. Thought I'd try it."

"Isn't it beautiful?" she said. "The giant Douglas-firs, the ferns, the birds, the quiet. I've been running in Forest Park for a year now and I'll never go back to the city."

"Not many people up here this early," he said.

His watch said it was eight o'clock and he'd been waiting for her since six-thirty. She usually started at seven-fifteen, but he'd always come earlier in case her routine varied.

"It's too far for people to come up here and get to work on time," she said. "I talked my friend into going with me a couple of days ago, but she normally runs in the early evening and doesn't like rushing to get dressed in the women's bathroom before work."

"What about you?" Trixie said.

"I'm lucky," she said. "I work for Adidas over on the North side. They have training facilities and a locker room."

He knew she was some kind of marketing expert from her Facebook page. He had driven by the Adidas headquarters a few times, trying to figure out which building she worked in. There were three of them, all part of the old Bess Kaiser Hospital complex on Greeley Avenue. One of the buildings was underground. He watched Connie rub her calf and became conscious of her watching him watch her. What was her game? Was she suspicious?

"What do you do?" she said.

"I'm between jobs."

"Oh, that's too bad. The economy is tough right now."

Did she feel sorry for him? "I'm okay." It was almost a shout. "I have some solid investments and I'm being a bit picky about my next opportunity."

He wasn't going to tell her his asshole father died and left him an inheritance. Or that his worthless mother killed herself six months later because she didn't know how to live without *the butcher*.

He thought back at the many beatings his father heaped upon him and how his mother stood by and didn't once intervene. *You had to learn to do everything he wanted so he wouldn't have a reason to hurt you.*

Of course she was full of shit. *The butcher* beat her as often as him. Even if you did everything perfect, *the butcher* still went off on you. The nicest thing his father ever did, the only good thing, was to die and leave them a few million each. Trixie was surprised he even did that. He was sure his supposed father would find a way to take it with him.

"I'm glad to hear it," she said. "What do you do when you find the right job?"

What did she say? The right job? "I work in the IT sector. I build firewalls for corporate America to keep hackers at bay." He smiled. "Don't want the wrong people getting in, do we?"

"My name is Connie." She extended her hand.

"I go by Brent." Trixie thought this pseudonym the proper millennium moniker for a girl like Connie. He took her hand and shook it.

"Nice to meet you, Brent. Maybe we could run together sometime."

"I'll be here tomorrow," he said.

Chapter 4

I had been thinking more and more about Steve lately. I missed him and wondered if our lack of intimacy was my fault. Maybe I needed to take the lead in our relationship and let him know how I felt about him. It was approaching the lunch hour, so I decided to call him and see if we could get together. Also, I planned to pick his brain about Facebook burglaries.

Steve works in the Portland Police Bureau's Central Office in the Justice Building downtown on Southwest Second. I suggested we meet at a Rose's Deli a few blocks away in the Wells Fargo Building on Fifth. By the time I found a place to park and entered the bustling restaurant, Steve had snagged a table and two Rueben sandwiches-- one of the few things we can agree on.

He stood and kissed me in the crowded restaurant. A few women in a nearby red booth chuckled. It wasn't a peck and it lasted long enough to make me self-conscious and then long enough that I didn't care what people thought.

He looked hot in an expensive looking new gray suit tailored to fit his Adonis-like body perfectly. He wore a red power tie against a blue dress shirt, and his brown hair looked newly trimmed. His steel-blue eyes sent a tremor through me like a thousand fingers massaging my body.

"I've missed you," he said, and smiled that boyish grin that warms my heart.

"Yeah, it's been a long time."

"I've got to testify in court at three-thirty this afternoon." He ran his finger up my arm, sending ripples of dopamine to my brain, and gazed into my eyes.

I'd like to take his testimony, I thought, preferably in an under-the-covers brief. "It's been too long," I said, sizing him up some more.

"I know. I've been so busy on this homicide case that I haven't had a chance to come up for air. The trial will last about a week and I'm on-call until it finishes."

I batted my lightly mascaraed eyelashes and tried to do the hair flip thing, but my hair length wasn't quite long enough to be an effective flirt tool. I wore a short black dress with killer high heels and a seductive scent of lavender and white peony called *Ange ou Demon* by Givenchy. The perfume brings out the demon in me. I've never been much of an angel. It's supposed to be for the woman who knows what she wants, and I was looking at him.

He noticed. "I have a few hours before court if you don't have any plans."

"Oh, I have plans." I took a delicate bite from my Reuben and wiped some mustard from the corner of my lip with my tongue.

Twenty minutes later we dumped our Rueben sandwich to-go boxes on a dresser inside the Hotel Modera, five long blocks from Roses. Had it been any further, we likely would have been littering Portland's streets with our clothes. Steve paid a ridiculous price for what would amount to a two-hour rental and we probed each other as discreetly as possible through the halls. In the elevator a retired couple watched unabashedly. Maybe they were looking for tips.

Once inside our room, he quickly found all the zippers, hooks, and other right places as we caressed each other onto the bed. I uncharacteristically whimpered as he touched my naked body. It had been two weeks since our last encounter so I pulled him onto me without shame. We writhed atop the bed covers and somehow managed to disappear into the sheets.

I was in mid-moan when I noticed our room door was ajar. What the hell, I thought. Let someone else close it. Our passion went on for about forty-five minutes before we called it quits. I took five minutes to catch my breath before I made a move to close the door.

But something came up as I threw the covers off, and Steve grinned at me mischievously. I knew then I wasn't going to make it to the door. He grabbed my breasts and rolled me onto him, and I just went along for the ride. After all, most men take a nap at this stage. I thought I'd better make the best of it while I could.

Lover Boy had conked out, so I decided to freshen up. About ten minutes into my shower, I heard a rapping at the door, and Steve poked his head in the steamy bathroom fully dressed.

"I've got to go," he said. "It's ten to three, and I have to be there in forty minutes."

"Can't you stay a little longer? At least until I get dressed?"

He stepped across the bathroom, cupped the back of my head in his hand and pulled me to his lips. It was a nice kiss. I reached to grab him and he stepped back to avoid getting his suit wet.

"I'd like to, but the D.A. gets testy if his witnesses don't show up on time."

A few minutes later, I stepped out of the shower wrapped in a body towel. My skin didn't need foundation, so I feathered the mascara back on, layered on some green eye shadow and balanced it with a light lipstick.

By my watch, it was three o'clock. We were only a few blocks from the courthouse so I knew Steve would make it on time. But it bothered me that because of the midday distraction, I'd forgotten to ask Steve about Facebook. I reached for my phone and hit the speed dial.

"Yello!" Steve sounded chipper for someone who just finished the equivalent of a double marathon.

"Hey," I said. "I meant to ask you something about a case I'm working on."

"Shoot."

I told him about my client and how I suspected her perpetrator used Facebook to case her home.

"I can see it happening that way. You should talk to Detective Sam Jacobs in Central. He's part of the property crimes unit. He also specializes in computer forensics."

I did a search of the room to find my clothes. The lodgings were semi-upscale and artistic, but not really romantic. I found my bra intertwined with the duvet, my dress hanging over a table lamp, and my killer heels playing dead on opposite sides of the floor. But my underwear and tights were missing in action.

I sighed and dressed the best I could, wishing I had worn a longer skirt. I finally found my tights on the other side of the bed. My black undies were nowhere to be found. Either some passerby stopped to ogle us during our lovemaking and stole them, or Steve took a souvenir. I shuddered and hoped an underwear junkie purloined them. I'd hate to think of Steve showing them to his buddies.

"Happens all the time," Detective Jacobs said, after listening to my story about Mar's break-in while on vacation.

He was a medium, thickset man in his late thirties and looked more like a prize fighter than a computer geek. Crime makes for strange bedfellows, I guess. He wore a white lab coat, unbuttoned and disheveled. Under it, I spotted a Glock 19 in his shoulder holster.

"We're getting more and more burglaries associated with people's online postings," Jacobs said. "Of course we don't have the staff to fully investigate burglaries, so often officers take a statement, record the losses and file a report. It's hard to do any follow up unless we make a connection."

This Facebook stuff was new to me because I avoided it in my own life, thinking it was kind of silly, and using it to rob homes hadn't happened when I was on the Portland Police Bureau.

"So do you ask victims if they posted news they would be away from their home on Facebook?" I sat across from him at his desk and thumbed the edges of a stack of unfinished paperwork.

He shook his head. "A lot of victims either don't think they did, or don't want to admit it."

"Are you working any active cases involving Facebook?"

"All of the detectives use Facebook as a matter of routine." He leaned back in a wobbly office chair and tucked his hands behind his head. "But most often to track gang activity or follow up on leads to see if anyone is stupid enough to incriminate themselves."

"Are they?" I asked.

"Sometimes." He winked at me. "We catch gang members bragging about everything from assault to robbery. One bozo posted a picture of his girlfriend with a ring he had stolen. I think both of them got time."

I was momentarily distracted by two computer monitors flashing images behind him. "Is there any way to trace robberies back to the criminals if they've used Facebook to find their victims?"

"Not easily." Jacobs frowned. "Most social programs have features which allow people to tell their friends where they are at the exact minute: on vacation, at a concert, out drinking, or at a restaurant. People get on their phone and update their status to announce where they are to their friends, unaware some unscrupulous people might also be watching."

"I don't get what motivates people to tell everyone what they're doing every moment of the day," I said.

"It's a social thing. People like to brag about themselves."

Like Mar, I thought. "So while they're out having a good time, one of their *friends* is back robbing their homes."

"They can even pull up Google Street View to get the neighborhood layout and see if a house looks worthy," he said.

"You should arrest Facebook and Google as accomplices." I chuckled at my little joke.

"It's just a sign of the times," Jacobs said. "Technology changes and so do the criminals."

"I want to find out who broke into a client's house while she was in Paris," I said. "She posted her itinerary on her Facebook page."

"We don't have the time or manpower to do detailed searches," Jacobs said. "It would require search warrants and some kind of online trail we could follow."

"So I'm probably out of luck as far as finding out who read her page and robbed her house . . ."

"Maybe not. Go down to records and tell the clerk I sent you. You might spend a few days sifting through records just finding a pattern. Then you'll have to determine if the victims have mutual *friends*. How you prove anything beyond that is the challenge."

For three days Angel and I slogged through more than a hundred police reports a clerk at the Bureau let me copy. We were looking to find a link between the burglaries and Facebook. Angel mapped the targeted homes within a one-mile radius of Mar Roy's home on a bulletin board by her desk in the lobby.

We ended up with a list of nine burglaries in a zone around Mar's home. Of the nine victims, we found five who had posted on Facebook. The other four had Facebook pages, but limited what we could see. We divided the victims between us and researched their Timelines. Of the four people I examined, I was able to view the Timelines of two people and they both had announced they would be away from home for an extended period of time. Three of Angel's victims posted about their trip.

"Here's one," she said. "A Mrs. Hillary Brown: 'We are so excited about our trip. Roger and I leave tomorrow and will see Greece, Italy, and France on a two-week cruise.' This is her fifth mention of their trip and there are scads of pictures posted in her European Vacation Album."

"I've got one too. His name is Joe Russell: 'I'm off for nine days of fun in the sun. If I can find a job here (the Bahamas), I may not be back at all. LOL!'"

"There's a privacy feature which limits browsing to their circle of *friends*," Angel said. "But these people apparently haven't bothered to secure their Facebook pages."

We had assumed the four people whose Facebook pages we couldn't view had limited their access to immediate friends. I wondered if they had done this before or after their break-ins.

I clicked on the page of another victim and nothing came up, but an icon of a kitten and a name. "I'm dying to know about the others. Did this one change her privacy features after she was robbed? How can we see more than their limited profiles?"

"Why don't we invite them to *friend* us," Angel said. "We are a private investigation firm. Maybe they'd like to have some security tips for their home."

"Wouldn't you want a *friend* like me if you were in their shoes?"

Angel nodded. "We could draft a message inviting them with a promise of posting weekly security tips." She walked back to her computer and started typing.

What if this was all a waste of time? We had spent the better part of a week following this angle and if it was a bust, we were right back where we started. How would Mar react to that?

I reread Joe Russell's post after he returned from the Bahamas: *"A great trip ruined. Got home and the place was a mess. Someone broke in and took all my sports memorabilia, coins, cash in the wall safe, and a bunch of other stuff. Luckily, I had my computer with me. All my work projects are on it."*

That's what the chump gets for announcing he's not going to be home for nine days, I thought. No mention if he had an alarm service or a house sitter. I looked up *Joe Russell* in the phone book. There were three. A Joe and two Josephs. I tried the Joe first, not expecting to get him at home.

"Hello," a voice said.

"Is this Joe Russell?"

"Yep. What can I do for you?"

"Is this the Joe Russell, who had his home burglarized three months ago?"

"Who is this?"

I told him who I was and how I was investigating a similar break-in ten blocks from his home. He seemed cautious and wanted some proof. I got the bright idea of referring him to my Facebook page, which Angel said was public.

A minute later he spilled his guts. "My alarm didn't do me any good. They disarmed it somehow. At least, that's what the alarm company said. They had a record of someone entering the house, but the jerk at the alarm company says someone entered the code."

"Did you give the code to anyone, a Realtor, or . . ?"

"Not a chance," Joe said. "My girlfriend doesn't even know it."

"Why? Don't you trust her?"

"I had a relationship with a girl for over a year. We broke up and she returned and trashed my place just for spite. I changed the code and now I don't give to anyone. I've had three relationships since then, so maybe it's still a good idea."

"Did you notice any suspicious activity in the neighborhood prior to your vacation?"

"This is a quiet area," he said. "Not much ever happens. Most of the people own their own homes. I live in a duplex, and my neighbor is eighty. I can't even throw a party."

"Maybe I could talk to some of your neighbors. It sounds like a lot of people might be home during the day. Maybe they'd notice if someone came around to case your home."

He let out a deep sigh over the phone. "Knock yourself out. I've already talked to everybody up and down the street. The only thing anybody noticed was a UPS truck cruising the area . . . There was one weird thing."

"What?"

"I found an empty cardboard box in my back yard. I thought maybe the thieves brought it to haul stuff away, but the cops said it was unlikely."

"How did they enter your house?"

"Back door. The alarm keypad was ten feet down the hallway. No damage to it. The friggin' alarm system just didn't work. I mean the door was kicked in."

"Someone knew the code," I said. "Or they knew a way around it."

Chapter 5

Jimmer pulled the brown United Parcel Service truck up to the front door of the retired cop's house. Eric, clad in a brown UPS shirt and matching shorts, hopped out of the open passenger doorway with a medium-sized package in his hands. It was big enough to be noticed and possibly too large to leave at the front door. Of course it was empty, so it was easy to carry around back.

Jimmer conjured up the plot of using one of his former employer's trucks for their neighborhood delivery ploys. He knew of some old trucks parked on the edge of Swan Island destined for decommission after twenty years of service. Whenever they needed a vehicle, Eric and Jimmer went to the isolated lot, hot-wired a truck, and drove it through the rickety gate protected only by an easy-to-pick padlock.

Once they actually drove out of Swan Island in a caravan of UPS trucks heading out for morning deliveries around the city. Eric cringed when Jimmer waved to other drivers dressed in one of the brown company uniforms he kept when his drug habit got him booted from the fleet.

Today Eric marched boldly up the front walkway of the retired cop's house with a package under his arm while Jimmer scanned the neighborhood for busybodies. Eric noticed the ADP alarm sign, staked in the ground by the front window, designed to let would-be burglars know the house was protected.

The sign would be enough to send most thieves on to an easier opportunity, but Eric knew that often homeowners changed and the new occupants didn't always renew the alarm service. They relied on the sign to scare away potential thieves and lived with a false sense of security.

Eric fiddled with the storm door in front and found it locked. He would take the package around back where it would be secure. Of course not many of the UPS drivers did this anymore, but not all of them were as conscientious as Eric.

He surreptitiously peered through the front window and glimpsed a large flat screen television through partially open blinds as he passed around to the side of the house. He closed the gate carefully and surveyed the back yard. The lots were large and fences blocked the view of nosy neighbors. A couple of well-placed trees ensured privacy for the owners and for him too.

He bypassed the dining room window and spotted an alarm module between the blinds and a sliding glass patio door. There was no sign of anyone inside the house.

He dropped the empty box on the patio and went to a bedroom window. Again, he found the telltale plastic modules designed to sound the alarm if someone separated them by opening the window. Eric guessed there were motion detectors in the home too.

The window blinds were drawn, but there was a slight crack. He peeked inside and was rewarded with a dresser mirror's reflection showing him the rest of the bedroom. He spotted a smaller flat screen television and a jewelry armoire. The furniture was high-end and the portraits on the wall looked like original oil paintings. Everything in the room looked upscale. Policemen must be paid better than he thought, Eric mused.

Two short beeps resonated from the street. It was Jimmer's signal something was amiss. He walked along the other side of the house, hidden from view by a fence separating two properties. He hurried to the front gate and peeked over the top. Jimmer, still in the truck, leaned out of the door and spoke to someone.

Through the aisle connecting the two entries to the truck, Eric noticed a red flashing light. He also heard the steady humming of a large vehicle. He stepped on a garbage can, for a better look, and spotted the front end of a Fire Rescue Truck. Firefighters, not cops. He opened the gate and walked casually toward Jimmer.

"I'm sorry, I don't know. It should be here somewhere," Jimmer said.

Eric jumped into the cab and looked down at the flustered face of a firefighter, dressed in heavy protective pants, a black Portland Fire and Rescue T-shirt, and gaudy yellow suspenders.

"How can you not know the address?" the flustered guy said. "You probably drive this area every day."

"How can you not know where you're going," Jimmer said, just as cocky. "You're a fuckin' fireman."

"We have new communications equipment and it's not working," the firefighter said. "What's your excuse?"

"He's new. I'm training him." The last thing Eric wanted was for these guys to get suspicious or to talk to the cops after they hit this place. "What's the address?"

"Fourteen hundred Northwest Foley."

Eric leaned across Jimmer's lap and could see the guy's badge. His name was Jasper. He also noticed Jasper's face had turned red. He was glad he had looked at the Google map of the area the night before.

"Common mistake," he said. "You probably want Foley Court. You have to go back out on Miller Road and it wraps around on the other side of those trees." Eric pointed at a stand of trees that backed the housing development, providing green space.

Jasper didn't thank him. He jumped into the rescue rig, made a U-turn in a cul-de-sac, and they sped off toward Miller Road with lights flashing. Eric was glad they didn't use the siren. The whole neighborhood would have seen them.

"Shit," Eric said. "Did you have to piss him off?"

"I was just messing with the guy," Jimmer said. "He thinks he's 'all that' 'cause he's a fireman. Hell, he was lost. Am I supposed to depend on him if I have a heart attack?"

"We're up in the West Hills," Eric said. "There are all sorts of obstacles to block wireless transmissions up here. He probably couldn't call back for instructions or maybe his locator's on the fritz. The point is, we don't want people to notice us and you're practically drawing a bull's-eye on our backs."

"Whatever," Jimmer said. "How'd the place look? Anything good?"

"Yeah," Eric said. "But now I think we'd better pass it up."

"Why?"

"Look over there."

Jimmer looked in the direction Eric pointed and saw a middle-aged woman dressed in sweat pants standing outside her doorway.

"Morning, ma'am," Jimmer said. "Nothing to worry about. Wrong address. No one dying in your neighborhood today."

Eric slugged Jimmer in the shoulder as hard as he could.

"What did I do?" The woman retreated inside her home and Jimmer put the truck in gear and drove away.

Trixie was trapped with no way out. Red strobe lights flashed ahead of him and the bile rose in his throat until he could taste the acidic foul stench. He scanned the area for an escape route, but he was stuck in a cul-de-sac and any exit would have to be on foot. He tried to tell himself he wasn't in any real danger.

After all, it was only a fire truck. One of those small boxy things the paramedics drove. Yet, it and the UPS truck blocked the whole street and they didn't seem in any hurry to move. The two drivers were arguing about something.

Suddenly the damned driver of the fire truck advanced towards him, spun around the cul-de-sac, as he sat parked at the curb, and looked right at him. A clear identification if anyone questioned whether he had been in this neighborhood. Then the fucking UPS truck turned around in the cul-de-sac and zoomed past him too. At least this time he'd had the sense to duck down in his seat.

His mind raced to a scientific term he had read called the butterfly effect. It referred to the simple fluttering of a butterfly's wing causing a change in the weather system somewhere a thousand miles away.

Trixie had his own interpretation of the butterfly effect. He believed it was a simple, innocent action by one in the company of others that forever linked them in some catastrophic way. He always tried to avoid contact with others when he was working.

He had not been successful with Connie because there had been some kind of chemistry between them. He knew it was a mistake to not follow through with his plan to kidnap her, but he couldn't help himself.

This is why he was scouting another victim in this idyllic little neighborhood of middle-class homes with dogwoods, azaleas, and rhododendrons systematically placed on each lot. Now he feared the butterfly's chain of chaotic events had begun because of his inadvertent contact with Connie. He never had contact with women before he abducted them. It was too dangerous. They might tell someone and it could create a trail back to him later.

He knew how chaos worked because he had experienced it so often in his childhood when his father came home drunk looking for someone to blame for his pitiful life. Little Bruce would shrink, hoping he would be so small *the butcher* wouldn't be able to see him. Sometimes it worked and *the butcher* went after his mother instead. This caused Brucie so much pain that he would disassociate and a part of him would turn into a butterfly, named Trixie, and hover over the top of them, looking for an open window to escape.

But there was no escape. Eventually his father would call out for Brucie. "Where is that worthless piece of shit hiding? There you are. What's so damn funny?" Brucie couldn't help smiling at times of danger. It was a defense mechanism he employed to tell himself everything was going to be okay. Smile and maybe it would put *the butcher* into a good mood. He was only six-years-old. Wouldn't his dad think he was cute?

His father would take off his belt and begin whipping it across his back and butt. When he was sober enough to think about it, he would remove Brucie's shirt and pants and flail on his bare skin.

Trixie would fly above the scene and watch, hovering above the pain zone, flapping his little butterfly wings trying to escape this monstrous beating on the helpless little boy below. Trixie knew how to avoid the pain. Just fly above it. The only problem being, Trixie and Brucie were still connected in spirit and body. Eventually Trixie's wings would tire and he would alight on poor little defiant Brucie.

When *the butcher* left the room, Trixie would nurse little Brucie's emotional wounds and his feeling of grief at the little boy's plight would bring a tear to Trixie's eye. Only a single tear at the sadness that a grown man, a father, would treat his son this way; not a stream of tears because of the pain. Brucie and Trixie would not give *the butcher* that satisfaction.

When Trixie and Brucie became too defiant, the old man, flustered at his inability to break the little boy, would lock him in a storage cabinet in the garage. Barely enough room to squat, Brucie would shift his little frame into a position where he might find some small comfort among the fumes of leftover paint rags and solvents on the shelves above. Fortunately, there were plenty of air holes in the cabinet to allow him to breathe some fresh air.

In his imagination, Trixie would take little Brucie on his little butterfly shoulders and they would escape through a knothole in the cabinet door. Trixie would fly Brucie out of the garage and they would sweep over the neighborhood, spying on normal people going about their business without any inkling of the plight of the little boy in the padlocked storage cabinet in *the butcher*'s garage.

Once, they saw Brucie's mother working in the garden outside. She was dressed in a gay red dress, her yellow hair flowing in the breeze, planting petunias in a row under the dogwood tree and among the purple azaleas and peppermint colored rhododendrons. She stopped to talk to another lady in a gay green dress. His mother removed her garden gloves and the two chattered like little brown squirrels, as if they hadn't a care in the world.

Trixie dive-bombed them, trying to get their attention. Hoping they would follow him into the garage and find little Brucie. But they ignored the little butterfly as if he didn't exist and went on about their chattering.

Eventually, when *the butcher* would pass out, Brucie's mother would come to the garage. He would hear the key turn in the padlock and feel her cold hands grasp his contorted little body and help him straighten it out after seven or eight hours of squatting.

If you would only try to do things perfectly, maybe you wouldn't find yourself in so much trouble, she would say. She would give him some leftover dinner, usually the fat from his father's steak, and he would gobble it down like a hungry pug dog, happy with scraps.

Trixie's hands and the back of his neck felt clammy. The firefighter and the other person on the UPS truck had both looked in his direction before leaving. The UPS guy even pointed at him. He could feel little Brucie panicking inside him. They were back in the cabinet in the garage again. "It's okay," he said to little Brucie. "I'll take care of you. We're never going back in that box."

Trixie had considered doing away with the witnesses. How would he track them? What were the risks associated with killing two UPS drivers and a firefighter? When he saw the nosy lady at the front porch staring at the three drivers and noticed two women talking on the sidewalk further down the street, he realized he couldn't remove all of the neighborhood witnesses. Both trucks had their engines running and it created a low rumbling noise easily heard from nearby residents, who also had likely peered through their windows.

His best bet was to get out of here. He started his Prius and rolled out behind the UPS truck close enough that the driver couldn't see him in his side mirrors. He slunk down in the driver's seat, and wished he could become the small butterfly again and whisk little Brucie away from this mess.

It felt good to get back to work. Billie Bly, on the job after months of self-pity. I walked up the street of perfectly aligned ranch homes, trying to decide which house to try first. I was following my first lead to a home that might be a future target of our Facebook burglars. I wanted to check with the neighbors and see if they noticed anyone suspicious or out-of-place during the past few days. I would give them my P.I. card and ask them to call me if they spotted any strangers lurking about.

I was going through Mar's *friend* list a few days ago and scanning them for others who might have been burgled, when I ran across a name I knew from high school, Daril Rogers. But the spelling was wrong. It should have been Daryl Rogers.

It occurred to me that maybe someone was friending Mar by asking for an invite using a name to someone she knew in high school but with a slightly misspelled name. I *friended* Daril and since I was supposedly in his high school class, I was accepted. Daril didn't do any posting on his Facebook page, but his Timeline suggested he was active in pursuing new *friends*.

From there I only had to read through his *friends'* postings to see if anyone was talking about going on a vacation or being out of town. And this led me to a home up the street of one Mr. Jack Springer, 1330 Northwest Foley Street. Springer was a retired cop and probably knew better than to discuss his vacation on Facebook. His wife, Lucy, should have known better too, but she had described their Maui trip faithfully each day on Facebook.

About a block ahead, I noticed a UPS driver talking with a firefighter. The firefighter waved an arm in the air and the UPS driver seemed amused. I watched for a moment, mesmerized by the scene. The firefighter became more animated, his face flushed red. I decided to wait until they were done. The UPS driver likely saw all kinds of things in this neighborhood and I wanted to talk to him.

The UPS truck would have to turn around in a cul-de-sac up ahead, and pass me on the way out.

"Can I help you with something?"

I turned and saw a woman in her early forties lugging a half-full metal galvanized watering bucket. She was trim and short, in white culottes and a tight-fitting yellow T-shirt, which clung to her oversized bosom.

I went into my spiel about wanting to form a neighborhood watch. I flashed my P.I. badge and explained a nearby resident was a friend of mine and wanted to organize the neighborhood. It was a flimsy cover, but people will believe anything if you appear sincere.

"I hope you have better luck than I did," she said, brushing her red bangs from her eyes with a free hand. "I tried a couple of times to get a neighborhood watch started, but people always say they're too busy. Plus, they know I'm always watching."

"Watching for what?" I asked.

"We get a lot of activity in this neighborhood. Gardeners, remodelers, carpet shampooers." She put down her bucket and shook my hand. "My name is Sally Brown. I try to keep an eye on things around here, but it's awfully hard."

"So, you get a lot of strangers?"

"Most of them have a reason for being here. But that doesn't mean someone still isn't casing the neighborhood."

I heard a roar and saw the fire truck racing toward us, lights flashing. It sped past as Sally walked to the front porch of her ranch style home with green vinyl siding and a Cape Cod window. I smiled toward the fire truck as it passed, but its driver and passenger were intent on being somewhere else.

Sally returned with a small wire-bound notebook. On it was a list of vehicles by make and model, license plate, and vendor name in some cases. Each subset of vehicles was headed by the day's date. I watched her go back a few pages and figured she got about eight vehicles a day down on paper. On today's date she added the fire truck and its city license plate.

"That's impressive," I said. "Can I take a look?"

I scrolled through the pages during the previous three-week time period and found several of the vendor trucks had been in the neighborhood for three to five days. Sally saw me studying the trucks listed and smiled.

"Mrs. Smith was remodeling her kitchen. It was a two-week job. The Henderson's had rotten subfloor in one of their bathrooms. That took a few days to repair. These contractors show up one day and tear everything up and return another day to make it pretty again."

As she spoke, the UPS van roared past us before I could summon the driver. The two of them appeared to be arguing about something. The truck was followed closely by a blue Prius.

The driver, in his mid-thirties with a cap pulled over his eyes, slunk down in his seat, but suddenly looked up at me with an expression of what I interpreted as disbelief. The Prius swerved to the middle of the street after he passed and then weaved back behind the truck.

"Got it," Sally said. She took the notebook from me and scribbled the make and model and license plate of the UPS truck and then screwed up her face. "The Prius had no rear license plate. I couldn't see the front plate because he was so close to the truck."

"Really?" I gazed longingly at the distant Prius and saw Sally was right. No license plate. Not on the car, or the window, and no temporary sticker in the window either. "That's odd."

"It's a bit suspicious," Sally agreed. "I'll make a note to keep a watch out for it in case he comes back. Did you see what he looked like? I was too busy spotting plates."

I gave her the partial description of what I noticed: Caucasian man wearing a baseball cap, mid-thirties. I neglected to tell her something about the guy had creeped me out.

"Please call me if you see anyone casing the neighborhood," I said. "Especially that house."

She looked where I pointed. "Why the Springer house?"

"It has a similar layout to my friend's house," I said. "You see, she was burgled two weeks ago. I have reason to believe the thieves might strike in this area again."

"Really?" Her green eyes sparkled and she licked her lips in response. "I'll have to go through my notes. Maybe I should expand my perimeter. I can walk the neighborhood."

"I wouldn't take on any more than you are doing," I said. "Just watch this block. There are others watching their neighborhoods already. I'll call you when we set a neighborhood watch meeting," I lied.

I gave her my business card and as I left, it occurred to me I had given Sally meaning and purpose of some kind. I felt sorry for any crooks that might cross her path. I also felt uneasy about the Prius without the license plate. The driver had seemed dismayed at seeing me, I realized. I wondered why?

And there was another nagging feeling. A feeling I missed something important.

Chapter 6

What the hell was Billie Bly doing there? How had she found him? Did she follow him? It was all Trixie could think about. He knew it was her. He'd spent enough time studying her picture and he'd never forget that *no nonsense* facial expression.

He should have been in a good mood, but he was miserable and anxious. After talking with Connie the day before, he had run with her up at Forest Park this morning, and she had actually suggested they meet for drinks after she got off work.

This created his first dilemma. What if she told someone at work about him? So what if she did? He had given her a phony name, and she didn't really know anything about him to tell anyone. He debated whether to go ahead with his plan to take her to his basement where they could have some fun, or maybe try dating her and see where that led.

The anxiety created by this unexpected development had prompted him to scout another potential candidate in an attempt to soothe his nerves. Mary Johansen wasn't as exciting as Connie, but she had plenty of potential. She came from an upper-middle-class family and was spoiled rotten by her father.

Mary had two brothers who both smoked dope most of the time and were practically homeless, to hear her tell it on Facebook. She had married poorly and after her recent divorce, had moved back home with her parents on Foley Avenue. She had a fiancé named John Benson, but it didn't matter to Trixie. He had no plans to marry her.

He found her parents listed in the phone book, and he knew by her profile that she worked at Murder by the Book over in the Hawthorne business district. The bookstore was a little hole in the wall. He didn't want to risk being noticed in the store with Mary, so he decided to see where she lived on the off chance she might be home working in the yard or washing her car. It was a long shot, but Trixie needed to work off his nervous energy.

He thought about getting out of his car to see if he could locate Mary's bedroom, but there were too many nosy neighbors and a fire rescue truck and a UPS truck blocked his escape route.

It was only when he finally was able to leave the neighborhood, he had spotted *her*. He had raced home to his computer to make sure he was right and there she was on his *friends* list. Billie Bly. She was definitely the same blonde he'd seen gabbing with one of Mary's neighbors. He wondered if she had somehow tracked him when he *friended* her on Facebook.

Trixie didn't believe in coincidences, but he did believe in his version of the butterfly effect. Somehow, by following her on Facebook, he had linked their lives together. First Connie and now Billie Bly. His world was spinning out of control. Maybe she was meant to be one of his projects. Little Bruce spoke from somewhere inside him: *She knows something. I'm afraid.*

It was almost time to meet Connie. Trixie got out of his car and swiped his debit card in the city's green box to get a parking receipt. She would be along soon and he wanted to be ready. He looked down Third Avenue at the flurry of activity as people exited buildings and made for their car, or bus, or the Max light rail. They were too busy thinking about getting home from work to notice him.

A few happy-hour types ducked into Huber's Café, a half block ahead of him, where he would dine with Mary. He watched as a blonde and a redhead pushed through the café's front door. The blonde had possibilities, he thought. He didn't like redheads.

The two reminded him of his older sisters, Aimee and Mandy. They had always been pampered and loved, where he had always been the object of ridicule. His father doted over them, never raising a hand. When he was drunk, he would give them money and send them to the store to buy a treat so they wouldn't be around to see his temper when he lit into Brucie or his mom.

His mother began entering his sisters in beauty pageants at an early age. He thought of all of the competitions he was forced to attend because his mother didn't want to leave him alone with *the butcher*. Once, during a competition, his sisters put him in a dress and added rouge to his cheeks and smeared on lipstick. He remembered how they laughed at how cute he was and how he felt special because of the attention.

During one competition, Aimee pushed five-year-old Brucie out onto the stage in front of an audience. The crowd laughed and someone said he looked *so cute*. He pranced around the stage like he had seen his sisters do and curtsied to a round of enthusiastic applause and laughter.

His mother ran out on the stage and pulled his arm so hard it hurt for a week. She swore at him under her breath and dragged him behind a curtain. "You little brat," she'd said. "You made a laughing stock out of us. I'll tell your father and he'll spank you good."

But she didn't tell his father. And his sisters, who escaped any shaming messages or spankings, continued to make him wear dresses at home. They would laugh and tell their friends about it on the telephone as he waited for them to clean him up before their father came home.

It all came to a head, he remembered, one rain-soaked day when *the butcher* came home early from the law office where he was a partner. He had lost a big criminal case and already slurred his words when he walked through the front door at about three in the afternoon.

And Brucie, wearing a multi-colored ruffled frou-frou dress, a feathery red boa, one of his mother's red wigs and red high heels, ran from his screaming sisters and right into *the butcher*'s legs. He looked up wide-eyed at the six-foot-three, two-hundred-fifty pound behemoth of a man in his business suit and smiled the best he could with red lipstick lips.

Suddenly he was alone with the authoritarian. Aimee and Mandy were no longer in the hallway, only their laughter lingered. *The butcher* looked down at him, puzzled at the comic little boy and then showed some sort of recognition, as if he had seen something of himself in the boy.

He removed the red wig and bent over to look Brucie in the eye. "You look ridiculous. Go upstairs and take those clothes off before your mother sees you. And don't ever let your sisters dress you like that again."

That was the end of it. No explosions. No beatings. And his dad didn't drink the rest of the night. Trixie remembered coming downstairs after scrubbing the makeup off and seeing his father sitting in his easy chair, staring through the picture window, looking sad and lost.

"Hello, Brent?" A rapping at the car window brought him out of his childhood memories. Connie stood bent over, squinting through the passenger window of his Prius. She wore her strawberry-blonde hair on her shoulders as opposed to the ponytail she sported while running.

He got out of the car and she returned his smile. He noticed her blue eyes seemed to sparkle and when he saw her dressed in a charcoal business suit, he was glad he decided to wear dark slacks and a nice dress shirt with his charcoal sport coat. We're actually color coordinated, he thought.

"You look nice," she said. "I was afraid I'd be overdressed. I had this business presentation today and couldn't get home to change."

"I like it," he said. "I think you look great."

She smiled and took his arm and they walked down the block and into Huber's. Three giant arched mirrors hung on the wall behind the bar and reflected a concave ceiling with more smaller etched mirrors in three sections overhead. A waiter motioned to a plain dark wood table, with a white linen tablecloth and two matching chairs, across from the blonde and redhead he'd seen enter earlier. The women were accompanied by a couple of businessmen, drinks, and happy hour appetizers, but the blonde seemed to be scouting the bar for a better deal.

"Have you ever had their Spanish Coffee?" Trixie said.

"No. What's in it?"

"Rum, Kahlua, coffee, Triple Sec and I think whipped cream and a bit of nutmeg." He knew the ingredients because he'd been here once before, and he hoped the floor show might be entertaining for his date.

"Okay, I'll try it," she said.

It took him ten minutes to get the attention of a server. The place wasn't busy yet, and Trixie had noticed the little tart of a waitress flirting with a guy in a three-thousand-dollar business suit. He ordered two of the overpriced $10 Spanish coffees, calamari for himself, and a Caesar salad for Connie.

"Derrick will be by in a minute with your drinks," the waitress said. Trixie figured that meant they wouldn't see their appetizers for another 30 minutes.

They made awkward small talk for a few minutes until Derrick broke the tension with a creative presentation of the Spanish coffee. He offered up two small circular glasses and poured one-fifty-one rum in them with outstretched arms from somewhere near the ceiling while he held the glasses at ankle level. This was followed by a long stream of Kahlua cascading into the glasses in the same fashion, but seeming to break the laws of physics by being poured at a forty-five-degree angle.

"That's marvelous," Connie said. "How do you do that?"

"I could tell you, but then I'd have to kill you."

"That's my line," Trixie said.

Derrick made another creative move and added the Triple Sec, poured some coffee from a carafe, and topped it off with whipped cream and sprinkled nutmeg over the top.

Trixie was impressed, but mostly happy Connie was entertained. He tipped Derrick five dollars and took a sip of the concoction. It was good, he thought, but clearly the value of the drink was in the entertainment.

"I'm glad you suggested this place," Connie said. "It's been a rough day and this takes the edge off a bit."

They ordered dinner and the conversation flowed freely. By the time the meal was finished, Trixie felt like he had known Connie all of his life. She was easy to talk to and although he remained guarded about certain aspects of his life, he did share some things about himself that didn't completely suck.

He told her about his high-powered criminal attorney father and how he was expected to meet his father's impossible standards. He told her about their spacious upper scale home in the West Hills, mentioning his sisters and how they were pampered. He explained his mother's need for order in the house to please his father. He didn't tell her that momma's darling, Aimee, was in a psych ward back East or how her perfect Mandy married a bum who spent all of her inheritance and how now she was a crack addict.

"It sounds like you've had a trying childhood," Connie said. "I can identify with that. My parents tried to get their self-worth through me. They bought me nice clothes, sent me to private schools, expected perfect grades, perfect boyfriends, and gave me extravagant parties to impress their friends."

"Sounds a lot like what my parents did with my sisters," Trixie said.

"All I wanted was their love," Connie said. "It was the one thing they couldn't give. I tried to get their love by meeting all of their expectations, but I was never good enough."

Trixie thought Connie *was* good enough. But she brought up feelings that made him uncomfortable. He didn't think he could let himself get close enough to love her either.

"I don't see them anymore," she said. "They're too toxic. Everything they have to offer has a condition on it. My dad wanted me to be an accountant and my mother wanted me to find a husband and make babies. I had to do my own thing and, of course, they were both disappointed, always harping on me to do what they wanted."

"I'm glad you didn't give into them," Trixie said. "You deserve to be happy."

It sounded so stupid when he said it. But he felt she expected him to say something and he just blurted it out. Her face changed and he saw a tear leak out of her eye. He must have hurt her feelings. Had he ruined the evening?

"Would you like to go home with me?" she said.

"Oh, do you need a ride? Sure," he said.

"Well, yes, I do need a ride. But I'm asking if you'd like to spend the night with me."

"Oh," he said. This was different. He thought back to the blonde and the redhead at the bar and how the blonde had finally noticed him and given the go-ahead signal. He wished it had been another time. She was definitely the type of one-night stand he would enjoy.

"I'd like that."

She smiled at him and he grinned back. A few minutes later she hung on his arm as they walked down the dark street to his Prius. He helped her in and walked to the driver's side. Before he opened his door, he allowed himself a small pleasure.

He turned away so Connie wouldn't see it, and he chuckled to himself. Life was full of surprises as she would soon find out.

Chapter 7

The last person I wanted to see walked through my front door as Angel and I were discussing how to track down cyber-burglars.

Chris Johnson wore tight-fitting Chinos and a black body shirt hugged his sculpted physique. Ray-Bans rested on top of his black gelled hair, and he displayed a quiet confidence I hadn't noticed during the early days of our relationship.

I use the word *relationship* loosely as it was my purse, which was the object of his affection the first time we met. I was entering a department store downtown during the Christmas season, and he was trying to relieve me of said purse. I was an off duty cop at the time and my gun was in my purse, so I resorted to slamming his head in a revolving door seven or eight times.

Chris, meet Billie, the tough bitch; Billie, meet Chris the slime ball.

Chris, The Creep, as he became affectionately known, sued both me and the city, even though I was off duty at the time. A judge awarded him a million dollars of my money and the city ponied up another $500,000 to make him go away.

Fortunately for me, or maybe unfortunately, Chris declined to pursue his award against me because afterwards I saved his life. His attorney wasn't quite as generous, so I'm still making payments to him.

The unfortunate part of his generosity is that now he's always hanging around the office.

"Hi, Billie," Chris said. "Angel says you're working on a *B and E* and she thought I might be able to help you."

I rolled my eyes at Angel. She thinks he has a crush on me. I wasn't keen on her asking him for help, but maybe I *could* use someone with his insight. He says he's gone legit now and maybe that's why he's always hanging around. He doesn't have anything better to do.

"I hear your bad guy is on some line. Facepage, something or other."

"I take it you don't go online much." I should point out Chris is not the brightest bulb on the Christmas tree, which can work for or against me, depending on the circumstances.

"Nah, I used to have a computer once. Well, to be honest, I had a closet full of them. They're harder to fence than you would think."

"Most crooks don't fence things anymore Chris."

"Well, they're harder to pawn too. The cops make pawn shops take I.D. and that can be awkward. When I turned honest, I took 'em down to the Free Geek recycling store."

"Shit, Chris. I mean crooks sell all that stuff on eBay and Craigslist nowadays."

"I know that. I was just pulling your leg," he said. "Now tell me about these Facepage guys."

"Facebook!" I said. "Facebook!" This would be one of those times the dim bulb would work against me. I explained to him how I thought some online crooks were looking on Facebook to find people who wouldn't be home so they could rob them.

"Oh," he said, his head bobbing up and down as I scrolled down a Facebook page. "I can see where this would work to case a house all right. Of course you would want to make sure your mark was really out of town. Then you'd want to be sure no one is house sitting or feeding the dog. There's always the neighbor who is asked to check on things. Would be good to check and see if the neighbors are home during the day. If not, that's when you hit the place."

"How would you do that? During the day, I mean?"

"Find a place with plenty of cover. Lots of bushes or trees and a narrow side yard with a tall fence. Oh, and no alarm if you can help it. When I first started in the trade, I would open a window and find a safe place to hide outside. You know, to see if it's really hooked up. A lot of 'em aren't. If there's no noise and no cops, then I would come back later and take my time."

"I thought you guys passed on homes with alarms," I said.

"There's two types of guys who do *B and E's*," he said. "The old style guys like me, who try to make a living by being careful and planning a job out. And then you have the junkies, who smash and grab. Unless they're high, they'll avoid a house with an alarm.

"What good does it do to steal stuff if they can't get their fix because the cops bust in on them. If they're high, they don't worry about cops as much."

I smiled. Chris may not be up on the latest technology, but he could be helpful with the psychology. I wondered if my suspect was a druggie or a career criminal.

"How would you scout the neighborhood?" I asked.

"You gotta blend in," he said. "You can't stroll down a street without drawing attention."

"So how do you blend in?"

"Depends on the neighborhood. I once delivered free newspapers to a bunch of houses, but people stopped and asked me how much for a subscription." He frowned at the memory.

"It never occurred to me to check the prices. Heck, I just paid a dollar to open a metal newspaper stand and got a whole stack of them. At first I told people too much and then I quoted a price that must have been too low because people started wanting to buy subscriptions from me. I never did get a chance to find a house to steal from. Too many people would have remembered me anyway.

"I guess the best way is to pretend to be a worker of some kind. A friend of mine wore coveralls and put "City of Portland" magnet signs on his truck. I know another guy who bought an old heating and cooling truck."

"I met a lady who operates as a one-person neighborhood watch," I said. "She had a list of vendor's trucks that came into the neighborhood. She even had then categorized as to how long they stayed."

"Stick with the ones that come in for twenty minutes or less," he said. "There *are* workers who can't pass up an opportunity to come back and rob a sweet place, but you're telling me you think your crooks are finding their marks on Facepage, uh, Facebook?"

"Yeah," I said.

"If they're just interested in casing a joint they've already identified, they'll be in and out in less than five minutes," he said. "That's all it takes to determine whether a target is safe to hit and if there is anything worth stealing."

"So if a truck spends half a day or more working, it's probably not someone I should worry about," I said.

"Unless she's a meter reader for the gas company," Chis said. "I know a gal who sewed herself a meter reader uniform with a name tag and the gas company logo. She wandered from house to house pretending to read gas meters and finding houses to rob for her boyfriend. Both got into drugs and got busted. Too bad. It was a great scam."

Angel buzzed the intercom on my phone: "Billie? Have you got a minute? I found something I think is important."

Chris and I went to the reception area and drew up chairs on either side of Angel so we could view her computer monitor. I noticed Chris placed himself so he was facing the front door in case someone unexpected should show up. Like the police, I guessed. Old habits linger.

"I found some possible future victims our Facebook burglars might be watching," Angel said. "These people are currently out of town, and they just happen to be *friends* of some of the people who were robbed. She showed Chris one of the postings.

"How many people can see this?" he asked.

"All of their *friends*, about a hundred in this case," Angel said. "But this person allows anyone to view her page so it could be in the millions."

Chris grinned and shook his head. "Oh, if only I wasn't retired from the criminal life."

"This is Tamala Reich." Angel pointed at her profile photo. "She's twenty-five, single, and works at Leman and Schmidt law offices downtown as a legal aide, according to her profile."

"Nice looking chick," Chris said. "Might have to accidently bump into her during lunch and introduce myself."

I rolled my eyes. "Just stick with the investigation at hand. I don't need to hear what's on your sleazy mind."

"I wouldn't waste my time hitting her place," he said, after Angel scrolled through some of her photo albums."

"Why not?" Angel asked. "I found her address online using Google search. You could easily check out where she lives."

"Look at the pictures," he said. "She wears costume jewelry. The pictures in her living room are cheap prints you might find at Goodwill. Her bracelet is plastic, and she really seems to be into the party scene judging from all of these bar pictures with her friends. She probably spends all of her money on booze and food."

"I don't see our suspect, Daril, as one of her *friend*s," I said.

"Maybe he has more than one phony name," Angel said. "He could be going through online high school yearbooks and choosing names at random."

I nodded.

"How about this one, Emily Gunderson," Angel said, clicking the mouse to another Facebook page.

"Ugh," Chris said. "That face could flush the Taliban out of hiding."

I chuckled. "Her earrings look like diamonds, maybe a full carat on each side."

Chris squinted at the computer screen. "Can't tell, but I doubt it. Let's see some more."

Angel scrolled through her Timeline. Emily had three children, the oldest one a freshman in high school. She divorced three years ago, and was currently on vacation at the Oregon Coast with her kids. It was her first vacation in five years. Even I could see as a single mother, she spent all her money on her kids and basic survival. A trip to the beach spent at a friend's manufactured beach home was about what her budget could afford.

"Look at the furniture," Chris said. "A lot of kids stuff, a bean bag chair, bunk beds, toys all over the house. Nothing worth *my* time."

"Your time?" Angel said. "I thought you were retired."

"I am," he said. "But this Facebook page stuff could come in real handy if I decide to unretire."

"Here's another one, Sylvia O'Connor," Angel said. "They left town today. Not much to go on in the way of pictures. She only has one album with four pictures."

Chris scanned the profile and the photos and watched carefully as Angel scrolled through her Timeline. "That *profile* thing I saw earlier. Can you find hers?"

Angel found it and scrolled down a ways.

"Jackpot," Chris said. "She's a patron of the Portland Art Museum and she encourages her *friend*s to join. That means she donated money. Look here: she renewed her season tickets for the Oregon Ballet Performances. Can you go back to that picture of her hugging a friend?"

Angel found the picture and double clicked on it to enlarge it.

"See that painting on the wall?" Chris said. I'll bet that's an original because Sylvia wouldn't have a print on the wall if she's a patron of the art museum. It's a painting by a guy named Gianni

Larosa, called *David*. I know because I saw a picture of it in a catalogue of oil paintings a cell-mate of mine had. He specialized in art theft. Larosa's stuff goes for a minimum of a hundred thousand dollars."

I had him take a look at the Lucy Springer's Facebook page to see what he thought of their home as a target. He scrolled through the pages and frowned a few times. He read and reread Lucy's wall posts and read her daily posts from Maui.

"I can't tell," he finally said. "Not from the pictures; she doesn't have enough of them. They seem to be retired with no kids to support. The guy was a cop so at first glance I'd give him a wide pass."

"At first glance?" I said. "I sense there's *a but* in there somewhere."

"Yeah," Chris said. "I've never knocked over a cop. It would be sweet." He smiled. "Something I could brag about to my buddies."

"You think our perps would be tempted?" Angel asked.

"Maybe," he said. "It would depend on if the score was worth it. I'd have to case the place and see what's worth stealing. And a cop would surely have an alarm system, so I'd probably pass . . . unless . . ."

"Unless what?" I said.

"Unless I bunked with someone in prison who knew how to bypass alarm systems," Chris said.

"Have you?" Angel's eyes seemed to sparkle and she smiled at Chris.

"Of course. There's not a lot to do in prison. You either become better at your trade or you spend a lot of time exercising with weights. I did a little bit of both."

"So you think someone would check out the house in person?" I said.

"There's not enough information to tell us if they have anything of value. They might, but then there's the alarm system. I'd want to scope it out and see if it's something I could by-pass."

"I was just there and I've had an uneasy feeling ever since I saw a guy without a rear license plate on his Prius trying to sneak past me behind a UPS delivery truck."

"Prius?" Chris said. "I don't know too many guys in my line of work driving a Prius. And not having a license on your car would get you pulled over by a cop sooner or later. You wouldn't want that to happen with freshly stolen goods in your car, not to mention the occasional *B and E* tool stashed in the trunk."

"You're right. I've been focusing on the wrong person. I think it was the way he looked at me. I should be looking at the two guys in the UPS truck. Why does it take two guys to deliver in a neighborhood?"

"A delivery truck is a natural way to case a house," Chris said. "You drop off flowers at the front door or leave it in back somewhere and you're out of there in five minutes."

"Shit!" I said. "Joe Russell found an empty box in his back yard."

"What?" Angel asked.

"When I talked with one of the victims, he told me he had asked his neighbors if they had noticed anyone suspicious lurking around while he went on vacation. He said nobody noticed anything beyond a routine UPS truck in the neighborhood. Russell said the only other odd thing was an empty box he found in his back yard."

"I don't get it," Angel said.

"It was the UPS driver," I said. "The empty box was a prop. The guy pretended to take it around back so he could case Russell's house. And those two UPS drivers were parked right in front of the Springer house yesterday."

"Who are you calling?" Angel asked.

"The nosy neighbor across the street. I want her to check and see if there is an empty box in the Springer's back yard."

Chapter 8

Eric found it hard to concentrate on the Hologram Quarter Conceptual Computer design with Jimmer tramping into his bedroom every fifteen minutes wanting to rob the Springer house.

It amazed Eric how a computer the size of a quarter needed scores of blueprints that spread out would cover the entire floor of his bedroom. Eric could see creating the interactive hologram for a display screen and keyboard is what stumped Robert Roy. Finding a light source so small was a major obstacle. The simple computer design would fit into a small chip while accessing a virtual hard drive and its programs in the cloud.

By tapping on a holographic keyboard or putting a finger to the virtual display, computer commands would be sent back to the miniature computer and the appropriate action to the prompt would follow. It was a marvelous concept with one major problem.

Robert Roy's concept involved utilizing digital light techniques used in older projection TVs and some HDTVs. The DLP design used micro mirrors to spread the light over the huge TV screens, but the concept couldn't be developed inside the space of a quarter without causing overheating.

Instead of relying on rotating mirrors to make images, Eric devised a fractal pattern which would divert light into thousands of designs and pictures as the images were spun through the various patterns selected by the computer chips.

In theory it would work. But Eric did not have the resources to build the fractal structure let alone the computer. He dearly wished he could meet Robert Roy and often thought of returning the computer design to its inventor with his suggested improvements. He sighed and downloaded his latest improvements of Roy's design to a thumb drive.

"Are you still working on that thing," Jimmer said, again interrupting him. "We need to make up our minds which place to hit. It needs to happen tomorrow 'cause I'm almost out of my vitamins."

That's what Jimmer called his crack cocaine. Vitamins. As if it would have a soothing effect on Eric or something. Hell, Eric didn't know what went through Jimmer's mind half the time anymore. The guy he knew from grade school and this current version of Jimmer were two different people. Jimmer lied about everything now, and he would do whatever he had to do to get his vitamins.

"I think we need to go with the O'Connor place," Eric said at last.

"I know you do, but I want to hit the cop's house," Jimmer said. "I got this plan. I'm going to take a dump in the middle of his living room."

"Shit, you've lost your mind," Eric said. The last thing he wanted was to be associated with this inane stunt.

"I'm going to make a statement. Then I'll post a picture of it on Facebook."

"Yeah, post it on Facebook and go to jail," Eric said.

"I won't be in the picture," he said. "No one will know I did it."

"You're high. It'll be on your Facebook page, idiot."

"I'm not getting high," he said. "I'm getting well."

"We're going to do the O'Connor house. We hit the bedroom, score on her jewelry and you've got enough to keep you in vitamins until you're ready for rehab."

Jimmer pouted. "I want to do the cop. No cop, no rehab."

"We can do the cop later," Eric said. "Give the neighbors a chance to forget about the UPS truck and the mouthy guy who argued with a fireman and the little old lady. Besides, that hill is too steep. It wouldn't be a good idea for the escape plan I have in mind."

"It would work," Jimmer said. "You don't think I have any brains. You think you're the only one who can plan this stuff. Well, go ahead. You do the old biddy's house. I'll do the cops place and we'll see who's smarter."

Eric sighed again. Maybe he should let his friend get caught. It might work out for the best.

People say I can be stubborn and they may be right. But this time I had a premonition, and I wasn't going to let anyone talk me out of it. Certainly not Chris or Angel.

I was sure the Facebook burglars were going to hit the Springer house sometime in the next couple of days. I'd spent the wee hours of the morning sitting on top of my sleeping bag among lizards, spiders, and probably mice in a designated green space on the west side of Miller Road. Across the street was the house that abutted the Springer residence, the next street over.

Chris said many robberies occur during the daylight hours. When I told him how it would be impossible to get by the nosy Sally Brown, he shrugged. "Any nosy neighbors on the back side of her home?"

There weren't. Chris suggested the burglars would simply enter from the rear through a neighbor's yard, climb the fence and break in the back door.

"But I think they'll go for that Sylvia dame's house," he had said. "The payoff is better. The place sits back by itself at the end of the block so there aren't any neighbors who might hear broken glass or even see a truck pull in the driveway."

Angel had agreed with Chris. "We should stake out the O'Connor place. I'll bring my designer Pink Lady .38 Special for protection."

Although I was sure I was at the right place, after four hours of staking out the ex-cop's house, I was tired, hungry, and itchy from sitting among the grass and weeds. I decided to head home for a quick hot shower and to give my butt a chance to uncramp from sitting on hard ground.

Sally Brown *had* found the telltale empty box on the Springer's back porch and her discovery told me I was on the right track. Angel and Chris weren't moved enough to join me in my stakeout, Angel going so far as to agree to go with Chris to check out the O'Connor home.

"Hey babe," Steve said, as he swept through my front door. It was the second time in a week he had worn a suit. It was blue with a faint bluish pinstripe design. Usually he might wear a sport coat and dress shirt without a tie. Today's red power tie looked expensive.

"What's the occasion?" I asked. "Are we getting married or something? Is there a funeral I forgot?"

"I just bought this suit and I recalled the last time I dressed up I got lucky. So I thought maybe it could encourage a repeat performance."

"That's it? No lunch or dinner or sweet talk? You think all have to do is blink those big brown eyelashes at me and I'll tumble into bed with you?"

"It's been known to happen," he said.

"Sorry Hon, I've got a stakeout I have to be at in less than an hour."

He turned his head at me sideways and grinned.

"No way," I said. "Maybe you can handle a daily double, but it puts me out of business."

"You could help me celebrate," he said.

"Oh?"

He smiled, displaying his perfect teeth. "I've been assigned to a joint task force with the FBI. We're investigating a series of missing women in the Portland-Seattle area. I'm meeting with a Seattle detective and a couple of Feds later."

"Big case?" I asked.

"Seven women, either missing or found dead in the last two years," he said. "One survived, but she died before she could be much help. We're starting almost from scratch. Most of the early work will be research and cross-correlating leads we've developed thus far."

"Sounds like fun," I said. "So is this why you bought the suit?"

"Yeah." He brushed lint off his sleeve. "I don't want to play second fiddle to the Feds. This should be our case, and I don't want them thinking I'm their glorified coffee runner. The suit helps with my credibility."

"I'd love to be a spectator in that pissing match," I said.

"I have other plans for you."

He pulled me into him. His cologne scent was a mixture of champagne, key lime pie, and lemon crème. He smelled good enough to eat, but I suspected he wanted *me* to be the main course.

"Sorry, you have to go. I have to go to work and so do you."

"I'll be available later this afternoon if you change your mind," he said. "I've arranged a standing deal with the manager of the Modera Hotel in exchange for some security advice."

Woof. I wanted him and he knew it. But I also wanted a paycheck and a bonus, and I felt I was close to getting it if I kept my boobs in their holster.

"We'll see how things go." I pushed him out the door as Chris and Angel came up the front steps.

"Hi Steve," Angel said. "You're looking hot today." Her eyes met mine and a wry smile crossed her face. "Did we interrupt something?"

Steve smirked. "Almost . . . but she has things to do." He blew me a kiss, got in his car, and drove off.

"We've got big news." Angel closed the door behind us. Today she was testing the fashionistas by wearing a transparent black blouse over a purple bra, with a purple dress, and spandex bronze body nylons with splotches of black tattoos. She had transformed her hair from brown with blonde highlights to raven black with streaks of purple and orange. She added sparkly lilac eye shadow and frosted mocha lipstick to draw attention to her face.

Chris paled by comparison. He wore gray slacks, a gray knit shirt, and black dress shoes. He held in his hands a brown box.

"I'll bite," I said, "what's in the carton?"

"We found a clue to support our case for the O'Connor digs," he said.

"And it's in the box?" I asked.

"Sort of," Angel said. "We went over this morning to check it out. Chris says it would be an easy mark for a crook."

"The alarm system sucks," Chris said. "It's ancient. Should have been replaced twenty years ago. I by-passed it in less than a minute. We went in and out without a hitch."

"Oh my god! You didn't steal something? Is it in the box?"

They stared absurdly at me and laughed. "It *is* the box," Angel said. "We found it on the back porch and it was empty like at the Springer house."

"But they didn't need a prop," Chris said. "They could have backed a UPS truck into the driveway and unloaded half the house without anyone noticing. The lots on that street are huge. The next nearest house is half a block away."

"And there are trees and bushes everywhere," Angel said. "The driveway goes back a hundred feet. Plenty of privacy if you want to rob someone."

"When did you two decide to do the *B and E*?" I asked.

Angel crinkled her nose. "After you ran off to do surveillance on the Springer house. Chris wanted to go last night, but I wasn't about to go into that dark house with *him*. Even with my new snub-nose revolver. It would just be too creepy."

"So we met early this morning," Chris said. "She had some real expensive jewelry lying around, and I'll bet there was even better stuff in the wall safe."

"You need to forget about the safe," Angel said.

"You should talk," Chris said. "She was in the lady's closet trying on all of her evening dresses and then she got into her bracelets. If I'd brought my stuff, I could have opened that safe in a couple of minutes.

Great. Somehow I got Bonnie and Clyde together. "Christ, if that place *does* get hit, your fingerprints are all over it."

"Oh, Chris brought latex gloves for us to wear," Angel said. She opened her purse to show them to me.

"Is that yours?" In her purse I spotted an antique gold bracelet with exquisite gemstones mounted between intricate etchings. "It can't be yours; it looks too damn expensive."

"Oops," Angel said. "I forgot to take it off and accidently left the house with it. We were halfway home when I noticed it on my wrist."

"Give it to me." I took the bracelet from her and wiped off her fingerprints and mine with a hankie, then wrapped it in the hankie and tucked it in my purse. "If she took something then you must have too," I said to Chris.

"It was an accident too," he said, pulling a Rolex out of his pocket.

I shook my head. "I have two choices. I can call the cops and have you two arrested . . ."

"Uh, I'd be interested in the other choice," Chris said.

"You two are going to cover the Springer house, and I'm going back to return these items."

"Billie, don't you think you should wipe my prints off the watch," Chris said.

"Maybe," I said. "But if I do you'll owe me big. You corrupted Angel."

"She's no angel if you ask me. I only grabbed the Rolex on the way out when I saw the bracelet on her wrist."

I sent the partners in crime to stakeout the Springer house after getting them to promise they would not go inside. Angel grumbled about sitting in a field in her dress and grabbed a couple of blankets, then grumbled some more about having to lie in the grass with Chris, who seemed amused by the whole thing.

After they left, not relishing having to break into the O'Connor place, I had a longing for Steve and thought about calling him back.

Chapter 9

Eric and Jimmer rode up to the back side of an old Portland English cottage on odd looking bicycles. Their two story target house, with its masonry chimney and exterior, and rolled thatch-style roof, might well have been in England as Portland.

Eric's plan was to use two delivery bicycles they'd borrowed the day before from a local soup selling business. They had removed all of the racks and the heater that kept the soup warm from a big-boxed three-wheeler and similarly dismantled everything on the front-loaded tub of the sleek two-wheeler, built for speed, or maybe special deliveries, Jimmer guessed.

The business advertising on the sides of each bicycle gave them legitimate reasons for being in the neighborhood, delivering soup door-to-door, if anyone noticed them. Only in Portland, the bicycle capital of America, would this ruse not attract attention. They parked the bicycles near the front porch.

Jimmer checked his watch. It was 9:30 a.m. He held a small battering ram and a crowbar he'd brought with him, watched Eric untangle the wires on his alarm buster gadget he called his gizmo, and wondered why his best bud would risk jail for him. He felt guilty involving Eric and often thought about going out on his own. He knew if he did, he'd wind up on the street and probably die with a needle in his arm.

He wanted to quit the drugs, but the urge would overtake him and he would forget his friend and all his good intentions in an attempt to smother the thoughts and feelings of his leftover childhood. His missing dad, his drinking mother, and her boyfriends who cycled through their lives leaving them both emotionally bereft.

The beatings, the drugs, the sexual abuse. It all became too much for Jimmer and so he took to drugs to survive. Thankfully Eric had been there for him or he might have killed himself when he was 16. Eric persuaded his mother to let Jimmer move in with them, but that only lasted for a few months. When Lois found out about his drug use, she booted him back home to his fucked up mother and the men she tried to use to fix her.

But Eric stuck with him. Encouraged him. Still sticking, still encouraging. Jimmer knew he was damaged. *Not good enough. A bum who will never amount to anything*, as his mother and her countless boyfriends always reminded him.

What good would rehab do? It would only open the floodgates of mental anguish which would surely kill him. The drugs took away those feelings. Made him feel good about himself, if only for a while. Drugs kept him alive.

The drugs and Eric were his life preservers in a sea of loneliness.

"Ready?" Eric said.

"Huh?" Jimmer looked at his buddy, smiling at him with the gizmo in his hands. "Yeah, I guess. Maybe we shouldn't do this."

"You say that every time. Let's do it."

"Yeah," Jimmer said. "Let's do it." He took the small battering ram and smacked it in the sweet spot where the deadbolt held the back door tight. It resisted the first two times, but on the third try Jimmer put his weight into it and the door crashed open.

Eric raced down the hall and quickly removed the face plate to the alarm box. Jimmer watched as Eric hooked two clips to some bare wires and punched a button on his creation. A series of numbers flashed in his hands as the minicomputer searched for the correct password.

His bud's invention first looked for traces of memory of past password selections, the easiest and fastest way to bust the alarm. That took seconds, but if it didn't work, Eric would resort to trying thousands of combinations, usually another twenty seconds would be plenty of time.

But shit, this was an antique, Jimmer thought. He had expected a more elaborate system in this expansive home. He continued counting: thirty seven, thirty eight. Shit, they only had maybe another twenty seconds and then they'd have to think about aborting.

"It's slow," Eric said. "This old system doesn't respond the way the new ones will. I have no idea if it's even going to acknowledge the password if I find it."

"You can do it," Jimmer said. "I know you can."

Eric smiled at him and pulled a couple of wires from his pocket. "I'll just bypass the relay," he said. "I shouldn't have even messed with my toy. I should have just bypassed it since it's so old."

"We're running out of time," Jimmer said.

Eric took a deep breath and was about to unhook his gizmo when it beeped. "We're in," he said. "It worked."

"Never doubted you, bud. Now let's see what goodies they left for us."

"We'll go out the front," Eric reminded him. "Just a couple of guys making a living selling soup."

"Hopefully, twenty-four carat soup." Jimmer laughed at his pun.

Angel and Chris arrived at the green space at 10:35 a.m. and trudged a hundred yards through wet grass and gopher holes so as not to be seen. Angel laid out the blankets and she and Chris sat on them and began peering through two sets of binoculars.

Angel was damp and bitchy and Chris wondered why she was pretending to smoke a cigarette. Then he remembered something Billie had said about Angel quitting smoking after 20 years, and how sometimes she forgot herself and lifted a pretend cigarette to her mouth.

He chuckled to himself. "Want a light?"

"Shut up!" She slugged him on the arm and it hurt, but he was having too much fun to notice. "You're the one who got us here."

"Maybe if I'd had a cigarette, I wouldn't have lifted the bracelet," she said. "Besides, you're not getting paid so why are you here?"

"Maybe I want to get into the P.I. racket. This is good experience. Maybe Billie will take me on as an associate."

"We're called operatives. You have a crush on her, don't you?"

"Nah. I might have once because she saved my life and all, but I've got my eye on another gal. Like I said, I want to learn the business." Chris lifted his binoculars to his eyes. "I thought I saw something. Guess not."

"This is a wild goose chase," Angel said. "We both know the O'Connor house is the sweeter score."

I was so angry with Chris and Angel I could have spit. I was sure the burglars would hit the Springer house while I was busy covering their butts. I was still thinking dirty thoughts when I passed by the house on King Drive in my little red MG. There was a vacant house behind the O'Connor place, and I thought about cutting through its yard to the O'Connor back door, but why bother? Angel and Chris were right. I could pull right into the driveway and I doubt anyone would notice.

My next concern was how to bypass the alarm system. Chris gave me a quick tutorial. He said in a worse-case scenario, I should run up to the bedroom, drop the merchandise, and take off. It would take three to five minutes for the cops to show.

I turned into the driveway under tall Douglas-firs, beginning to feel calmer about not being seen, when two guys flushed from the front of the house like pheasants from tall grass. It caught me off guard because they rode delivery bicycles. The unofficial motto in this town is *Keep Portland Weird* and these two lived up to the billing.

"What the hell?" I said.

"What the hell?" the husky one yelled as he veered around my hood.

They zigzagged past my car and peddled like mad to the street. The suddenness of the spectacle startled me and I popped the clutch, stalling my MG. I tried to restart it, but the ignition whined.

I recognized the bicyclists as the delivery guys from the UPS truck in front of the Springer's house two days ago. The one who swore at me was built kind of chunky with a carefree attitude, laughing as he sped by on a three-wheeled bicycle with an attached yellow trailer. The sign on the side said *Soup Cycle*. The other, a scared stringy thin guy, was right on his friend's heels.

I got out of my car and ran to the curb in time to see them hot-tailing it down Southwest Salmon Street and heading for the downtown area, where in a matter of minutes they would lose themselves among the workday clamor.

I ran back to my car, said a little prayer to Myrtle, punched the clutch, put my foot on the gas pedal for a two-count and forcefully turned the ignition key. R-R-R-Vroom and Myrtle started up. I worked the gear to reverse and slowly backed up, not wanting to stall again.

Chris and Angel had been right. I thought about calling them, but that would have to wait. I was in hot pursuit and anyway they needed to pay for their crimes a little longer. I turned down Salmon Street and spotted the two cyclists about seven blocks ahead going 30 miles-per-hour downhill.

I raced down a hill and swooped under a low hanging sky bridge that connected a parking garage with the Multnomah Athletic Club. I blew a stop sign at 20th Avenue and a guy in a red pickup hit his brakes, laying rubber in the intersection, and blasted me with his horn. Myrtle shuddered as I negotiated a panic swerve, and I was sideswiped with a litany of swearing I hadn't heard since I was on the police bureau.

The momentary distraction made me lose sight of the guys on the soup cycles. "Shit, they must have turned somewhere," I muttered.

Except now, I'd picked up a tail. The red pickup, a shiny new Dodge Ram with Devil Horns on the front chrome grill, roared its muffler as the driver, a big ugly guy with black slicked-down hair, swore out his window at me.

I flipped him off and crept down another block, frantically looking for any sign of the soup cycles, with the guy in the pickup almost kissing my bumper.

I had to stop for a red light on Eighteenth and used the opportunity to look north and south. It was a two-way road separated in the middle by light rail tracks and a Max station on a brick island to the left of me. There was no sign of the soup cycles.

The pickup also stopped. The guy getting out of his truck and walking toward me. I hit the gas pedal and as the light changed and roared into a 20-mile-per hour school zone, the red brick walls of Lincoln High School whizzing by me. Luckily, all students were in classes.

I could see the bicycle bandits about three blocks ahead now, but the guy in the Dodge Ram swerved alongside me and shook his fist. We jockeyed for position on the two-lane-one way street before I managed to jet ahead and cut in front of him. I lost him at an intersection when pedestrians jaywalked in front of him and the light went red as he waited for them.

By the time I approached Thirteenth Avenue, I'd lost sight of them again. I slowed and scanned the grounds of a church and a large masonry building, with pink-tinted windows and a large dome on top, to see if my suspects had ditched their bikes.

I was at the core of downtown Portland now, and I turned my head back and forth, like I was watching a tennis match, looking to see if the burglars were trying to hide in a parking lot or behind a stopped truck offloading a delivery.

On Tenth Avenue, I was sure I'd lost them. On a whim, I took a hard left on the one-way four-lane street and scanned the area, hoping the pissed-off guy behind me had gotten it out of his system.

I reached the Multnomah County Central Library at Yamhill and began to experience a churning in my gut when a metallic flash caught my eye. The three-story Georgian-style brick and sandstone building occupies a full city block. There are about ten oversized arched windows, three center ones with mini balconies, on the second level. A dozen steps lead to massive maple doors at the front entrance.

A flash of chrome radiated from some greenery on the south side frontage. I swerved over two lanes, resulting in more horns bleating at me, and pulled into a motorcycle parking spot.

I hopped out of my MG and ran over to a wheelchair walkway leading to the front doors. It zigzagged into a small patio area behind a large birch tree and some rhododendron bushes. The two abandoned soup cycles were parked in the alcove. I opened the back of the large trailer and discovered their loot: a small painting, a smattering of trinkets and jewelry, two handguns, an iPad, some cash, and more clutter in the back of the box.

I walked back to my car where the guy from the pickup stood, kicking Myrtle's side door with his big shit-kicking boots. I grabbed at his black leather jacket, and he spun on me and sneered.

"You shouldn't be driving lady. I just got my rig out of the body shop and you almost crashed it again."

"My mistake and I'm truly sorry," I said. "I'm a P.I. and I'm chasing some bad guys, so if you'll accept my apology I'll be on my way." I took a small revolver and a switchblade from my purse in the front seat.

The guy staggered back. "Sorry Lady, I was just so upset. I just got it out of the shop."

I also grabbed the Rolex and the bracelet, still wrapped in my hanky, and walked back to the bicycles. The Dodge Ram, license plate B-RUDE, roared away and I made a mental promise to Myrtle to take care of him later. I tossed Angel and Chris's ill-gotten gains into the soup cycle's trailer. Then I stabbed the three tires on the soup tri-cycle and the two on the smaller blue delivery bicycle.

I walked up the steps to the library, the gun tucked into the back of my blue jeans, and I pulled the tail of my striped blouse out to hide it. The switchblade went into my pocket. Inside, I entered a great marbled hall with high ceilings and tables and books everywhere.

This was not going to be easy.

"Are you looking for something . . . or someone?"

I turned and met a carbon copy of me, except with copper hair instead of blonde. About five-nine, she had a trim if somewhat muscular figure. She wore unflattering brown slacks and matching shirt with a brass badge, and a big gun on her hip. A name badge said *Brenda, Multnomah County Sheriff's Deputy*. She wore a blue topaz stud in the cheek of a pleasant if not pretty face.

"Did you see two anxious men, Laurel and Hardy types, about nineteen or twenty years of age, run by?"

Brenda smiled. "Just a minute ago. They went up on two. What's your deal?"

"I'm private." I showed her an I.D. I always carry in my pocket. She nodded and handed it back.

"What's up?" she said. All business now, her fingers on the handheld radio rover clipped to her shoulder, ready to call it in.

"Those two guys just robbed a house up on King Drive," I said. "I've been looking for them on an unsolved and literally stumbled upon them coming out of the house. The stolen loot is outside in two stolen soup cycles."

She looked at me, puzzled. "Are they armed?"

"I don't think so. Don't know for sure."

"I'll call it in. You stay here. I don't want any trouble in here."

I'll be quiet as a cat." I was already halfway up the steps to the second floor. "Just want to keep tabs on them until help arrives."

I should have asked her how many exits there were in this place. I spotted the skinny worried perp at a computer station and moved in quietly until I was directly behind him.

"Have you reserved that computer, young man?" My voice was autocratic and formal. "I think someone else has signed up for it." I hoped he hadn't seen me at the house long enough to recognize me. I knew his buddy got a good look when we almost collided in the driveway.

"Uh, sorry," he said. "I just thought it wasn't being used." He stood up and turned, intending to move past me.

"Sorry young man." I grabbed his arm. "We have procedures. You will have to come with me and fill out the proper forms downstairs. We must have records of all users."

"But I wasn't here more than two minutes. I didn't even have time to log on." He looked like a deer in the headlights and for an instant I felt sorry for him. Then he bolted. I chased after him down the stairs. He took them six at a time and I'd spotted him fifty feet, plenty of time for him to make the front door.

A brown blur came at him from the sideline, and I watched dumbfounded as Brenda and the skinny kid rolled across the floor, Brenda hugging his legs. She whipped out a nylon cord, her knee on his back, and wrapped the make-do bracelet around his wrists like a calf roper at the rodeo.

The husky kid, stood nearby with a look of shock on his face. I skidded up to him on the slick marble floor and pinned him against a wall. "You got any more of those bracelets?"

As we waited for the cops to send a transport car, I questioned the two Facebook burglars. The one called Eric listened carefully, jerking his head occasionally when I told him I was onto him for stealing from a client of mine.

"You actually tracked us down using Facebook?" he said. "I didn't think the cops were that smart or I would have used better precautions."

"I need to know if you've kept any of the things you stole from my client on Southwest Jackson Street," I said.

Eric's eyes lit up. "The ditsy gal who tells everybody how rich she is? Once we read some of her posts, we knew we had to teach her a lesson. And it sounds like she could afford it the way she bragged."

"Her name is Mar," I said. "She's an old high school chum of mine. Her husband developed a new computer system and you stole it. She wants it back."

"Really?" His eyes narrowed. "You represent Robert Roy?"

"That's why I chased you for the last mile."

"Would you do me a favor? There's a USB drive in my pocket. Would you get it out for me?"

I was skeptical about this. Anything on him was evidence. My reluctance must have shown.

"It has Robert's computer designs on it. It's on my home computer too, but this way you can get it to him. It's a really cool idea, and I'd like to make sure it doesn't get lost."

He turned his side toward me. I patted him down to make sure there were no needles and tweezed the memory stick out of his jeans pocket with two fingers. I didn't want the thing to get lost in the system either.

"Keep it to yourself," I said. "I'm breaking the law."

"I won't say a word." He let out a deep sigh, as if releasing a huge burden. "I thought about returning it myself, but didn't want to get caught. Tell him to check out my improvements; they should solve his overheating problems."

I palmed the memory stick as two sheriff's deputies arrived and took Eric and Jimmer to a patrol car. What a waste, I thought, as Eric disappeared into the back seat.

"Nice blindside tackle," I said to Brenda as she returned from the squad car.

"I used to play football with the boys at the park on Saturday afternoons," she said. "The Eric kid told me they've been finding their victims on Facebook and you tracked them down."

"I got a little lucky, but yeah, we had it narrowed to two sites they might hit. My assistant tried to tell me it would be the house up here. I was focused on another location. The only reason I went up there was to follow up on some, uh, scouting she had done earlier this morning."

I remembered Angel, with Chris, still sitting on the dirty, wet, buggy field in her new dress. "I should call her and tell her she was right."

"Would you like to debrief?" Brenda asked. "I'm due for a break and there's a pretty good coffee shop across the street."

"My adrenaline rush seems to have fizzled," I said. "I could use some caffeine."

Angel could sit in the field a little longer. They're both lucky I was able to add the bracelet and Rolex to the loot Eric and Jimmer stole. No harm done. I figured the crooks would have taken them it they'd been there to take.

Chapter 10

Trixie lost control last night and now his life would never be the same. His date with Connie hadn't gone the way he had planned and now another of his victims had surfaced. He sat up in bed, staring at the newspaper headline: *Woman's Body Found by Hikers*.

"It's always either hikers or dogs," he muttered under his breath. Bodies weren't usually discovered by law enforcement searchers, he knew. But dogs being walked were the number one reason bodies were unearthed and hikers or hunters seemed to be a close second.

The story said Christine Crawford had been discovered five days ago. Why did the police sit on the story so long? He mashed up the newspaper and threw the wad across the room. He thought he hadn't left any clues. Yet the tremors within him forecasted the possibility of trouble.

He needed to kill again to regain control. He couldn't stop thinking about that nosy P.I. he had added to his possible date list. Why had she shown up at the same time he was scouting Mary Johansen's house? He had picked Mary as a replacement in case Connie hadn't worked out, and quickly abandoned that plan after the P.I. made him.

"Hi sleepyhead," Connie said. She held a tray in her hands with coffee and a plate of bacon and scrambled eggs. "I figured anyone who worked as hard as you did last night would be hungry this morning."

"It's late," he said, looking at his watch.

"I called in well," she said. "I felt too good to go to work."

"I should get going," he said. But he stopped short when he became aware he was naked under the sheets.

"Not shy are you?" She set the tray on an end table near her bed. "Not after last night, I hope. You were amazing."

"You . . . you didn't mind me being a little rough?"

"I like a little adventure," she said. "I *am* a little sore and I have a bruise or two."

When she turned and faced him head on, he saw a bruise on her neck. "I'm sorry. Sometimes I get a little carried away."

"You told me when to say no," she said. "I didn't mind. It was exciting and gave me a rush. I've been looking for a little spark in my life for a long time. I thought you might be *it*."

"Why would you think that?" Not having been in a position of dating a woman he had planned to kill, Trixie felt somewhat awkward and definitely out of control. Because he remained cautious, lest he might say or do the wrong thing, he thought he might have come across as a bit dull.

"Well, aside from your ruggedly handsome face and your well-proportioned physique, she said, laughing, "there's something about your eyes. They seem worldly, like they've seen and been through a lot in life. I pictured you as some kind of adventurer."

If she only knew. His stress started to melt away even as he thought he could take her right here, right now and do whatever he wanted. All he would have to do is go to the trunk of his car and get out his extermination kit, come back and bind her mouth, arms and legs with plastic cable straps and the fun could begin.

"I burnt the bacon and the eggs are runny," Connie said. "Would you like to go out to brunch instead?"

She leaned over him on the bed and her nylon robe slipped open. She was lean and muscular, and her milky-white thighs climbed up and over him as he closed his eyes and lost himself in her scent.

"Maybe later." He pulled her cool body onto his.

Brenda Towne joined me with her freshly brewed Cappuccino and a Hummingbird Muffin. We sat at a small table in a place called Case Study Coffee, presumably because it was across from the library.

I sipped from my Caffe Mocha and took stock of her. Her copper hair seemed to shine in the brightly lit area, but I was fascinated by the bluish gemstone stud in her cheek.

"You like it?" She touched it playfully with an index finger. "I got it last week. I wanted to be more approachable since I'm working closely with so many people at the library."

"The sheriff's department allows that sort of thing? I know the Portland Police Bureau doesn't. Not on the job."

"I wouldn't wear it on active duty." Brenda said. "But I got permission for when I'm on library duty. There's not much chance of getting into a fight or anything. In fact, today was the first time I had to take down a suspect. I usually wind up babysitting homeless people who come in to use the bathrooms. Other than that I'm a presence. If I run into trouble, I call for backup."

"How long have you been working the library beat?" I asked.

"Too damn long," she said. "I need a chance to prove my chops and they won't give it to me."

"How long have you been on the job" I asked.

"Two years next month. I was only supposed to do this for a couple months, but I got into a beef with my commander and I've been exiled. I think he's hoping I'll quit."

"Don't," I said. "You've got the makings of a good cop."

"I think so. What's your story? What made you go private?"

I told her how I roughed up Chris Johnson by rattling his head in a department store's revolving door when he tried to steal my purse, the resulting lawsuit for police brutality, and my forced resignation.

"I read about that in the paper," she said. "Weren't you off duty?"

"I was doing some last minute Christmas shopping." I took a healthy swig of my coffee. "Ironically, he dropped his lawsuit against me because he thinks I saved his life a while back. Now he hangs around my office all the time. My assistant, Angel, thinks he has a crush on me."

"You can get a restraining order," Brenda said between sips. "Sounds like a wacko."

"He's harmless enough, but I seem to attract weirdos. If I get rid of him, another will just pop up to take his place. With him, I know what I've got."

"I guess," Brenda said. "At least you've got a man hanging around. I get pretty lonely some nights."

"You've got to be kidding. You're having a hard time meeting a guy?"

"I'm too intimidating for a lot of men, and I don't want to date cops. I get enough hardline attitude and macho bullshit on the job."

"I kind of miss it." I thought of Steve and the crap he used to give me when we were partners. Now that I wasn't on the police bureau any longer, I needed some of that macho bullshit.

"You ever thought of moonlighting?" I asked.

"I do some private security work sometimes, but it's Dullsville."

"If I ever need to hire an operative . . .?"

"Call me." She handed me her business card. "But try to make it interesting."

"I'm not sure what I'd pay. It would depend on the job."

"I don't care about that so much."

"We should get together sometime and tour the bars," I said. "Find a nice man for you."

"I wouldn't mind that either," she said. "You're not seeing anyone?"

"I am, but I'd just be your wing woman. I think Steve would understand."

She shook her head. "I've never known a man yet who did."

"What's wrong with you lately?" Chris chewed on a piece of straw and raised his hand to shield his eyes. The sun was directly overhead and they'd been sitting on Angel's blanket in a green space for two-and-a-half-hours waiting to be relieved by Billie.

Angel had been lost in thought for the past thirty minutes and Chris was frustrated. He wanted her to talk to him, but she barely noticed he was alive and when she did she always said something snide to him.

"Man troubles," she said after a moment of silence. "Earl's been avoiding me lately and he won't tell me why."

"Is that so bad?" Chris said. "I never thought he was good enough for you."

Angel turned at him and someplace between a tear and a smile she said, "Thank you. I'm starting to believe you might be right."

Good, she was talking to him now. Chris wanted to get all the dirt. "When did he start avoiding you?"

She sighed. "I might as well tell you. Billie's not going to want to talk with me for a while. She and I went to Jakes Crawfish a couple weeks ago. I saw Earl outside after we got our table, and he was with a woman."

"What did Billie say about it?" Chris asked.

"She didn't see him, and I was too embarrassed to tell her."

"Maybe she was a cousin or something." Chris wondered why he said that. The sooner Earl was out of the picture, the better.

"I don't think so. I excused myself to go to the powder room and followed them. He grabbed her ass twice and kissed her full on the lips before she got into his car."

"You were stalking them?"

"Shit. What would you do if you saw your girlfriend messing around with another guy?"

She pulled at the blanket, trying to get off its corner, where the wet grassy field surged toward her. She took a tissue from her purse and dabbed at the beginning of tears in her eyes.

"I wouldn't like it," he said. "Did you confront him?"

"*Hell, yes.* Of course he denied it. He said it must have been someone who looked like him."

"Fat, bald, with a naked lady tattoo on his arm?" Chris said. "How many guys fit that bill?"

Angel slugged Chris in the arm. "He's not bald or fat, he's a bit husky and his hair is starting to thin a bit. And he wore long sleeves that night so his tattoo wasn't showing."

Women, Chris thought. "Did he stick with that story?"

"He finally admitted being with her, but he said it was a case he was working on and he wouldn't be able to see me until it was finished."

"And you bought that? I still don't believe he's a P.I. He's a tow truck driver and uses that line to pick up chicks instead of cars." Chris waited for her to slug him again, but she turned away and he realized she was crying. "Hey, I'm sorry. I didn't mean to hurt your feelings."

"He asked me to trust him and I told him I would. But I don't think I can. That woman is all I think about day and night. He's sleeping with her, I just know it."

"There, there." He put his arm around her shoulder and she shocked him by leaning into his embrace. "I'm sure things will work out." Now he had his arm full around her in a hug and she didn't pull away.

"That man's got me acting crazy. First, I break into a ritzy home and steal an expensive bracelet, and now I'm letting you console me."

"Yeah," Chris said. "Crazy."

"I think I took that bracelet because I'm pissed at him. I'm acting out. Billie will never forgive me. I put her license and reputation in jeopardy."

"Well . . . her P.I. license, maybe, but she does a pretty good job on her own with her reputation."

"That's true," Angel said. "Chris? Will you do me a favor?"

"What?"

"Will you kiss me?"

Chris tried to act nonchalant by picking up another a piece of straw and sticking it in his mouth to suck on. He swept a few strands of weeds from the plaid blanket, taking his time before answering her.

"Would this be just to get back at Earl?"

"Absolutely. You don't think I find you the least bit attractive do you?"

"You don't?"

"No, and besides, I know you have a crush on Billie."

"I do?"

"It's written all over your face."

"Angel?"

"What?"

"Yes, I will kiss you to get back at Earl. It will be my pleasure."

She leaned into him and kissed him passionately. He knew makeup sex was really good, but now he was wondering how good revenge sex might be. Before he could find out, Angel's cell phone rang and she stopped to answer it. He spread out the blanket better so they could lie down on it when she got off the phone and pulled her from a sitting position to lie beside him as she talked.

"No kidding," she said. "Okay. I've got a situation to wrap up here and then we'll head back." Angel pouted at Chris after she put her phone in her purse. "Billie says she caught the Facebook burglars."

"Is that right?" he said.

"Yeah, she even said she wouldn't have caught them if it weren't for us."

"Did she find them at the O'Connor house?"

"Yep," Angel said.

"So why are you upset?"

"I don't know. I guess I'm confused. Billie didn't sound mad at us. In fact, she sounded happy."

They lie side by side on the damp blanket, looking into each other's eyes. Angel gave him a wary look. He was losing her.

"We were talking about that rotten scoundrel, Earl," Chris said.

"Yeah." She sighed and kissed him.

Chris smiled. Revenge sex. Damn, he was on a roll.

Chapter 11

It had been two hours since I called Angel with the news of the capture of the Facebook burglars, and she still hadn't returned to the office. I decided to call Mar and set up an appointment with her and her husband at three o'clock to give them the good news.

I was thinking about tracking down my absent assistant when she phoned me with some story about her dress being full of grass and stickers and having to go home and change clothes. Chris was with her and they wanted to eat lunch before she returned.

Not much was going on so I started playing games on Facebook. I decided to quit, because one game wanted me to pay to play and it wasn't cheap. As I closed out the page, I noticed the newspaper I'd brought in from the front porch. The lead story was about a woman's body found by hikers. Her name was Christine Crawford. She was young, blonde, and very dead.

As I read the story, I realized this woman might be one of the victims of a serial killer that Steve and his FBI friends were trying to track down. It was hard for me to fathom what goes on inside a serial killer's mind. I knew the murders were usually a result of an abusive childhood and that somehow the killer was trying to assert control in his or her life.

On a whim, I decided to see if Christine Crawford had a Facebook page. It took me a few minutes to decipher the Facebook search parameters, but eventually I found her page. She hadn't activated her privacy controls so her posts were visible to me, as was the high school she graduated from. There was even a map I clicked on to find she lived somewhere in inner Northeast Portland.

The last entry on her Timeline was more than thirty days ago, coincidentally, the day she went missing: *"Jeff had to cancel at the last minute, so I'm going hiking by myself,"* she wrote.

I scrolled further down until I saw an earlier post: *"Jeff and I are going to hike the Marquam Trail to Council Crest Tuesday. It's a moderate hike, about 6 miles. We are trying to get in shape for some steeper hikes next month. Most of it goes through Marquam Nature Park above the Veteran's Hospital in the West Hills."*

I read back through her postings for a while, but most of them were of fairly inane stuff. However, some of the twenty or so pictures she posted of herself were mildly risqué. Not that they revealed everything but many of them were suggestive in her poses and her dress. She had a nice figure and appeared to be proud of it. In some photos, she wore skimpy hiking shorts and loose halter tops. Her legs were muscular but her blonde hair obviously came out of a bottle, because her black roots needed a touch up.

One photo was of her and a young man with unruly brown hair, a neatly trimmed beard, and fairly developed muscles. In a selfie, she was lowering her halter top toward him for a peek as he leaned in. Christine's comment on the picture: *"Jeff likes to ogle me; it's why I keep him around."*

I shook my head. All of this was open for anyone to see. Upon further reading, I learned she'd worked at as a waitress at Huber's Cafe, a downtown restaurant, where Jeff was a cook.

I've eaten there before, I thought. That's the place that serves the Spanish coffee. I wondered if I'd met Christine there. Maybe Jeff was the guy who did the fancy gyrations while serving the coffee.

"I'm in the middle of something," Steve said. "Can I call you back?"

I knew the *middle of something* was probably a joint task meeting with the FBI about Portland's serial killer.

"I just wanted to share some information with you that may be pertinent to your investigation," I said.

A sigh resonated from the other end of the phone. "Make it quick."

"Did you know that the day Christine Crawford died, she'd posted where she was going on her Facebook page?" No response. "I'm telling you this because it might have led to her death if someone had been stalking her on Facebook."

"I'll pass that information along," he said. "I'm sure someone has already gone over her social sites."

"How many victims have there been so far?"

"Five with Crawford" he said. "There may be a sixth if I don't get off the phone soon."

"Is someone listening?" I said.

"That would be the case."

"Can you text me the victims' names?"

"I'd rather share that information in person."

"Oh? Will we have a chance to get together anytime soon, with you so busy and all?"

"All I need is some motivation," he said.

"Are you sure you'll have time for some motivation?"

I heard him make a choking sound at the other end of the line. "Maybe, if you'd make the arrangements and let me know when."

"I'll start making plans now."

"To show good faith, I'll text you when I have time," he said. "We can talk about it more when we meet."

"Sounds intriguing. I hope you can enlighten me."

"I'll do my best." I heard him chuckle before he disconnected.

I hung up the phone just as Angel, finally back from her three-hour lunch, poked her head in my office. "Mar and her hubby are here. Should I show them in?"

I nodded and a minute later Mar and Rob were sitting in two chairs across from my desk. Rob was not what I expected. He was good looking in a nerdy kind of way with curly blond hair and black framed glasses over his blue eyes. He wore slacks and his muscular biceps bulged under a short-sleeved blue dress shirt. His red tie was mostly hidden by a black sweater vest.

He gazed around the room and smiled at a picture of me with my four brothers in uniform, taken when I was on the police bureau.

"I invited you here because I always like to give good news in person," I said.

Rob's eyes suddenly focused on me. "Did you find my computer?"

"The police are conducting a search on the suspects' apartment this afternoon, and I'm hopeful it will be recovered." I slid the USB drive Eric had given me across the desk. "In the meantime, maybe this will alleviate some of your fears."

He looked at the flash drive and then up to me, his sharp eyes weighing the possibilities. Mar looked at it stupidly and frowned. "What's that thing?" she said. "Did you get my wine back?"

I did a mental eye roll and ignored her. "Eric is the person who stole your computer, and he's kind of a technical whiz himself. He gave me this storage device when I caught him trying to rob another house in the West Hills."

Rob nodded as I talked. He was starting to get it.

"He wanted me to make sure you got this back, Rob. He felt guilty stealing it and was hoping to find a way to return it to you."

"What about my wine?" Mar said.

"Martha, will you shut up about the damn wine for a minute?" Rob said. "Miss Bly, what is on the flash drive?"

"It appears to be some designs you developed for a hologram computer," I said.

"Could I use your laptop to check it out?" he asked.

"Help yourself." I spun my laptop around to face him. "Eric said he had an idea of how to solve your overheating problem."

Rob peered up skeptically from the computer screen. "He what?"

"He seems to be a pretty bright young man who made some mistakes because he was loyal to a childhood buddy with a drug problem."

Rob turned his attention back to my computer and punched a few keys, followed by furious clicking with my mouse. His blue eyes brightened and his taut lips widened into a wondrous smile.

"My design," he yelled.

"Mar, I think most of your wine should be recovered," I said. "Although I wouldn't be surprised if the boys drank a few bottles of it. Eric's friend, Jimmer, seems to have little control where drugs and alcohol are concerned."

"Oh, well here I was thinking of myself again when Rob has been frantic these past few weeks. I'm just glad you caught these crooks and got his designs back."

"Yes!" Rob shouted. "It's all here." He scrolled through some screens and clicked the mouse feverishly. "What's this?" His eyes narrowed. "This might do it. What was the name of this person who gave you my design?"

"Eric," I said. "Eric Williams."

"Too bad he got mixed up in crime. He might have had a real future in computer technology."

"I have some advice for both of you." I had their attention now. Success can have that effect.

"Rob, you need to find a way to back those plans up so if you lose one set, you don't lose everything."

"You're right," he said. "I was so paranoid I didn't want to save it to a cloud drive. I had a backup drive at home, but the thieves stole it too. I'll have to find a better way."

"Yes, you need to take better care of your things so you can't blame me," Mar said.

"Mar, dear, I have a suggestion for you too." She turned to look at me with raised eyebrows as if to say *what could anyone hope to teach me*?

"You must quit posting all of your private information on Facebook," I told her. "People can read it and know when you are out of the house at one of your appointments or on vacation. It's an invitation to rob you."

She thought about it for a minute and nodded. "They don't warn you about those things when they invite you to have a Facebook page."

"That's your responsibility as a grownup," I said. "You have to watch what you write. And it would be a good idea to change your privacy settings so the whole world can't see what you post on your page."

"I'll help her with that," Rob said. "If I hadn't been so distracted on my project, maybe I would have noticed it before."

Mar wrote me a huge check and Rob hugged me three times from my office to the front door, and they walked down my front steps arm-in-arm. For some reason, instead being envious of Mar's success, I felt happy for them.

Chapter 12

Trixie woke up early, glad to be free of Connie after spending nearly the whole of yesterday with her. She seemed a bit clingy after their last sexual romp, but he supposed that was normal in a new relationship. He wasn't sure because he didn't know what normal was.

Now that she was gone, he had time to fret again about his situation. Anxiety welled up within him like a dam about to overflow. The apprehension began the day he had seen that meddlesome private investigator while he was checking out the house Mary Johansen lived in with her parents. He was sure Billie Bly had somehow traced him and although he knew it was next to impossible, he couldn't shake the feeling.

He dressed and brought coffee and a bagel to eat in the car. The other thing creating anxiety in his life was his newfound interest in Connie, or rather her newfound interest in him. Somehow she had thrown him a curve and instead of becoming his prey, he had been entrapped by her. She was everything he might want in a woman: beautiful, exciting, and submissive. And like him, she suffered from a bad childhood. He could never remember feeling empathy for anyone, but he had felt it for her.

These new feelings took him outside his comfort zone. His life had always been orderly. His method of subduing his playmates assured him he was in command and he felt safe as long as he was in control.

Now his life seemed to be spinning and it was essential he regain control. It was either through Connie or a new playmate. And as much as he fought the urge, he knew the only woman who could bring order back into his life would be that bitch, Billy Bly.

He parked his car at the curb outside a five-story apartment building off Burnside Street, a block from Zupan's Market, and opened his laptop. It took only a minute to scour through dozens of wireless connections before he found the one not needing a password.

Under one of the several Facebook pages he had created under assumed names, he began trolling for potential playmates. First up, was the elusive Mary Johansen, whose house he had been checking until Billie Bly interfered. Mary was a fitness nut and lived at home with her parents. He hadn't even needed to *friend* her because she had no privacy controls.

Trixie found Mary's *friends* list and scrolled down through their pictures. She had quite a few attractive *friends* and most of them posted their own profile pictures instead of a cat or dog or a frog.

He selected one who was attractive and well-built. She had also neglected the privacy features so Trixie viewed her posts with interest:

Janet Domingo:

Whew. Got up at 4 a.m. today to practice for Dragon boat competition. Don't know what's harder, rowing or getting up early enough to be on the water at sunrise.

12 hours ago.

Janet Domingo

No rowing practice tomorrow, so I'm partying tonight with some girlfriends. Maybe I'll get lucky. Hear there are lots of available men at The Outrigger in Vancouver.

2 hours ago

Trixie liked the fact that she worked out and her profile picture was hot. Her profile said she was 28 and graduated from

Washington High School in Michigan. A geographic change, Trixie knew, was either due to a move with a boyfriend or husband, or to get away from a bad family life. Janet's Timeline indicated she had been in Portland for five years and Trixie was willing to bet it was to get away from family.

She posted party pictures where she was obviously very drunk, pictures of her in rowing gear, and one of her sipping a Margarita with a come-hither look as she glanced over the salted rim of a glass.

She wasn't perfect, but she would do. According to her Facebook post, she would be at *The Outrigger* tonight. With luck, she would kiss her frog and meet her prince, Trixie thought. A dark prince willing to release her from all of her demons.

Trixie sighed and went to Billie Bly's Facebook page. All he could see was the one lousy picture of her serious and stern face that seemed to say *don't mess with me*. It turned him on in a way none of the others did.

He scrolled down her Timeline and noticed she had scheduled an event in a few days. It was a self-defense class for women. He wondered if they would mind observers and made a mental note to check it out.

The morning newspaper on the car seat pulled him out of his daydream. It featured a photo of two young men being pushed into a cop car. Two women stood in the background, a cop and a blonde. He picked up the newspaper and squinted. The blonde looked familiar.

He read the story and chuckled at the part where two young men had used Facebook to find victims for their crimes.

"Imagine that," he said.

He read further until something stopped him cold: *Billie Bly, a local private investigator, assisted police in apprehending the serial burglars. "I had been staking out a house and got lucky," Bly said. "It was my assistant, Angel Peterson, who led me to the house and they just happened to run out as I arrived."*

Trixie read on and learned Billie Bly had been working on the case for the better part of two weeks. She apparently sifted through Facebook friends of some of the earlier burglary victims and picked a few potential targets to watch. The news article said she had hoped the burglars were also following friends of their victims.

A lesson to be learned, Trixie thought. He felt calmer, realizing this P.I. had not been tracking him. They had both been scouting neighborhoods and simply bumped into each other. Was it merely a coincidence? He didn't believe in coincidences. He and she were somehow linked now because of the butterfly effect. He knew they would meet again and preferred for it to be on his terms, not hers.

"I think," he said to himself, "it's time we meet. I need to be able to see more of you. Do you have a playful side? Does your picture do you justice or are you better looking? It would really turn me on if you were bossy. My mother used to be bossy. Not with *the butcher*, mind you, she took everything out on me."

He wanted to meet this Bly woman in person. He thought again about the self-defense event she posted about on her Facebook page. His anxiety increased and he didn't know if he could wait.

"I wonder . . ."

The morning after I had closed the case on Mar and Robert's burglary case, Angel came in late and out of sorts. She forgot to make the coffee and spent the morning staring vacantly at her computer.

Her hand whisked to her mouth several times a minute trying to deliver the cigarette, which no longer rested between her fingers. She caught herself, swore, and muttered something under her breath.

When the phone rang, she nearly jumped out of her chair. I watched her surreptitiously through the beveled glass window from my office. Even her outrageous fashion sense seemed to have deserted her. Instead of wearing garish mismatching colors she wore a simple brown dress and sensible flat shoes rather than red-spiked heels. Her eye shadow was a muted coral that Mar might have worn.

She entered my office after she got off the phone and seemed positively demure. "We have a client, a Mr. Benson, who would like to meet with you this afternoon." She turned and sighed and began to close the door that separated our offices.

"Angel?" I called.

"Yes?"

"What time will Mr. Benson be here?"

"Oh, about two o'clock. Oh my, did he say two or three? I can't remember."

She looked worried and I couldn't tell if it was about Mr. Benson's appointment or something else. I watched her eyelashes flutter as she mumbled something to herself.

"Did he say what it was about?"

"Didn't I tell you? He wants to know if his girlfriend is cheating on him."

"Angel, is there something bothering you?"

"Me? No . . . I just seem to be having an off day. I'll be okay."

"I thought by now Chris would have dropped by to say *I told you so* about his being right about Eric and Jimmer choosing the O'Connor house."

"Oh, I hope he doesn't. I mean, it wouldn't be right to rub it in."

I looked at her sideways. "Are you upset with me for making you sit in the field yesterday?"

"No!" she huffed, and stormed out of my office.

I was about to follow her when Steve walked through the front door. He stepped into my office and looked back over his shoulder. "What's wrong with her?"

"I don't know. I tried to ask her and she ran out."

"Was she crying?" he asked.

"I've never seen her cry, but she's up to about two packs a day if she was still smoking," I said.

"I thought I'd take a chance you wouldn't be busy," he said. "Maybe we could sneak away for an hour or two and go over case facts on the serial killer."

He wore another zippy suit, this one brown with a blue gingham tie. His brown hair was combed front to back and held in place by gel. I couldn't help myself. I stood and ran my fingers through his hair to muss it a bit. I knew he wanted to look good for the joint investigative team, but I thought he took himself a bit too seriously.

"I can't leave," I said. "I have a client at two o'clock, or maybe it's three, and I have some other work I have to do in the meantime."

"How about we talk business first?" he said. "Then, if you can get rid of Angel for a while, I'll take you upstairs to inspect my new Armani boxers.

"Hmm. Much as I'd like to put my inspector tag on them, I don't think I can get Angel to leave. She seems to be hiding out here today."

His eyebrows sagged and his lips pouted. He handed me a slip of paper. "Here's the list of the four missing or dead women from the Portland area. The Seattle PD wouldn't authorize the release of the names of the three dead women up there yet. They're still processing the graves."

"Graves?"

He nodded. "The killer dumped them all in the same location. Their Detectives think he wasn't familiar with the area, so he kept returning to a spot by the Nisqually Reservation near Ft. Lewis. They're still investigating the area and don't want sightseers."

I looked at the list of Portland victims: Wendy Meyers, Cynthia Miller, Carol Spence, and Donna Timberlake. Each had a *before* and *after* death photo accompanied by vital statistics.

"You said one of these women escaped from the killer, but died before she could be of any help," I said.

"This one." He pointed at Wendy Meyers. "She didn't really escape. He left her for dead and she crawled to a road where somebody found her. She died the next morning, but not before she told police she had been kidnapped by a white male in his thirties. She wasn't able to give a better description. It was dark, and he attacked her outside a local bar. But she *did* say he bragged about how he'd killed ten women before her."

"So you know you have a serial killer," I said.

"We suspect he stalked her for a period of time before abducting her."

"Christine Crawford isn't on this list," I said.

"You asked about the others, these are the others."

"Did you read her Facebook page on the day of her disappearance?" I asked.

"I looked at it. She said she was going hiking and where she was going on the day she was murdered."

"I'm surprised you checked," I said.

"I'm a cop. Of course I checked."

"I piqued your curiosity."

"That's not all you piqued."

"What did the task force think?'

"Like I said, they were unimpressed. Your idea is up on the board with a hundred other theories we're bouncing around right now."

"All of the murdered women had Facebook pages, didn't they?"

"Yeah," he said. "But everyone is on Facebook these days. There is nothing to indicate someone might be looking at their pages and stalking them."

"Didn't they all post their where-a-bouts on the day they died?"

He rolled his eyes at me. "But three of them had privacy controls in effect. I checked. It's unlikely some random stranger would be able to gain access to each of them."

"Did you investigate to see if they had any mutual *friend*s?" I asked.

"I haven't had time. We have someone who will follow up on it eventually. We don't have a lot of manpower yet and there are too many other solid leads we need to follow."

I nodded absently, turning over possibilities and scenarios for tracking down a potential Facebook stalker. I was one-for-one in catching bad guys on Facebook and right now I felt I was on a lucky streak.

"I know that look," Steve said. "If you turn anything up, come straight to me. Don't try to handle things yourself."

"You don't really believe I'd turn anything up, *do you*?"

"No, but crazy things seem to happen to you, and I want to make sure you don't get mixed up with this guy. He's dangerous and ruthless, and he's killed maybe as many as fifteen women if his boasts to Wendy Williams are true."

"I'll keep you updated," I said. "If you promise to take me seriously."

Chapter 13

"John Benson?" I reached across my desk and shook the hand of a thirty-something well-built man with sandy brown hair, blue eyes and fair skin. He had an impish smile with a bit of nervousness to it.

"I'm glad you could meet with me on short notice," he said. He sat in a chair opposite me, brushed one hand through his perfectly coiffed hair, and offered a charismatic smile.

"I understand you think your girlfriend might be cheating on you," I said.

"My fiancé. We're supposed to be married in a month and lately she's been acting strangely."

"How so?" I narrowed my eyes at him.

"She cancels out on me a lot. Sometimes she gets a phone call and leaves the room to talk--she never used to do that." He slammed his fist on my desk for emphasis.

"And lately she's too tired for sex or has some other lame excuse. We seem to see less and less of each other now and she always has a reason, except . . . well, she never has been a good liar, so it's painfully obvious to me when she's deceitful."

"Has it occurred to you," I suggested, "that she's probably busy planning her wedding and all of these excuses may be legitimate. A wedding takes a lot of planning and can be very stressful."

"But the lying?"

"Maybe she doesn't want to hurt your feelings," I said.

"I might be able to believe that, except . . ."

Benson's eyes became steely serious, and I felt he was trying too hard to convince me.

"Mary was seen with another man downtown last Friday night by a friend of mine. She told me she was with a cousin from out of town. My friend saw this man with his arm around her downtown. He became curious and followed them to a restaurant."

"Which restaurant?" I asked.

Benson thought about it for a moment and a slow smile came to his lips. "I think it was called Huber's. Yes, it was definitely Huber's."

"Is that all? Did your friend follow her in by any chance?"

"Yes. He watched them from the bar for a few minutes, but had to leave shortly afterwards because he had an appointment."

"Did you see anything else incriminating?"

"Me?"

"I meant your friend."

"Shit yes. He said they were pretty chummy. Mary was flirting with the guy and my friend thought the dude might have groped her, but the light wasn't good and he wasn't sure. He didn't know the guy was supposed to be a cousin or maybe he wouldn't have followed them in. He was acting on my behalf, you see."

"Maybe," I said. "Or maybe you don't need friends like that. What do you want me to do?"

"I'd like to know . . . to be sure that our lives together will have a chance to be happy. As long as this nagging thought is in my head that she might be cheating or have cheated on me in the past, it will make it hard for me to marry her."

"I can understand that. You'd like peace of mind entering your marriage."

"You've got it," he said.

"I can follow her for a while and see what turns up."

"Great," he said. "I have a picture of her. You can call me at this number any time." He handed me a wallet-sized photo of an attractive woman, with blonde hair and a flirty smile, and added a business card indicating he handled investments.

"You will have to pay me a week in advance," I said.

"Is that typical?" he asked.

"It is for this type of case. Sometimes the client doesn't like the answers I find for them and they become reluctant to pay."

"I see. You think I won't pay you for bad news?"

"It's been known to happen. But let's hope I bring you good news."

"Will cash be good enough?" He pulled out a money clip and counted out ten one-hundred-dollar bills.

I tried not to blink. "Um, that will be thirteen hundred, plus any expenses I incur."

His face turned earnest and he peeled out five more hundred-dollar bills. "I expect nothing but the best service for this amount of money."

"And you shall have it."

"I don't doubt it," Benson said. "I saw the article about you in the newspaper today. You seem like you might be a tiger once you get involved in a case."

"I'll do my best. I'll need your fiancé's full name." He looked me over like *he* was the tiger, sizing me up for lunch, and the tone in his voice implied a sexual vibe I didn't like.

"Mary Johansen," Benson said. "Here's her address." He took a notepad from my desk and wrote an address on it. "She lives with her parents right now to save money for our wedding. I told her it wasn't necessary, but she's insistent."

I ushered him to Angel. He signed our standard contract, received a receipt for money paid, and strolled confidently out the front door.

"Thinks a lot of himself doesn't he?" Angel said.

"You noticed it too?" I studied the picture of Mary Johansen in my hand. "Most clients come in rattled and nervous if their partner is cheating on them. He was a little anxious, but I didn't get the feeling it was because his fiancé was cheating on him."

"Really?"

"No. It was more like you've been acting today. Like he was afraid I might find out something about him."

"Half of our clients are holding things back," she said, avoiding eye contact. "If they told us the truth, we'd never earn any money. Their cases would be solved overnight."

I smiled. "And what are you holding back from me, dear one?"

She manipulated a pen between her fingers until it eluded them and fell to the floor. "I . . . nothing. I'm just tired."

"Angel, I've been watching you all day. You're smoking like a fiend, if you were still smoking. You jump out of your chair every time the phone rings and when I mentioned Chris earlier you retreated into a shell for the rest of the morning. What happened? Did you and Chris get into an argument? Are you afraid your little thefts might get you into trouble? I covered for you, you know. I put your little stolen trinkets in with the rest of the loot those boys took."

A tear came to her eye. "I appreciate your efforts, but I just can't tell you. Not now. Not ever. It's just too terrible."

"Anybody home?"

Chris Johnson walked through the front door with a fistful of white daisies and handed them to Angel.

"Nothing but the best for my girl."

"They look remarkably familiar," I said.

Angel took the flowers and looked at them, then at Chris, then me. Her face flushed and she shook her head. She thrust the uneven bouquet of Shasta daisies into my hand and wiped the tear from her eye.

"This is a nightmare," she said. "I'm not your girl. This never happened. I never want to see you again."

She brushed past Chris and out the front door with her purse in her hand and a phantom cigarette between her fingers.

"She forgot her lighter," Chris quipped. "She'll be back. Once you've had Chris, you always come back.

I looked at the flowers in my hand. "You picked these from my front yard."

He shrugged. "I was inspired."

"What did you do to her?"

"Me? Nothing. It was her idea. I just went along for the ride."

"Chris!"

"We had sex out in the field. We got bored and she was mad at Earl because she saw him with another woman."

"What?"

"It's true," he said. "Earl told her she was a client or a stakeout, or some such bull. Did you know he's a P.I. too? I thought he was just a tow-truck driver, but apparently he just does that when business is slow."

"You had sex with Angel?"

"It was revenge sex. I know makeup sex is always supposed to be hot, but revenge sex is even hotter. In fact, I was hoping she was still pissed enough at Earl for another round. I was so tired I've been off my feet most of the day, but I'm back now."

"Why are you telling me? I don't want to know this. You're too icky. Why would Angel ever have sex with you?"

"I told you. She was mad at Earl for messing around with another woman. She wanted to get even. I didn't even think I liked her because of the way she always talks trash to me and throws vases and dishes in my direction. But I've had time to think it over, and I realized maybe it's her way of saying she likes me."

"No, it's not, Chris," I said. "She really doesn't like you. Take my word for it."

"I think I like her too," he said. "And I know I like the sex. She's smoking hot. The way she talks, the things she knows how to do. You've got a real sex goddess working for you. That friggin Earl is crazy to step out on her, and I'm going move in while the moving is good."

"What? You're talking like an idiot. Get out of here." He looked at me sheepishly as if I hurt his feelings. Who knew he had feelings? I picked up a small chair and poked him with its legs, pushing him toward the door.

"Don't be mad. Be happy for us. We may even move in together."

I swung the chair at him and he yelped and made for the door. He managed to open it, but not before I clipped him on the arm. I raised the chair again, but he was down the steps and halfway to his car.

"And don't come back. If you do, I'll shoot you."

Chapter 14

Trixie entered *The Outrigger,* a Vancouver nightclub on the Washington side of the Columbia River. The decor was dated, with floral carpet and a 1970's angular architecture. Inside were huge schooner masts reaching toward the vaulted ceiling and supporting square rigged sails, complete with yardarms.

The nautical theme was accentuated during the evening hours when darkness conspired with a loud band and strobe lights to bring the place alive, teeming with young people looking for a good time. The place was jumping and Trixie was already making plans for a return visit soon.

He was still waiting for Janet Domingo and her friends to arrive. They had been chatting on Facebook all day so he knew they planned to meet early enough for the uninspired happy hour menu of mozzarella sticks, Buffalo wings and sweet potato fries. It seemed a poor diet for a dragon boat enthusiast, and Trixie wondered if Janet would choose the Chicken Caesar Salad or throw caution and her training regimen aside tonight.

A few women had gathered at a table away from the noise near an expansive window overlooking the river. He thought he recognized one of them from her Facebook picture, but it was too dark to be sure. He was more than a little interested in this group of women because the elusive Mary Johansen indicated she would also attend.

This might be a problem if Billie Bly took her responsibilities too seriously and began her new job tonight by tailing Mary. It would be easy enough for her to stumble on the scene if she went to Mary's Facebook page and noted she planned to meet friends here.

It also occurred to Trixie that it might be too big an opportunity for Bly to pass up, as several of these women indicated they were here to meet men. Maybe Mary *was* stepping out on John Benson.

He had thought himself so clever when he made the appointment with the P.I. earlier this afternoon, pretending to be Mary's fiancé, and hiring her to find out if Mary was cheating on him. It all seemed perfect. He was finally able to meet Billy Bly face-to-face.

It was risky because if she *had* been trailing him, all kinds of things might have gone wrong. But she didn't seem to recognize him at all and that alone was worth the risk. From then on, he'd played the victim pretending to hire her to follow his fiancé. She would call him on his disposable cell phone to report in. If she checked Mary Johansen's background, she would see Mary was engaged to John Benson, just not *the* John Benson she had met.

There were no pictures of John Benson on Mary's Facebook page. It was what gave Trixie the idea of impersonating him. John had no Facebook page; Trixie had checked. Nor was John on *Linked In* or any other popular social websites. One thought had occurred to him. What if Billie saw Mary and John together? It would happen eventually. What would she think?

She would track John Benson down eventually and realize she'd been played, but by whom? In the few days that would take to happen, he would be ready for her. It would make things sweeter in the end. A little mystery he had created for her--one they could share--before she died.

The band quit playing and the lights came up, snapping him out of his musings. He looked over at the table of women again and spotted Mary.

His years of attending his sisters' competitions paid one dividend. He became fascinated by the makeup they applied and taught himself how to create disguises. He had taken the precaution of donning a fake mustache and a goatee, and further changed his appearance with brown contact lenses over his blue eyes. He spray-tanned his face and arms and wore boots with built up heels to make him seem a few inches taller than his actual five-foot-eleven inch height. Although he was there for Janet, Mary would have been a good target if he hadn't brought Billie Bly into the fray. But Mary needed to be in play for Billie's little investigation.

A tall blonde with dangling earrings and strawberry-red lipstick, dressed in slinky black miniskirt, strode up to the women and exchanged greetings before sitting down. He recognized Janet Domingo immediately from her Facebook photo. Trixie supposed her hair was naturally black and she had colored it. One Facebook photo showed her eyes as brown, but in all of the other pictures her eyes were green. He guessed she must use tinted contacts, maybe to disclaim her Spanish heritage.

The women huddled together near a window. The four of them were attractive and very intimidating as a group. It would take a confident man to burst through the alliance and ask one of them to dance.

The band, now bathed in blue light, started playing another tune. Trixie rose, confident in his ensemble of faded blue jeans, a white dress shirt, collar unbuttoned, and a tan leather jacket. He walked over toward the quartet without missing a beat.

He ignored Janet and smiled at Mary. "Would you like to dance?"

"Oh, I couldn't." She showed him a tiny diamond on her ring finger. "I'm engaged."

"Lucky man," he said. "But I won't hit on you, I just want to dance."

"Go on," Janet said. "It's just a dance."

"I guess it would be okay." She got up from her chair and took his hand and he ushered her to the dance floor, a cheesy stainless steel remnant of the seventies.

"I saw you when you arrived and I've been building up my courage for the past thirty minutes to ask you to dance," he said. "Just my luck you're already engaged."

"You're quite the sweet talker, aren't you?"

"Is that what you think? I was being sincere."

She moved around him, not touching, but gliding dangerously close as she danced. "Sorry. But this *is* kind of a pickup place. I wouldn't have come, but my fiancé is out of town, and my friends wore me down."

"I'm glad you did. Even if it means I only get one dance with you."

"You keep talking like that and you might get more than *one* dance," she said, flirting with him now. He liked that. Apparently he had not been far off the mark in his concerns to Billie Bly.

"I'm Brent," he said.

"I'm Mary."

Seeing her up close and in person, he wished he had not used her as part of his ruse with Billie Bly. She was tall and well-built with shoulder-length blonde hair, blue eyes and an infectious smile. She wore slacks and a silk blouse tied up to bare a toned stomach.

They talked about mundane things, but she agreed to a second dance. He spun a story tailored to win her over a little at a time, acting a bit embarrassed when she flirted with him. He gave her a little teaser about a successful lifestyle, and she wanted to know more. He made her work for it, appearing modest, yet still confident in himself.

After the second dance, he walked her back to the table, thanked her, and kissed the top of her hand. "Best wishes on the upcoming wedding," he said, and walked away.

As he left them, he heard a cacophony of female voices back at the table, querying Mary about him and giggling. They were so easy to read, he thought. Now he would sit and wait for a while to see what would happen next.

Back at his table, nursing a microbrew a waitress had brought him, he surveyed the crowd to see if anyone new had come in. He didn't see Billie Bly, but it was early and she might show up later. Eventually a few men approached Janet's table and asked her and some of her other friends to dance. A few times he spotted Mary gazing at him and quickly turning away when she noticed him looking in her direction.

It was about nine-thirty and Billie Bly still had not shown. Good, he thought. If she had, he would have quietly slipped out a side door. It was a good omen and he planned to take advantage of the situation. The four women had been talking and giggling. Two of them paired off with other men and Janet rose and walked across the room toward him.

"I was hoping you might come back and ask me to dance," she said. "Since you didn't, I decided to take a chance and ask you."

"Not much of a chance," he said. "No guy in his right mind would turn you down."

She smiled and offered her hand, wriggling it.

"Why don't we talk for a few minutes first," he said. "It's hard to hear each other in front of the band, and I'd like to get to know you."

"If I'd known, I'd brought my drink."

"Don't go back for it. I'm afraid you might get picked off by one of these other rascals before you made it back." Trixie waved a waitress over and ordered her a Margareta.

"So if I'm so popular, why didn't you come over and ask me to dance?"

"I started to a couple of times, but some other guys beat me to it."

114

"Are you scared of a little competition?"

"In a place like this? Not really. Most of the people are here because they're desperate."

"Well, I never!"

"Don't get me wrong. You've got to put yourself out there somehow to meet someone new, but sometimes when I go home, I feel slightly tarnished. I tell myself I won't do it another time and a month later here I am again."

"I see what you mean. Yes, it is a lot of work for very little reward."

"Exactly," he said. "So if I'm a little ambivalent at times, it's just that I don't want to become a person that isn't me. I've decided to take some time and observe people to see if there's anyone who might appeal to me on an individual level."

"Someone you have something in common with," she said.

"Yes. That's why I suggested we talk first. You can't get to know someone with loud music blaring in your face all night."

They talked for an hour about her rowing routines on the dragon boats, his love of kayaking, her work, her boss, his investment business, her dreams, and his dreams. If one had been listening, it would appear they were an ideal couple. Trixie planned it that way.

Eventually they got up and danced. Trixie had taken lessons a few years back so he made Janet look better than she was and, when they lulled into a slow dance, she nestled herself against him like they were long-time sweethearts. After a while they were both hot and sweaty and this fit into Trixie's plans.

"Shall we go outside for a walk along the river to cool off?"

"I guess so. But maybe I should tell my friends first. I've pretty much ignored them most of the evening."

"We can join them after," he said. It's a beautiful evening. We'll be back in fifteen minutes."

"My purse."

He sighed. "Of course."

She went to her table and made small talk with her friends. There was more giggling and she eventually returned carrying a small clutch purse. They stepped into a mild evening and a warm wind blew from the Columbia River, caressing their faces. She interlocked her arm in his and snuggled against him as they continued down a sidewalk, the black waters of the river in front of them and a full moon above.

"It's a nice night," Janet said.

"It can only get nicer," Trixie said.

"Did you like Mary?" she asked. "I noticed you two seemed to hit it off when you danced with her."

"She's okay," Trixie said.

"I only thought maybe you liked her." She remained quiet for a minute. "She seemed to like you."

"Oh?" he said. "Did she talk about me much?"

"A little," she said.

Trixie could see her sly glance, checking him out. "She's attractive, but I really wanted to meet you."

"Then why did you ask *her* to dance?"

"Sometimes it's nice to have a good referral before an interview," he said.

"An interview? Is that what you think this is?"

"In a way," he said vaguely. "I need to get my phone. I left it in my car."

"Why do you need your phone now?"

"I forgot to leave a message for someone. Come with me. My car is just over there in the parking lot."

He took her hand and guided her toward the parking lot, but she stopped after a few steps forcing him to release her arm. "It will only take a minute," he said.

"It will spoil the mood. And I'm still trying to figure what you meant by that *interview* remark."

He put his arms around her slim waist. "You were so beautiful that I was afraid you might say no. I chanced it with Mary because there was nothing to lose if she rejected me. I was building up my courage and trying to be suave with her so she might say something nice about me to you and your friends."

"You don't seem the type to be self-conscious," she said.

"I'm usually very confident," he said. "But for some reason with you I feel like a gawky thirteen-year-old."

"You know how to turn a girl's head." A slight smile revealed itself in the moonlight. "You go ahead to the car without me. I'm going to stay and enjoy the view."

Trixie tried to appear disappointed. "You're sure?"

"The call you have to make. Is it to another woman?"

"Sadly, no. I don't have your phone number yet. It's a business associate. I told him I'd give him the okay on a deal we're working on, and I forgot to call him. He's probably been trying to reach me all night."

"I'll be right here. Just don't make me wait long."

Trixie didn't make her wait long at all. A few minutes later he surprised her with a kiss. Before she could react, he stuffed a rag over her face and made sure he avoided the sweet smell of chloroform. She panicked and fought as he adjusted the rag to cover her nose and mouth.

He had tried other methods of abduction. Once he used a stun gun, but his prey wriggled on the ground and made it too hard to detach the prongs and get her to her feet. The chloroform kept them on their feet and gave them the woozy look of someone who'd had too much to drink.

"Don't fight," he said. "It won't hurt you."

She gasped and fought for breath, just as the others had. He scrutinized the parking lot for witnesses and seeing none, pivoted her toward the parking lot and waited for the chloroform to take effect.

A minute later she swooned and staggered. This was all he needed. The full effects of unconsciousness could take several more minutes.

Her panicked behavior turned to the demeanor of a person who had taken too many drinks and he acted as a steadying influence and steered her stumbling gait toward his car. He clicked his car key fob with a free hand to open the hatchback. The Prius had a remarkably large rear compartment, he mused, and rolled her dazed body into it.

He had parked at the edge of the lot where it came closest to the sidewalk along the river. It was far enough away from the bar that there shouldn't be any potential witnesses. Seeing none, he grabbed a roll of duct tape and masked her mouth, then tied her wrists, and finally her ankles. She barely reacted except for a slurred sentence before he taped her mouth.

"Why aaar're yooo. . . dooing thus?" she slurred.

Janet's reaction stirred a memory from his past, one he'd tried to suppress for years, and it jolted him. *Why are you making me do this Daddy? I don't want to!*

Shut up and do it. This will make you a man instead of a namby-pamby girly boy with feathers around your neck. Take the ax and do it.

Trixie pulled the cover over the Prius' cargo area and snapped it to the seat headrest to hide Janet. He closed the lid to the hatchback and surveyed the parking lot once more to make sure there were no witnesses.

His dad would have been proud of him. He wasn't a namby-pamby little boy anymore.

Chapter 15

Angel hadn't come in to work yet and I was feeling down again. The burglary case pulled me out of my doldrums for a while, but now I was back in the present and alone with my feelings.

Memories resurfaced of the day I got my brother, Darrin, killed. Contract killers had left me for dead in a dank warehouse and miraculously, I had survived the ordeal. I had talked with Darrin about quitting my gig as a P.I. the day I was released from the hospital and he had given me the pep talk I needed. He made me feel almost good about myself again until I caught a flash of light from a parking garage across the street as we left the hospital.

I knew what it was. But I couldn't react quickly enough to warn the others. Before I could say the word, *sniper,* shots rang out, and Darrin stepped in front of a bullet meant for me.

He died on the sidewalk and that memory sent me back in time to another horrific event-the death of my father. He, too, was killed on a sidewalk in downtown Portland. It happened in front of a restaurant where he'd just eaten lunch. His killer, a mentally unstable homeless person, still resides in a state-run hospital.

My mother died a year later of a broken heart and that left my older brother, Dan, as our surrogate father. I was fourteen when my father died and I guess I have been in minor depression ever since. Because I didn't know I was depressed, I've used excitement in my life as a form of self-medication, according to my therapist.

My depression resurfaced a bit last night and I opted not to follow Mary Johansen to The Outrigger in Vancouver when she posted on Facebook she was going out with some girlfriends. It seemed more satisfying to stay home and isolate with homemade margaritas.

It would have been the perfect opportunity to find out if she was cheating on her fiancé. A pang of guilt stung me for not following through, and I tried to rationalize my apathy against my dislike for Benson. Something about him seemed off and, although I couldn't put my finger on it, I already liked Mary and hoped maybe she *was* cheating on him.

From her Facebook postings, I felt I knew her better than Benson. Reading someone else's static conversations and feeling close to them? Explain that to me. Fortunately, Angel deigned to honor me with her presence and I shifted my concern to my somewhat fragile assistant.

"Brought you some coffee from Starbucks," she said. "Sorry I'm late."

She'd colored her hair again. Today it was the same shade as mine, an honest blonde with no garish color splashes. She wore a purple wool dress with shoulder pads, a forties-style nostalgia appearance, probably bought at a vintage shop. No sparkles in any of her make-up--eye, cheek, or lips, and barely any eyeliner. She would have been shunned by any self-righteous hipster, hippie, or Goth devotee. Usually she combined all three looks, but the blonde hair is what struck me first.

"Your hair looks a lot like mine," I said.

"It was supposed to be platinum, but Sheila got the color wrong. I'll have to wait a while before I can color it again. Sheila says my hair is becoming brittle."

"No wonder. You change your hair color every other week."

"You could use a bit of a makeover yourself," she said. "Look at you. Blue jeans and a flowery blouse. Tomorrow probably jeans and a white blouse. Next week, maybe you'll add a jean jacket to your ensemble."

"I like to feel comfortable," I said.

She rolled her eyes and started to walk away.

"Chris told me some weird stuff after you left yesterday."

Her shoulders tightened and she turned to face me. "What did he say?"

"He professed his love for you," I said.

"What?"

"He went on and on about how you two rolled around in that dirty field and how he thinks maybe he loves you."

"Eewe," she said.

"You can say that again."

"What did you say to him?"

"I told him to take his slimy talk and get the hell out of here, and if he ever came back I'd shoot him."

"Thanks." She gave me a hug. "You know that won't keep him away."

"I just wanted to give him something to think about until I could talk to you and find out the truth."

"I don't know what happened." Tears dribbled down her cheek. "We had some fun in the O'Connor house and even though I was entirely wrong to steal that bracelet, and I'm profusely sorry I did it and put your reputation at risk, it *was* kind of exciting at the time. And I realized for the first time, maybe Chris wasn't as slimy as we thought he was."

"He does have a streak of loyalty in him that can be endearing," I said.

"Maybe that's it. For some damn reason I mentioned I'd seen Earl out with a slut and he agreed Earl was an ass. Then he continued to agree with me and said Earl didn't deserve me and I was too good for him."

"Earl stepped out on you?" I sometimes wondered about him, but it was a touchy subject with Angel so I avoided it.

"He said it was business, but it's been over a week and he still hasn't called."

"Maybe he's afraid. Maybe you should phone him."

"There's no way I'll put myself out for him again."

"So what happened with Chris?"

"He was so sweet and understanding, and we were so close and being so intimate with our feelings."

"Well, *you were*," I said.

"It was revenge sex." She sighed. "I used Chris to get back at Earl, and I feel so guilty about it. There's no way it's going anywhere."

"Are you sure he didn't use you?"

"Maybe. But I led him on."

"It sounds like he wants to make an honest woman of you."

"I'm so ashamed. Billie, do you think less of me?"

"We all make mistakes," I said. "I'm not going to judge you."

She hugged me again. "What am I going to do with him?"

"My experience tells me he's going to hang around like a puppy dog until he tires of you or finds another distraction."

"I don't suppose . . ."

"What?"

"Would you shoot him for me?"

"So now that your case is over, do you find yourself sinking back into your depression?" My analyst, Dr. Anne Sizer, peered over her bifocals and cast a suspicious glance at me. Her brunette hair was packed tightly in a bun and she wore a conservative brown business suit indicating a no-nonsense approach to counseling.

"I guess," I said.

Dr. Sizer revealed a sardonic smile and snapped back to attention. "Tell me what feelings you had while you were working on the Facebook burglaries."

"I don't know. Why do you always ask how things make me feel?" At the moment I felt she was throwing out an often used line designed to make me do all the work. When did she plan to punch the time-clock?

"I ask you how you feel because you aren't in touch with your true feelings and, therefore, you don't know what you want out of life."

"I'm feeling down," I said.

"How did you feel while you were working the case?" My eyes roamed around the room, searching a reproduction of a *Van Gogh* hanging on the wall for an answer. "I guess I felt excitement," I admitted. "There was something new happening in my life and it challenged me to prove myself."

"And how did you feel when the case concluded?" Dr. Sizer asked.

"I told you. Depressed."

"Why did you think you feel depressed?" she said.

I reflected. "Because the excitement is over?"

"And?" she said.

"I'm right back where I started?"

"And?"

"Nothing has changed."

"So you merely postponed your feelings," she said. "Took a vacation from them?"

"And I feel so guilty about Darrin," I said.

"You didn't cause your brother's death." Dr. Sizer adjusted her bifocals. "He chose to sacrifice himself for you. You had no control over the event."

"That's the problem," I said. "I can't change what happened. No matter how many times I go over the day he died, no matter how many things I think I could have done differently--he's still dead. If it's not my fault, why do I feel so bad?"

She put her notepad on her lap and removed her glasses. "You won't like the answer."

"Try me."

"Attempting to control the outcome, mind-racing everyday-- hoping things will come out differently, making yourself feel guilty-- all of these actions are tied to your ego. Your ego wants to protect you."

"Whaaat?" I cried.

"There is a certain comfort in mind-racing, Billie. It's something you are used to doing. I'll bet you've done it all your life."

"Angel says I'm a bit of a worrier," I said.

"Your payoff is that it keeps you from dealing with present day problems. It keeps you in denial about your real problem."

"That I feel guilty?"

"No, dear. You have chosen to make yourself feel guilty by making yourself the victim."

"I don't do any such thing."

"You're doing it now by denying it. The victim in all of this was your brother. He died. Yet, you're the one choosing to feel sorry for yourself."

"I don't have to listen to this." I stood up and grabbed my purse. "You don't know what you're talking about."

"I could be wrong," she said, still sitting with the notepad on her lap. "But is there a chance I might be right?"

"No," I said.

"Then why are you becoming so defensive? If I'm wrong, it shouldn't offend you. In fact, you should be able to dismiss it with a chuckle."

I sat down in the upholstered chair and tried to laugh it off. I couldn't. She had stung me and my instincts told me there might be some truth to what she'd said.

"So, do you have any ideas on how to get out of your depression?" she said.

"I've got another case, but it's a stinker. A boyfriend is worried his fiancé is two-timing him."

"How will that help your depression?"

"It gives me something to do besides feeling sorry for myself."

"But keeping busy also helps you avoid your feelings."

"There *is* something else that's been nagging at me. I have a feeling that a serial killer is using Facebook much in the same way these kids were using it to rob houses."

"Now it sounds like you're looking for excitement again."

"Maybe. But I can't ignore this if lives depend on it."

"You're a good person, Billie. Try to be aware of your feelings, especially when you jump into the victim role. Tell yourself that you aren't a victim and ask yourself why you put yourself in that role. It's primarily why you fall into these depressions."

A tear streamed down my cheek. "If I knew that, I wouldn't be here."

Chapter 16

After my appointment with Dr. Sizer, I headed to the Justice Center downtown for a pre-arranged visit with Eric Williams. Angel had checked on his status and found he was still in jail and the judge had set his bond at $2,000.

I wrote a check out for the clerk after the paperwork was finished in the Justice Center a few floors below the jails. Oregon is one of four states that doesn't use bail bondsmen. The court acts in that status.

I spent another twenty minutes waiting in a secured room for his arrival. When the door opened, Eric looked much younger than the last time I saw him. He was thin, almost skinny, and stood an inch taller than my five-foot-ten frame. His thick brown hair caressed soft facial features and his brown worried eyes searched the room.

"Hi." The young man looked more like a little boy as he sat in a chair the guard suggested and rapped his fingers nervously on the metal table separating us.

"Hello, Eric. How are you holding up?"

"It's not like I thought it would be," he said. "It isn't so scary in here, but Jimmer is in another area, so it's not a lot of fun either."

"Why hasn't your mother bailed you out?" I asked.

"My dad won't let her. He's teaching me a lesson, I guess. They've been on me for a long time about hanging out with Jimmer. This is their 'I told you so' moment, I guess."

"You two have quite a history, don't you?"

"Since third grade," Eric said.

"That's a long time. I can see why you remain loyal to him."

"Yeah, well, Mom and Dad have always been there for me physically, but not so much emotionally. I mean, it seemed like I was always in their way. Jimmer and I could talk about anything."

I nodded. "How would you like it if I bailed you out?"

"You? I don't understand. You put me in here."

"I could use your expertise on a case I'm working on," I said. "If things work out, I might be able to put a good word in for you at your trial."

"What about Jimmer? Could you bail him out too?"

"I think Jimmer needs the help that a good judge might provide him through rehabilitation." I said.

"But he can still get that at trial."

"Jimmer would be in the way--a distraction. Right now he needs some structure and the more real this experience is for him, the better chance he will have of turning his life around."

"You're probably right. It's just that I worry about him."

"I gave the flash drive to Mr. Roy," I said.

"That's cool."

"He was very excited to get it back, and he seemed interested in your design ideas."

"I'm glad. I wish I could work with him on it. Now it looks like I'll never get a chance."

"Don't give up too easily," I said. "Life is full of surprises and you're still pretty young."

He offered a sheepish grin. "So what do I have to do to earn my freedom? I suppose you're having some problems with your computer system."

"I need you to teach me everything you know about Facebook."

"All you need for that is a book," he said. "Why bother with me?"

"Because I don't have the time to study. I have a killer to catch, and I need you to help me catch him."

"For real?" he asked.

"For real." And I told him about my suspicion that a serial killer was trolling for victims on Facebook.

I paired Angel up with Eric and a new laptop computer I purchased for him on the way to my office and left them to set it up. Then I sat at my desk and tried to imagine how I was going to tail Mary Johansen and determine whether or not she was cheating on her fiancé. The whole idea revolted me. Why was I doing these slimy cases?

If I was a better P.I., I could pick and choose my cases and kick the John Benson's to the curb. But because I needed the money to pay my bills, I'd accepted this one. Spying on an innocent woman probably.

I decided to check her Facebook page again and see if I could learn Mary's plans for the day. Her account was open to anyone who wanted to view her posts.

Mary's latest posting caused quite a stir among her friends.

Mary Johansen
I had a good time last night with the girls, but a little concerned about a friend who left early without saying goodbye.
Like • Comment • Share

Trudy Holbrook
I'm worried about Janet too. She didn't show up for work this morning and she didn't call in.
2 hrs - Like - Reply

Beth Anderson

Her car was still in the parking lot next to mine when I left last night. Maybe she went home with Brent.
1hr - Like- Reply

Trudy Holbrook
I've been calling Janet all morning. She doesn't answer her cell phone.
1hr - Like- Reply

Mary Johansen
Brent seemed okay when I danced with him. I'm going to go out to The Outrigger on my lunch and see if her car is still there. Maybe she stayed over with Brent and lost track of time.
1hr - Like- Reply

Beth Anderson
I called the police just now, but they said she hasn't been missing long enough. Stupid Police! I'm going to meet you at The Outrigger!
36 mins - Like - Reply

Trudy Holbrook
I'm coming too. Leaving now.
26 mins - Like - Reply

"Shit," I muttered. I had not only missed an opportunity to catch Mary doing the nasty, but I may have missed something bigger. I didn't even want to admit to what I was thinking because it felt like I was reaching for that *excitement* drug to pull me out of my depression again. Yet, I couldn't deny it was a possibility.

"Angel, I'm going out," I said.

"What's the rush? We're just getting set up. Don't you want to give Eric anything to do?"

I stopped short. "Yes. I want you to check out Mary Johansen's Facebook page. It's still open on my desk. You'll see why when you read down. Eric, I need to know who might have monitored it yesterday other than people who posted there."

"I don't think that's possible," he said.

"Well, then you'd better damn well come up with a *Plan B*," I said, and slammed the door behind me.

On my way to Vancouver, all sorts of thoughts rushed through my head. Had Mary been cheating on John? Was Janet the victim of a crime or a prolonged one-night stand? If Mary danced with this guy, she must have gotten a good look at him. Could she or the others describe him to the police? If this guy was the serial killer Steve and the FBI were looking for, he had just made a tremendous mistake by allowing witnesses to see him.

I pulled into the parking lot at The Outrigger and spotted three women arguing near a late model Honda Civic. I pulled into a parking spot next to three other cars and got out of my MG.

"Hello ladies, is there a problem?"

"Do you work here?" A blonde in a gray business dress asked the question.

"I'm security for The Outrigger." I'm a great liar and this seemed to be the best way to start out. "Did you lock yourself out of your car?"

"This is my friend's car," The blonde said. "We're looking for her. She didn't show up to work this morning."

"And you are?"

"I'm Mary Johansen. We're all here because our friend didn't show up for work today. We were at the bar last night and this is her car."

"It's possible she met someone and went home with him," I suggested.

"But she would have told us," a redhead said. She wore black slacks and a white blouse. "I'm Beth Anderson. She would never blow us off or not show up for work without a phone call."

"What is your friend's name?" I asked.

"Janet Domingo," Beth said.

"Description?"

"She's tall and blonde," Mary said.

"And strong," Beth added. "She has muscles on her muscles because she rows dragon boats."

"Oh, and she has a dragon boat tattoo on her left shoulder," the third woman said.

"Can any of you describe the man she was with?" I asked.

"He was tall, about six-two and well-built," said the third women. I noticed she was slightly Rubenesque, with purple highlights in her raven colored hair.

"You must be Trudy," I said, remembering her name from Facebook.

"Yes, Trudy Holbrook. How did you know?"

"My psychic told me I would meet someone named Trudy today," I said. "You were my last chance in this group."

"Did your psychic tell you how to find Janet?" Mary rolled her eyes at me and crossed her arms.

"My psychic would like more of a description of this guy Janet was with."

"He had brown hair and a mustache and a goatee," Beth said.

"He wore faded blue jeans," Mary said. "I think his shirt was white. It was hard to tell in the dark with the strobe lights. It was a lighter color. He also wore brown dress shoes and a brown leather jacket."

"He had a nice tan," Trudy said. "I noticed it when he came over to us. He was really dreamy in a mysterious sort of way. He walked straight up to our group and asked Mary to dance. That takes nerve because we'd just shot another guy down."

"But the one she went off with passed inspection?" I was familiar with the safety in numbers concept they had obviously employed.

"Oh yeah. We encouraged Mary to dance with him," Beth said, brushing her hand through her red hair with a flip.

"So he didn't dance with Janet right away?"

"No, he didn't ask her," Trudy said. "It was kind of weird. She walked over to *him* like she was in some kind of trance. She sat at his table, and they talked for a while and then they got up and danced."

"She didn't even tell us she was going to ask him to dance," Mary said.

Trudy chuckled. "Just went over there stone cold and started talking with him."

"Mary, did you feel slighted when she went over to talk to him?" I asked.

"What do you mean?" she said.

"Were you jealous?"

"Me? Hell no. I'm engaged. I only went with him because he asked me so politely and the girls here told me I should have a little fun before I got married."

"When are you to be married?"

"Next month. On the fourth. Why is that important?"

"I'm just trying to understand the psychology. The guy comes over to ask you to dance and winds up leaving with your friend."

"So?" Mary said.

"Could be this guy have picked up on you because you were giving him signals. Did you encourage him at all?"

"No. I wouldn't do that to John. I love him too much."

"Did you tell this guy you were getting married?"

"I said I couldn't dance with him because I was engaged, and he said he didn't want to marry me; he just wanted to dance. He was a real sweet talker, willing to tell you whatever you wanted to hear. But he was polite, and we danced two dances before he walked me back to my friends."

"Did he mention his name?" I asked.

"Brent."

"Did Brent talk about any places he frequented or mention where he worked or lived?" I asked.

"I think he said something about investments," Mary said. "He mostly tried to charm me. I only danced a second dance with him because he was kind of nice to look at."

"Mary always did like a man with facial hair," Beth said.

"Okay, I need to be honest with you now," I said. "My name is Billie Bly, and I'm a private investigator. I have reason to believe your friend may have been abducted by this guy we'll call Brent."

"I don't get it," Mary said. "Did The Outrigger hire you?"

"No. I'm working on another case, and I think Janet's disappearance might be related to it. The good news is: I know someone at the Portland Police Bureau I can talk to and try to get the police to take Janet's disappearance seriously."

"That would be a huge relief," Mary said. "We've been so worried and the cops told us she wasn't missing long enough. The only way they can act now is if she has a medical need."

"With your help, I may be able to expedite things. My boyfriend is a cop." I took their names, addresses, and phone numbers and gave each one of them my business card.

"If you hear from Janet, or if you remember anything from last night that might help, call me immediately."

Janet's car was locked, and I didn't want to break in or contaminate a possible crime scene. I walked around it, peeking into the windows for possible clues as the three women drove off. A combination of anger and fear stirred inside me. The address Mary had given as her residence was a block away from the house of the retired cop's house I had staked out on Mar's burglary case.

I pulled out my notebook and looked at the information John Benson had given me. It was the same address, only a block from the Springer house at *1330 Northwest Foley Street*. Why hadn't I noticed it when Benson gave me her address?

I flashed back to the two UPS drivers, Jimmer and Eric, to the nosey neighbor, Sally Brown, and to the guy in the Prius tilting his cap up to peek at me as he drove by. A wave of heat swept over me and my face flushed. I felt a dark force tugging at me like a magnet.

My gut told me the mystery man in Prius and Mary Johansen somehow were connected. Had the driver of the Prius been stalking Mary Johansen that day? If Brent was the guy in the Prius, why had he kidnapped Mary's friend, Janet Domingo?

And where did John Benson fit in?

Chapter 17

It was Saturday and Steve was working overtime on his serial killer case at the new FBI headquarters near the Portland Airport. I called and arranged to meet him for lunch a few blocks away at Dave's Famous Barbeque at the Cascade Station mall.

He was sitting in a wooden booth with a police report, ignoring a plate of half-eaten hot wings when I joined him.

"So, am I back in your good graces?" he said, not looking up.

"Depends," I answered.

"I don't have any time this afternoon, but . . ." He laid the report on the table and grinned at me.

"You have a one-track mind," I said. "I wanted to meet you because I might have a lead in your serial killer case."

"Does this have anything to do with your Facebook theory?" His eyes dropped to his report and he flicked a page.

"In a way. But it's completely by accident. I was reading a Facebook post on a different case and I sort of stumbled upon something."

He kept reading.

"A missing white female adult. She met a guy at the bar last night and ditched her friends without a word. She didn't show up for work this morning and her companions found her car where she left it at The Outrigger."

"The Outrigger's in Vancouver." He squinted at his report. "Not my jurisdiction."

"Janet Domingo lives in Portland. She works downtown. She missed work and her friends haven't heard from her. She's been missing for fifteen hours now and her friends are worried."

"Does she have family?"

"They live back East. I don't think they know anything about her disappearance."

"She hasn't been gone long enough unless there's reason to believe she's in danger," he said.

"You and I both know there's not a required wait time before the police can start looking for a missing person," I said.

"You and I also know people get distracted and forget to call their friends and family." He pushed the report aside and winked at me. "Sometimes they even run off and get married without telling anyone."

This was one of Steve's not so subtle hints that we should run away and tie the knot. I'm not so sure about our relationship so I ignored his comment.

"My gut tells me there's something wrong here. If you won't . . ."

"Settle down. Do you have her friends' contact information?"

"So you'll follow up on this?" I jotted down the names and numbers of Janet Domingo's fellow clubbers from my notes.

"I'm busy this afternoon, but I'll give it to one of my detectives. You're not making it easy for me. We'll have to call the Vancouver PD and get them involved and they're going to have the same reservations I do."

"You can tell them it's a priority case."

"There's an FBI liaison over there. I'll let him know it might be related."

"Thanks." I stood and gave him a peck on the cheek.

"Is there something else?" he said. "You seem . . . somewhat agitated."

"There *is* something nagging at me, but it's kind of complicated, and I don't know if I can explain it to you right now. I need some time to sort it out." I was thinking about John Benson and Mary Johansen and wondering if Benson might be the guy I saw driving the Prius in Mary's neighborhood.

"You always were the complicated one. Does it have to do with us or your case?"

"My case." *Us* was another problem I needed to figure out. "Maybe you could stop by later tonight and we could, um, talk about us."

"I'd love to, but if this bit of information turns into something I won't have time. I'll get back to you."

I sighed. It was probably for the best. Sex is just another distraction, according to my therapist. She says it keeps me from being in the present. But aren't you in the present when you make love? I don't get it.

Janet Domingo was past fear. She resided in a state of perpetual panic, her heart racing faster than her mind most of the night. Before Brent removed her from his car, he wrenched her mother's cameo ring from her finger, blindfolded her, and then carried her into some kind of box or cabinet. She wasn't sure where she was because she blacked out a few steps from the car.

But now she was crammed into a small space, sitting in an awkward upright position inside some sort of wooden storage closet. She was not alone. There were several items in the storage closet with her. Paint cans, brushes, plastic tarps, rags, and a shelf above her seemed to hold more items. There was some light now and she could see inside her space.

She had screamed all night and her throat was sore. To make things worse, fumes of paint solvent permeated the air around her and pierced her raw throat like prickly thorns.

There was a knothole in the door of the cabinet, but the opening was about the height of the shelf above her head and practically impossible to see through.

Janet had no misconception about her predicament. She knew she had been abducted with one purpose in mind. She would be raped, maybe tortured, and killed. What worried her most was the waiting. Why hadn't he already assaulted her? Why bring her here and leave her alone? She decided this was part of his game. He wanted her to fear him and be under his control.

As much as Janet didn't want to give him power over her, she couldn't stop her mind from racing. He controlled her completely and he wasn't even here.

She decided to try to get a glimpse through the peephole. Her wrists were taped behind her back and her ankles were tied too. She squirmed and wriggled like a caterpillar shimmying up a tree branch.

When her head hit the shelf above, she realized her eyes were still an inch below the aperture. She mustered some determination and pushed the top of her ahead against the board above her and it moved slightly. It wasn't nailed down. It was probably held in place by the weight of whatever rested atop it.

With that insight, she struggled to get better traction, using the side of the box for leverage, and pushed against the floor harder. This time the shelf gave way and her eye reached the knothole.

She spotted a rolling garage door and noticed some gardening tools against the wall. A concrete floor finished her snapshot before gravity forced her back into a sitting position on a small wooden crate.

If she could get out of this storage cupboard--for that is what her jail must be if she was in a garage--she could escape easily enough. She pondered her predicament for a minute, wondering how much time she had before Brent returned. She thought he might be at work, which could give her some time to break out. The odor of turpentine wafted from above, and she thought if she could tip the shelf at the right angle its contents might spill down. Maybe a tool or a knife would fall near her hands.

It was worth a try.

I watched open-mouthed at the transformation as Brenda came through the front door. The mannish deputy uniform was gone. She wore a light gray suit over a white cotton blouse. Her tapered slacks and a blazer stopping at her midriff revealed an hourglass figure. Her long copper hair, freed from the bun she wore on the job, bounced playfully as she walked.

Brenda Towne was ready for her first P.I. gig, the topaz stud in her cheek the only remnant of her cop job. She also wore a matched set of topaz earrings, with an extra three silver rings in one ear and three rings on her right hand. I felt a tug at my heart, envious of her beauty. I wished I could look that feminine.

My plan was to give Brenda the John Benson case, freeing me to work on Janet Domingo's disappearance. But as we sat across my desk, my eyes fixated again on the information Benson had given me.

"Is something wrong?" Brenda asked.

"It's this case," I said. "There's something about it that's off."

We stared at each other in silence because I didn't have an answer and she didn't know the question. I explained the coincidences of Mary Johansen's case and about my being in her neighborhood while investigating the burglaries, and how John Benson dropped into my office asking me to investigate her fidelity.

"Sounds to me like John Benson might be a prime suspect if there *is* a serial killer out there," Brenda said.

"I thought so too, except if Benson abducted Janet, wouldn't Mary have recognized him at The Outrigger? Hell, she danced with him. Also, the descriptions are totally different. Benson was shorter than the six-foot-two Trudy described. Brent had a tan; Benson was light-skinned. Brent had a beard; Benson was clean shaven. Even if Benson wore a disguise of some kind, Mary should have recognized something about her fiancé."

"What do you want me to do?" Brenda said.

"Stake out Mary. Find out if she's cheating on Benson. That's what we were hired to do. But you should look for anything that might tie Mary to this Brent character. Shit, maybe she's seeing him on the side and they're working as a team."

She took the Benson file from me and studied it. "I'll drop by where Mary works at the *Murder by the Book* bookstore and maybe start a conversation with her to see what I can learn."

"Brenda?" How could I tell her in a kind way? "Are you aware that you have a very brusque tone to your voice? It almost screams *cop*. Try a softer approach when you interview people for me."

A slow recognition appeared in her emerald eyes. "I guess I'm so used to being the no-nonsense cop, I didn't think about it. No problem. I'll work on my soft side."

"Don't get me wrong. It's okay to have that thick-skinned approach. Sometimes it's essential to this job. But in this situation, you don't want her to know you're a cop."

"Got it!"

I chuckled and she giggled. She is so much like me, it hurts. Maybe I could use this mirror image of myself to remind me to be a bit softer with Steve.

I walked Brenda into the laundry room where Angel had set up a command post for our Facebook serial killer case. It consisted of two folding card tables set up on each side of the room with an aisle down the middle to get to the washer and dryer.

Three computers occupied the tables with Eric straddling the aisle. He scooted back and forth on a swivel office chair, alternating between two laptops on one table and a desktop computer at the other makeshift desk. Facebook pages were displayed on the two laptops and the desktop revealed of some type of web page computer code. Eric hesitated between the two computers and began pecking away on a smart phone.

"How is the sleuthing going?" I asked.

"Slow and nowhere." Eric continued tapping on the smart phone.

"What are you looking for?" Brenda asked. No reply. She grabbed an office chair, straddled it, resting her arms on its back, and scooted next to Eric. "Aren't you supposed to be looking for a serial killer? Why are you on your phone?"

"I'm checking out our victims' social sites," he said, mesmerized by the phone screen. "Donna Timberlake posted on her iPhone's Twist app so her friends could see she was on her way to meet them at a bar. It shows her departure time, her route--including the street address, each minute along the way to the bar, and the time she would arrive. If someone wanted to hijack her, he had a map of her route and could have waited for her along the way."

"How would her killer be able to see it," Brenda said. "I'm assuming it would be viewed only by her social buddies."

"You would think so," Eric said. "But Donna also had the option of forwarding her Twist locations to Facebook."

"She didn't," Brenda said.

"Oh yes she did." Eric swiped his iPhone and a Facebook page appeared in place of the Twist map. "And her Facebook privacy controls allow the public at large to view her page. Of course she could have posted her location using Facebook's location app too."

"Do people do that?" Brenda asked.

"All the time," Eric said. "It's a prestige thing to brag about yourself and what you're doing. Many of today's social apps cater to those desires."

"Do you think this is how she was abducted?" Brenda said.

"You tell me. She never made it to the bar to meet her friends and she was never seen again." Eric finally looked away from his phone to Brenda and his face went white. "You're the cop who arrested me!"

"It's okay," she said. "You're legal now. At least until your trial."

"I thought you were Billie." He gazed past Brenda to me, standing in the doorway. I gave him the thumbs up. "You guys sound so much alike."

"She's going to be working with us," I said. "I told her about you helping me in the hopes it might carry some favor with a judge if we're successful."

"Yeah, well, I'm having my doubts about the successful part," he said.

"Why?" Brenda asked.

"This idea of finding someone who is stalking victims online is crazy," he said. "It can't be done."

"I found you," I said.

"That was dumb luck. And we weren't working as hard not to be found as this guy probably is. He slid his phone across the makeshift desk and tilted a computer monitor toward us. Do you realize how easy it is to become anonymous on the web?"

"Show me," Brenda said, combing her copper hair away from her face with her fingers.

Eric flushed and managed a smile. "Okay, picture this. Anyone can set up a fake Facebook page. All you need is an anonymous email account, which you can get at Yahoo or Google or some obscure service. Once you create a fake name, your page is born."

"Isn't that against the Facebook rules?" Brenda said.

"Sure. If they catch you. And then all you need is another email address, and you can create another Facebook page using another fake name. This guy we're looking for could have multiple Facebook pages already."

"Isn't there some way we could trace his Internet Protocol address?" Brenda asked.

Eric licked his lips and thought about it. "If this was an official investigation you could get a warrant."

"We'd have to have probable cause," I said. "And a name, which we also don't have."

"Yeah, and all that sounds like a pain," Eric said. He pounded the keys of his laptop and the rickety card table wobbled at the fierce attack.

Brenda leaned into Eric to observe the screen better, and her hair brushed against his shoulder. He continued to pound on the keys like a drummer performing a solo in the middle of a rock song.

"This investigation isn't an official one anyway," Brenda said. "If we learned something, we could take it to the FBI and maybe they could make something happen."

"If they'd take us seriously," I said. "Somehow I doubt they would."

"You guys are missing the point," Eric said. "If this guy has killed as many women as you say, he's learned to be careful. And if he's using the social media to find his victims, he's no dummy."

"What are you getting at?" I asked.

He quit pounding the keyboard and turned to smile at Brenda, still only inches away.

"If I was doing this, I wouldn't want to leave an Internet trail. I'd be stealing other people's Wi-Fi signals when I went on Facebook. You can drive up to any apartment building in Portland and there are probably as many Wi-Fi signals as there are people living there. Most are password protected but not all of them. And it's pretty easy to figure out someone's password by looking at some of the cute names associated with their Internet router. Sometimes the password is close to or the same as the name indicated by the signal. One of the larger brand routers uses the word "password" as its default password if you can believe that."

"So you drive up to an apartment, log on Facebook, look for targets anonymously, and surf the web," Brenda said.

"You got it," Eric said. "Except you can also log on free at Internet cafés, coffee shops, motels, and you could even go to the library and use their computers. If that's the case, good luck tracing a Facebook page to this guy's Internet Protocol address, and if you did, it would probably belong to some poor dude who's Wi-Fi he had hacked."

"Can you find his Facebook page?" I said.

"Doubtful. The best way to track him down is to scour the pages of the women he killed and see if we can find any common *friends* among them.

"So, do you think you can find him?" Brenda asked.

He shook his head and grimaced. "It will be like finding a needle in a bucket of needles," he said. "To make things worse, some of these missing women didn't use privacy features. That means anyone could Google them and look at their Facebook page and not have to be a *friend*. How do you find someone who isn't even listed on their pages?"

"You mean someone can view my page, and I wouldn't even know them?" I said.

"Everything you haven't blocked. Photos you upload, your posts, where you are, where you'll be, what high school you went to, where you work and the city you live in. It's a bonanza for the bad guys."

"I would think most women would protect themselves," I said.

"I noticed you haven't changed your privacy settings," he said. "You know Facebook's default settings are open for everyone to view. It's up to you to take control and restrict who can see you."

"But if I change my privacy settings the public won't be able to find me."

"You need a Business page," he said. "Maybe when this is all over I can help you convert it and set up a marketing plan."

"Isn't there some way of finding this guy?" I asked. "Time is running out for Janet Domingo."

Eric sighed. "There are one or two things I can try, but it will be time consuming and there is no guarantee."

"I have faith in you," Brenda said. "I know you'll come up with something."

Chapter 18

Angel tried to concentrate on what she was doing, but it was difficult at best with the elephant in the room she needed to ignore.

She had chosen to casual out fashion-wise, wearing only blue jeans and a white blouse with her new blonde hairstyle. She felt plain and frumpy outside of her peacock persona of colorful hairstyles, stiletto shoes, and unique outfits. Not many women could pull off Daffodil Yellow eye shadow, but she could rock it, along with black lipstick. Today she stuck with Boring Brown for the eyes and Even More Boring Pink for the lips. Not that those names would ever be trademarked.

She tapped away at her keyboard, attempting to appear industrious. *Let's see, 'event?' What was the name of it again?*

Was she trying to look plain to scare Chris away, or was she trying to look like Billy to attract him? She long suspected he had a crush on Billie. It was the only explanation for him hanging around the office so much. But now he had shifted his attention to her since their little roll in the grass.

"Event?" The word stared at her from the screen, waiting for an answer. *Self Defense Class*, she finally typed. Why was she starting a new event? She created this class on Facebook weeks ago. Fifteen people had already signed up. Billie was going to lead the class in three days. She merely had to remind people not to forget it and see if she could get a few more signups.

"Hey, when you're done, how about we go out to lunch? I'm getting hungry." It was the elephant again, foraging for food now.

"I'm busy," she said, "and I don't want to go out with you anywhere. Not dinner, not a movie, and certainly not lunch."

She looked up from the computer monitor she had been hiding behind and gave Chris Johnson her best sneer. He only smiled back, looking dapper in a vintage suit he had picked up at her favorite shop on Southeast Hawthorne Street. He had followed her there yesterday and even asked her opinion. When she tried to lie, telling him she didn't like it, he chuckled and took out his credit card.

"You have to be getting hungry," Chris said. "I am."

"I told you, I'm too busy to go anywhere today. I have too much to do getting ready for Billie's class. Get out of here and leave me alone!"

But she couldn't take her eyes from his groovy 70's Norfolk Hunting buttercup-tan three-piece suit. It had a mod disco look and the Norfolk hunting style belted back. The wide notched lapels and three saddle bag-style front pockets made her weak in the knees. An urge came over her to go out buy an outrageous horseback riding suit for herself. They could walk long the Pearl District's hoity-toity fashion stores and be the envy of everyone.

"I'm not asking for a date," he said. "I just want to show off my new duds. It would be more fun with you along. I could take you by your apartment, you could change into something a little more stylish, and I'll take you to the Chipotle Mexican Grill.

"It's too crowded."

"Okay, how about Andina?"

Shit. She loved Peruvian Food and Andina was so good. So--ick--romantic. It did have a bar. Maybe she could drink him under the table and leave him behind. She began to weaken. They could dash to her place for a quick makeover--he would probably try to get fresh--and be at Andina in an hour if she didn't give in to his come-on.

"You probably have to make reservations at lunch time." What was she saying? She couldn't go out with him. She used to call him Chris, The Creep. They all did: Billie, her brothers, and even her boyfriend, Steve. But no one seemed to call him The Creep after he helped Billie in her last case.

"I'll call Andina now," he said.

"Who you gonna call, creep?"

Okay, there was still one person who called him a creep. Earl Monroe closed the front door. Her Earl. The rat that stepped out on her with another woman claiming he was working on a case. He grinned, wearing khakis and a blue and white checkered button-down shirt over a generous belly.

A startled Chris turned. "The naked lady man," he said, staring at a tattoo of a naked woman on Earl's arm.

"Hi, Creep. What the heck are you wearing? Looks like a rubber suit. You finally get accepted to the loony bin?"

Angel forgot how much these two disliked each other. Chris once thought Earl had tried to run him over in his tow-truck downtown. Earl had resented the accusation, and she wondered if he was sensitive to Chris's making fun of his tattoo. She suspected Chris had picked up on her dislike of Earl's well-endowed naked woman and needled Earl by calling him the naked lady man. It's not that she didn't like tattoos. She did. Just not a tattoo of naked women in such a conspicuous place on his arm.

"What do *you* want?" she said. It was a weak question considering she was still mad at him for stepping out on her. Crap, that's what led to her revenge tryst with Chris. She should be absolutely ready to kill Earl for that alone. But she found it hard to feel anger toward him. Had she actually hoped he was telling the truth about being with that woman?

"I just wanted to talk." Earl stared at her head. "The blonde hair is a different look, isn't it? I almost thought you were Billie at first. So where were you going with the creep?"

"Chris asked me out to lunch, and he's not a creep."

"Yeah, and you *are not* invited," Chris said.

"Cancel it," Earl said. "We need to talk. I feel bad it's taken me this long to get back to you, but I've been sort of undercover. I wasn't even living at home. I moved into a condo complex down by the river and created a different lifestyle and identity for myself. I'd like to explain things to you now that the job is over."

"I don't know," she said, weakening. If she went out with Chris to lunch, he'd interpret it as an invitation to pursue her. But leaving with Earl would mean reliving the hurt and shame of his affair with that other woman.

"Where were you going for lunch?" Earl asked.

"Andina," Chris said. "A special place for a special girl."

"She's a woman, not a girl," Earl said. "And she deserves to be treated like a woman, not manipulated by an ex-con."

Chris unbuttoned his exquisite jacket and took it off.

"What are you doing?" Angel said.

"I don't want to get any of his blood on this jacket when I beat him to a pulp," Chris said.

Earl started unbuttoning his shirt, exposing a T-shirt underneath. "Likewise here, you creep."

"Now boys," she muttered, not knowing what to say or do next. Jeez, it felt like there were two bull elephants in the room now, flinging their tusks in the air. She was afraid she might be trampled in the melee. And yet, she experienced a rush of excitement.

Were these two men about to fight over her? How could she stop them? Did she want to stop them? Of course she wanted to stop them. Well, maybe she wanted to stop them. Who would win if she didn't? Who did she want to win? The questions came so fast they confused her.

"Stop it right now." Out of desperation, she pulled a thirty-eight from her purse and took a step toward them. "The first person who takes a swing, gets a slug."

They stopped, staring wide-eyed at her. This was followed by a pair of grins as they closed in on each other. Chris strutted like a bantam rooster and swung a haymaker, which Earl easily ducked. He was deceivingly quick for his size, she thought.

Earl countered with a thrust to Chris's stomach, which had little effect. This surprised her too. She always thought Chris was kind of a wimp. Chris and Earl danced and strutted around the small office pushing each other against filing cabinets. Their gyrations toppled furniture and scattered a bowl of candy set out for clients in the waiting area. Angel stepped back toward her desk, holding her gun at her side, her mouth agape.

In a minute it was over. Chris socked Earl in the eye and he staggered backward. But when he closed in for the kill, Earl retaliated with an uppercut to the jaw. Chris grimaced and landed on his back, semi-conscious.

Angel ran to him and cradled his head. "Chris, are you okay?"

He managed a smile and put his hand to a tender jaw. "Au'll be aw'right. Guave me a sec and au'll finosh him off so we can hauve luanch." His jaw was red and looked tender.

"You'll do no such thing. If either one of you throw one more punch I'll never speak to either of you again." That's what she should have said earlier instead of pulling her gun.

"Can we go to lunch and talk?" Earl put his blue and white checkered shirt on and buttoned it. "I need to clear the air with you. He'll be okay."

Angel stood and walked to Earl. He took her hand and smirked at Chris.

"What the hell is going on out here?" Billie had entered the room from the back of the house where she was working with Eric and Brenda.

"I was on the phone with someone and it sounded like all hell breaking loose."

She stared at the room. A settee turned over, candy and papers scattered everywhere, and Chris sprawled on the floor, carefully opening and closing his jaw.

"There was a bit of a skirmish," Angel said. "Nothing serious. I'll clean things up after lunch. Earl wants to explain something to me."

Billie nodded absently and knelt beside Chris. "I'd better get you some ice. That looks like a nasty bruise."

"Yood betta gat him soume too," Chris said, "His aye looks baud."

Angel noticed Earl's red and swollen eye, where Chris had tagged him, and held back a whimper. She ran to Chris, bent over and kissed him gently, full on the lips. "I'll be back after lunch and take care of you," she said.

Billie's mouth flew open. "What the . . .?"

Angel took Earl by the arm and ushered him toward the front door.

Earl stared back at Chris. "What, uh, why? What just happened?"

"I'll be here," the former creep said with an ear-to-ear smile, apparently no longer feeling the effects of Earl's blow.

Chapter 19

Brenda suggested lunch, but I wanted to check back with Steve to see if he had made any progress finding Janet Domingo. Eric seemed relieved when I said I couldn't go, and he trailed after Brenda with eager eyes and a pogo stick bounce that made me wonder if he'd developed a crush on the deputy.

I called Steve and made a date for lunch at one o'clock at Huber's Cafe downtown. I took a few minutes and sifted through Eric's notes consisting of hundreds of names printed in columns on legal-sized paper and with handwritten arrows connecting some of them. He told me he was looking for correlations between the victims and people who had *friended* the dead women. He highlighted a few women's names in yellow, but I couldn't make sense of any of it.

I pulled up my Facebook page and searched for Christine Crawford, the serial killer's last victim. She had worked at Huber's and it was another reason I suggested to Steve that we have lunch there. I hoped I might find an employee who could shed some light on Christine's death.

On a whim, I printed her profile picture with her boyfriend, Jeff, and tucked it into my purse. You can never overlook a boyfriend or a spouse, usually considered the prime suspect by police in a murder investigation.

Thirty minutes later, I spotted a parking space in front of Huber's, pulled Myrtle to the curb, and fumbled my debit card into a green machine for a parking time slip.

I ate at Huber's Café once about a year ago, but the stunning stain glass high ceiling in the main dining room still mesmerized me. A gentleman in a black vest over a white shirt and tie introduced himself as Mario. He was short with curly black hair and a professional manner.

"I'm meeting a friend," I said. "But before you seat me, could you help me with a few questions?" I handed him my business card and he squinted at it with tired brown eyes. He was short and young, close to the age of Christine, I guessed.

"Is this about Christine Crawford?" He tugged at a goatee. "The cops told me not to discuss her death with anyone."

"Mario," I said in an urgent tone. "Another girl has gone missing and there's a good chance she has been abducted by the same man who killed Christine. I'm working for some friends of hers who are worried sick and the police are treating it as just another missing person case. The sooner I track down this killer, the better for this other girl."

He shrugged. "How can I help?"

"Did you know Christine?"

Mario looked around the room as if for other customers entering the establishment.

"Yeah. But the police were here asking all sorts of questions. I just seated one of them in the back."

"It's okay. He's the friend I'm meeting," I said. "Is there someplace private we could chat?"

He nodded. "Heather, could you take over?"

A slim brunette, with bright colored tattoos on her arms and neck, nodded and came around the end of the bar toward the door. Mario guided me through the kitchen, where two cooks were creating salads and sandwiches on a butcher block table. He steered me into a break room, consisting of three chairs, a row of metal lockers, and a portable rack on wheels where uniforms and aprons hung.

"I can't talk long." He closed the door behind us and pushed against it to make sure the door was tight. "Business picks up in another few minutes."

"What did the cops ask you about?" I said.

"They wanted to know about Christine's relationship with Jeff Jones. He worked here with Chrissy. Was everything okay between them? Did they fight? Was he overly possessive? Did Chrissy ever talk about having problems with him? You know, the usual bull."

"What did you tell them?"

"They were, like, the perfect couple. He worshiped her and she thought he was a great guy. They had talked about getting married after they saved up some money. Jeff told me they wanted to open their own restaurant."

"Why did he cancel going hiking with her the day she went missing?"

Mario plopped on a three-legged stool. "The cops asked me that. He got called in to work for someone who was sick. No way he could have killed her. She called in after he got to here to tell him she was going on the hike without him."

"Was he upset about that?"

"Nah. He just laughed about it and said he shouldn't have answered the phone when work called."

"Did anything strange happen here in the weeks before her disappearance?"

He turned toward a clatter in the kitchen. "Sorry, habit. How do you mean?"

"Was Christine upset about anything? Did she have a run in with any of the customers or the staff? Just anything out of the ordinary, even if it didn't involve her."

"Chrissy got along with everybody," he said. "I think I need to get back to work. That ruckus is sure to bring my boss out of his office."

I thanked him and he guided me back through the kitchen. In the dining area an irate customer was scolding a waitress about something. She remained polite and said she would get his order right away.

Mario stopped so abruptly that I ran into him. "I'm sorry," he said. "But I just thought of something."

"About Chrissy?"

"It's something that happened with her, yeah, but I was thinking of Jeff. One night I saw him at a table arguing with a customer. When I asked him later about what happened, he said some guy was asking for the name of *the cute blonde waitress*, meaning Chrissie. Jeff got upset with the guy and told him we weren't allowed to give out employee names."

"So?"

"The guy was a smart ass, and he wouldn't take 'no' for an answer. Later, Jeff caught him talking to Chrissy by the cashier's desk. She was trying to be friendly with the guy, but Jeff said he could see she was agitated. He blew up and told the guy to get out."

"Why would he get so volatile?" I asked.

"I don't know," Mario said. "It wasn't too long afterwards that some maniac in a car ran him and his bicycle off the road on his way home from work. He was all banged up and his bike was totaled. He missed work for a week."

"When did this happen?" I asked.

"About a week after Chrissy disappeared. I don't remember the date."

"Did he get the make and model of the car?"

"I think he said it was a Prius."

"A Prius? What color?"

"Don't know. Jeff just said some jerk in a Prius ran him off the road. He didn't say what color."

Whereever I turned, it seemed I was hearing about a Prius. I knew I was on the right track, but I didn't seem to be getting anywhere.

"Did you tell the police about this?"

"They didn't talk to me that long. Jeff might have talked with them. You'd have to ask him."

"Is he here today?"

"He doesn't work here anymore." Mario's face saddened. "He quit a couple weeks after Chrissy disappeared. He's been pretty depressed since her disappearance."

"Do you have his address by any chance?"

"I can't give it to you, but I'll text him and see if he'll let me share it."

"That would be great."

I thanked Mario, and he took me to a back corner of the restaurant where Steve sat nursing a coke.

"Got here early," he said. "Flashed my badge and asked for a table in a quiet location."

"Taking advantage of your authority, huh?" I slid into the nineteenth century mahogany booth and placed my purse beside me.

"It *is* police business in a way," he said.

A waiter came and I ordered an iced tea. Huber's specializes in turkey entrees, so we both ordered a grilled turkey salad.

"Any luck with Janet Domingo's disappearance?" I asked.

"Nothing yet." He shifted his weight on the wooden bench seat and scanned the room as if looking for an answer. "We have a bulletin out on her. Missing Person's Unit has been advised. I gave it top priority. I can't do much more short of going to the press. We don't want her to turn up suddenly or alert a perp that we're on to him, if that's the case."

"Did you interview her friends?" I ran a finger through the rut-like veins on the dark table top.

"I sent officers to interview each of her buddies and her employer. Nobody seems able to offer much help. We're circulating a description of this guy and a picture of Janet to all patrol units."

"What does the FBI think?"

"I told them about your idea and it's up on the board with a bunch of other leads, but . . ." He grabbed my finger to stop me from picking at the table top.

"They think it's a bunch of hooey?" My face flushed. "Each victim had a Facebook page and each one mentioned a specific place and time they were going to be when they went missing. They might as well have given the killer a road map to find them.

"Speaking of which, there's a social phone app called Twist that charts a person's departure time, the route they will take, and where they will be each minute between the beginning and the end of their trip. Donna Timberlake used it and posted her route to her Facebook page the day she disappeared. She was walking and it was only ten blocks from her house. Our killer could have seen her post and abducted her along her route."

"Settle down," Steve said. "It isn't that the task force is discounting the Facebook angle, but we've got a good lead right now."

"Oh really?" I tapped my finger at the table's groove as the waiter brought my iced tea.

"We got a tip from a relative of one of the dead women about a man who was seen with one of them shortly before her disappearance."

"Which woman?" I asked.

"Cynthia Miller. She lived on the West side, not far from where Janet Domingo resides. She had been attending a fitness Aerobathon at the Southwest Community Center on Southwest Forty Fifth just before she disappeared."

"A fitness what?"

"It's like a marathon, but with aerobics," he said. "Afterward she made plans to meet a couple of her exercise friends at the Laughing Planet restaurant."

"And she didn't show up?"

"No, and it was only two blocks away. Her car was found later in the parking lot of the community center. She had parked on the opposite side of the building so they didn't leave together."

"What did her friends say?" I asked.

"They waited for a while, tried calling her, and then went looking for her. After a several hours worrying and a phone call to her boyfriend, they called the police."

"Boyfriend's name?"

"Scott Blanchard. We cleared him. He was at a Timbers game with some friends. Airtight alibi."

"Not to beat a dead horse, but my Facebook lead sounds more promising so far."

"We've identified the guy she was seen with earlier that morning. He's a former boyfriend who has been stalking her off and on. At this point he's our prime suspect."

"What's his name?"

"Sorry, that's on a need to know right now."

Great. So there's a person of interest now and he won't give me a name.

"He could still be using Facebook to stalk his victims. Maybe it's the same guy I'm trailing."

"Oh really?" He smirked. "Who would that be?"

"The guy I'm tracking on Facebook," I said.

The waiter brought our grilled turkey salads and we munched without talking for a few minutes, each of us thinking about what the other had said. Finally, Steve broke the silence.

"You got a name for your perp?" he asked.

"Brent," I said. "I'm assuming it's an alias, and I'm working on another possibility."

"No last name. Possibly an alias anyway, and you think we're wasting time with *our* lead?"

"I didn't say that. I think that maybe we're tracking the same guy and we could be of help to each other."

"You're going to have to bring more to the table than just theories," he said.

"I've got more," I said, jabbing my fork at him.

"Such as?" He chuckled.

"Okay, I've been holding something back."

He stabbed a piece of salad with his fork. "I'm listening."

I told him about my interview with the Sally Brown, the nosey neighbor on Northwest Foley, when I investigated the Facebook burglary. I filled him in on the empty cop's house, Eric and Jimmer in the UPS truck talking with the driver of a fire truck, and the guy in the Prius who pulled a baseball cap over his eyes and gave me a startled sideways look as he pulled out behind the UPS truck.

"Maybe he was a partner of your two burglary suspects." he said. "You should ask your burglar friend, Eric."

"You know about Eric?"

"Angel told me about him when I called the other day and how he's helping you."

"There's more," I said. I told him about John Benson hiring me to find out if his girlfriend is cheating on him."

"So?" He buttered a roll. "You must get plenty of those kinds of cases."

"Benson's girlfriend, Mary Johansen, lives three houses down from the cop's house that I thought might be Eric and Jimmer's next target. Three houses from where I saw the guy in the Prius. And now Mary's best friend, Janet, has been abducted."

"I don't get it." He took another bite of his salad and chewed it for a minute. "So you saw a suspicious person in the vicinity of one of the missing women's friend's house? It's a coincidence. One case doesn't need to be related to another.

"Think of this way," he said. "Benson asks you to investigate his girlfriend and when you're doing this you run across a crime being perpetrated against a friend of hers. There's no link except you noticed a suspicious guy during your burglary case. Like I said, he could be a silent partner with your friend. You should ask him."

He remained thoughtful for a minute, buttered another roll, and said: "It would make more sense if Mary Johansen was the one who went missing. Otherwise, I don't see a link."

"Facebook is the link," I said. "He could have found Janet on Mary's Facebook page, just as I did, and decided he liked her better."

"You got anything else?" He got out a notepad and pen and jotted down a few words in chicken scratches.

I'd been holding back my ace card. I told him what Mario revealed to me regarding Christine, Jeff and the troublemaking customer. He nodded politely, waiting for the punch line. Then I told him about Jeff being run off the road by the guy in the Prius.

"Could be another coincidence, but I'll make sure the team looks into it."

"And?" I leaned across the table and wrapped his blue tie around my index finger.

He grabbed at my finger and laughed. "Okay, I'll try to get the FBI to take your Facebook theory seriously. Do you have anything else to share?"

"Nothing tangible. Except the longer I work on this the more I have this feeling of impending doom."

"Doom?"

I unraveled his tie and straightened it. "I can't explain it, but it feels like someone is messing with me."

"How so?"

"You know how an expert chess player lures his victim into checkmate by pretending to make a false move?"

"The only thing I know about chess, I've seen on T.V. One person says: 'you sure you want to do that?' And the other guy smiles and takes his rook. Next thing happens, the first guy says 'checkmate.'"

"Well, I feel like I'm trapped in a game of chess, but I don't know the rules. It feels like I have some kind of connection with this guy I'm looking for. It manifests itself in these weird coincidences. Seeing that guy in the Prius, John Benson's relationship with Mary Johansen, her friendship with Janet Domingo, and now this Brent character. We all seem interlinked to each other somehow. These coincidences must add up to something greater than what I'm seeing. I wish I could figure it out."

"You've just got too much stress going on in your life." Steve displayed an impish grin and his brown eyes sparkled. "I know a cure for that."

I rolled my blues at him. "You have one cure for everything and it's always the same thing."

"So I'm not very original. You have to admit, it *does* relax you."

It was a reminder that my guilt and depression are never far away, even in the middle of an exciting case. I needed someone to take me from the darkness for a while. Even a few minutes.

"You still have that room option at the Modera Hotel?"

"Shit, yes," he said. He grabbed the restaurant bill and added a generous tip. He stopped in mid-signing, staring at the check.

"What's wrong?" I asked.

"I must have used that stress reduction line on you a hundred times and this is the first time it worked."

I put my hand over his and grinned at him.

"Honey, you could have said: 'You want to?' and I would have been ready for action. Although, it wouldn't hurt if you could come up with a new line."

He finished signing the bill and escorted me out of Huber's with my hand on his butt.

Chapter 20

Trixie waited at a table in the Happy Family Chinese restaurant, a few blocks from the Adidas headquarters on North Greeley Avenue.

Connie had raved about the menu, but she was late. He shook his head at the red lacquered tables covered with plexiglass and faded plastic flowers and wondered what she saw in this place. Its best feature seemed to be the seedy bar in the back room, where a small crowd of regulars headed after entering through the front door.

He had entered the so-called lounge and noticed a woman and two men drinking their lunch at the bar and another woman passed out on a table, a cigarette burning between her fingers. The unconscious woman reminded him of Janet back at his house.

He would leave her alone all day and tonight, until her nerves were frayed, and then begin making his demands with the implication he might set her free if she cooperated. He would make her repeat things his mother used to say to him as a child, and then he would punish her. When he tired of that, he would torture and berate her for his mother's misandry.

He sighed, bored with the game of punishing these women over and over but unable to stop himself. He had fantasized a *ménage à trois* with Janet and Billy Bly to spice things up a bit, but now as he thought about Connie's high threshold for pain and her willingness to please, he wondered if he might coax her to join him in the fun and games.

Would three women be too much for him to handle? Not if Connie were to become an ally. He had wondered from the night they first had sex if he could convert her. Her past indicated an abused and emotionally bereft childhood, which might make her easily manipulated.

It would be a huge risk on his part. He really liked Connie, but if she wouldn't go along, he would have to kill her too. He didn't want to think about that possibility.

His thoughts drifted back to Janet. He imagined her struggling to get out of the same cabinet, he had been locked in as a child. He imagined little Brucie in there with her, telling her everything would be okay, and then climbing on that magical butterfly's back and flying through the cabinet's knothole above the pain while his surrogate mother suffered the prolonged darkness and the paint fumes cutting at her lungs.

Connie entered the restaurant and caught him smiling to himself. She wore a short black skirt with a white blouse and sensible black shoes. He admired her bright red lipstick and knew she wore it for him. Her infectious smile eased his weariness and he returned her grin.

"You sure look pleased about something," she said. "Could it be me?"

"Could be," he said. "I have a present for you."

She scooted into the booth across from him and he fished a dainty cameo ring from his jacket pocket, he had taken from Janet the night before. He knew it had belonged to her mother because she posted a picture of it on her Facebook Timeline.

"This was my mother's ring," he said. "I remember her wearing it when I was little, and I thought it was a shame to be locked away in a box. I was hoping you would wear it so I could admire it again."

"Oh, I couldn't take it if it was your mother's," she said. "What if we were to break up for some reason?"

"Then you can give it back if it eases your conscience," he said. "But in the meantime, I can enjoy seeing it again on your lovely finger."

164

"I don't know . . ."

"Promise me you'll wear it every day so I can enjoy both of you, the ring and the person who is becoming special to me."

He watched her closely. He knew he had come on a little strong, but if she balked, he could make apologies for what sounded like a profession of love for which she might not be ready. But if she accepted . . . well, it might eventually lead to the relationship he hoped for.

Her face blushed and she took the ring from his hand and placed it on the ring finger of her right hand. "It's beautiful. I'll wear it proudly."

Things were going well. He wondered if there was a French phrase for a sexual relationship involving a man and three women.

Janet forced her head against the wooden shelf above her. It raised several inches and metallic objects rattled above her head. But when she lowered herself, the plank fell back into place on top of metal brackets.

The paint fumes were unbearable. They pierced her throat and inflamed her lungs. She was light-headed. Bluish translucent spots hovered before her eyes, and she thought she might pass out. She tried calming her breathing. Her hands were still taped behind her back, but her ankles weren't bound. They were, however, asleep from sitting in an enclosed space for so long.

I've got to be strong, she thought, if I'm going to get out of here. She guessed her captor must be away at work and this gave her a short time span to get away before he returned. When she thought about the ghoul returning, bile burned in her throat with the acrid turpentine fumes.

She wriggled her feet, attempting to get the blood circulating in her ankles and legs for better thrust. After a few minutes of the stretching exercises, she pushed as hard as she could, forcing every muscle in her body to contribute to the action.

The result was startling. Her head cracked against the shelf and raised it to a point where it stopped abruptly. She tweaked her neck and fell back in a heap. The shelf returned to the brackets, but this time some objects toppled off.

A screwdriver, some nails, and something wet spilled onto her head and lap. Her hair became drenched with paint thinner, and she coughed and tried to move away from the cascading fluid. She squeezed her eyelids tight as the liquid ran down her face, and she attempted to alleviate the sting from her eyes by brushing them against the shoulders of her dress.

She forced herself to cry, hoping the tears would clean away the caustic liquid. Her lungs filled with the pungent smell, but she pushed through the pain and, after a few minutes, she was able to open her eyes without as much stinging. She gazed toward where she'd noticed the screwdriver fall on her lap. She shifted her body and the screwdriver rolled from her thigh and onto a can of paint. She rotated her body toward the screwdriver, managed to snag it with two fingers, and manipulated it into her grasp.

The screwdriver gouged her flesh as she dug it into the duct tape. The tedious clawing eventually rendered her muscles useless, and she stopped to rest. The sweat from her brow once again rained the solvent into her eyes.

She cried again to flush the turpentine. As the pain gradually dissipated, she wondered if all of her gouging and twisting of the tape might have weakened it enough. She concentrated her strength to her wrists and tried to separate them. The gap between her hands widened, so she tried twisting the tape at various angles, and her skin seemed to rip with the tape. She pulled again and the tape stretched a little more.

She contorted her right hand and heard a tearing sound as the tape separated from her burning wrists. A minute later, she had the screwdriver in front of her and began attacking the cabinet door hinges with renewed vigor. This too, took wrist strength, but she ignored the pain and concentrated on escaping from her hell hole.

"You can do this," she said. "Just keep turning the screw. When you get out of here, you'll just open the garage door and run. You're almost there. Two screws to go."

When she finished with the screws, the hinges, pressed into the wood for so many years, resisted her efforts to dislodge them. She leaned back and kicked against the right side of the cabinet door. The hinges on the left door were still screwed in and the two doors were locked together in the center so when the right door finally gave away the two cabinet doors swung open like a wobbly gate.

Soft fluorescent lighting rewarded her efforts as she climbed out of the cabinet and staggered to the floor. She crawled for a moment searching for another burst of energy. "You can do this," she reminded herself. "Just get up, and take it one step at a time."

But when she managed to stand up and survey her surroundings, something felt wrong. The room seemed too small to be a garage. Yet it had a garage door. Janet guessed the room to be twelve by fourteen feet. She couldn't imagine a car fitting in it comfortably.

She went to the garage door, twisted the handle and tugged. It wouldn't budge. She looked to the floor, but see didn't a gap or any sunlight beneath the door. Of course it could be night. She'd lost all track of time. She stared at an overhead guide rail designed to assist in opening the garage door. It looked new and shiny, like the door had never been used.

Why did he make this room look like a garage? She surveyed the area again and noticed the usual things you would find in a garage. A hose, gardening tools, a stack of boxes on shelves, a workbench without tools, and a black and white-checkered linoleum floor. There was nothing here she could use as a weapon except the screwdriver she found in the storage cabinet.

There were no windows. The only door led inside to the house and it was locked. She couldn't remove the door hinges with her screwdriver, because they were on the other side of the door, so she started working at the lock mechanism.

Janet cried again, but not because of the stinging solvent in her eyes. She was overcome by her diminishing hope.

Trixie had tried to get Connie to skip work and come home with him for some fun and games, but she had a presentation scheduled with some of the asshole mucky mucks at Adidas.

It left him with an emptiness inside, he desperately wanted to fill. He decided he would move the timetable up with Janet instead of playing mental games to break her spirit.

He moved around his kitchen with fervor, opening a can of chicken noodle soup and heating it on the stovetop. He would leave her in the cabinet and hand-feed the soup to her. She would be helpless and grateful for something to soothe her throat, which doubtless would be sore from her screaming and the paint thinner fumes he had thoughtfully provided.

He poured the piping hot soup into a large blue mug, retrieved his jailer keys from a cup hook in the mudroom, and proceeded down the back stairs.

He had taken special care to recreate the garage interior in the basement. The attention to detail was incredible. It had taken him nearly six months to build the room. Hauling the garage door sheet metal down the stairs in sections was difficult. He mounted it against the wall in three pieces as you would a giant puzzle. He even installed a non-working door opener mechanism to affect realism.

Trixie had moved all of the remnants of the days he was tormented from his parent's garage to make a jail in the basement. This included the cabinet, in which his mother and *the butcher* had locked him in, and all of its contents, especially the paint solvents.

Everything had to be exactly the same, so his playmates could feel what he had experienced as a child.

It was necessary to move the garage into the basement so his playmate's screams would not be heard from the outside. He had also attempted to soundproof the room to lessen the likelihood someone in the house might hear a disturbing cry for help. It had not been tested so he hoped Connie would not hear Janet's cries when she visited.

As he stood at the door, key in hand, the smell of the chicken soup triggered him. He flashed back to another time in his childhood. He was in the backyard with his father, *the butcher*. His two sisters had been taken shopping by his thoughtful mother so they wouldn't witness the carnage.

His father, a tall man, loomed behind a tree stump with an ax in one hand and gripped his pet rooster by the neck. "It's time you became a man," he said.

"I don't want to be a man," Brucie said. "I'm only a kid."

"When I finish, this thing will run around the yard without a head. Your job is to catch him and hold onto him until he stops trying to run. I don't want him stumbling into a neighbor's yard."

"I don't want to, father, please?"

"You'll do it or I'll take this ax *to you*," he screamed.

He put Sampson's neck across the stump and in one blow the head was gone. He let go of the bird and it ran off like it didn't know it was dead. Brucie stared at his friend, running across the lawn with blood gushing from where its head had been. It was heading for the Larsen's yard.

"Get that damn bird," *the butcher* said, waving the ax at him.

Brucie tore off after Sampson, but the rooster veered and ran in circles. Then it stopped, pivoted, and came right at him. Brucie also turned and ran, his father lacing the back yard with profanities.

When he turned back, he saw his friend lying in the grass under the apple tree, kicking and shaking. He went over and picked the bird up by its neck as his father had instructed. He hugged its twitching body. His best pal, his only friend, was dead and he felt empty inside. He took Sampson to his father even though his intense hatred for the man bubbled up in his throat.

"You are completely worthless. There are two to go," he said, alluding to his sisters' hens, and he retrieved Madonna from her wire pen and placed her against the tree stump. Madonna had seen what had happened to Sampson, and she screeched and fought *the butcher* as much as a hen can fight a man.

He whacked her head off and watched the bird flail across the lawn. Brucie noticed the malevolent smile on his father's face and instinctively knew he was enjoying his control over the little boy.

He charged off after the confused Madonna, running in circles, and this time caught her right off and brought the struggling bird to his father. It wasn't until the chicken had stopped kicking and he laid it at his father's feet, that he noticed he was drenched in blood from the two killings.

It was caked in his hair, on his hands and covered his clothes, and there was still one more hen to chase. Janet. *Shit. That was the chicken's name. Same as the girl in the cabinet behind the door he was about to open.* His sister, Aimee, had named it after a friend.

Trixie had not seen the irony until this moment. As the keys to the door dangled precariously in his hands, he dropped them at the realization.

He had become *the butcher*.

His hand trembled as he picked up the keys from the floor. The thought raced through his mind again as he began to unlock the door. He had become *the butcher*. The man he hated. How had this happened? He opened the door, dazed by the epiphany and stepped into a replica of his upstairs garage.

"What?" The cabinet door sprung from its hinges, lie wide open. He started toward it and instinctively turned around.

A wild-eyed Janet Domingo came at him with a screwdriver and stabbed him in the shoulder. The cup of soup he carried crashed to the black and white squared laminate floor, and Janet came at him again. She jabbed at him with the damned screwdriver. *Where in the hell did she find that?* He put his hands up to protect himself.

"Die you fucking monster! Die!" She stabbed him in the chest, and it felt like she nicked his heart.

She came at him again. He backed away, tripping over his own feet, and tumbled to the floor. She pounced on him like a puma in the wild, wielding sharp claws. He fought her attempts to stab at his face, allowing his hands once again to be his only shield.

"Please, don't hurt me," he cried out in a voice he recognized as the scared nine-year-old his father had traumatized.

Janet hesitated and he grabbed her wrists and threw her off him. He stumbled to his feet, staggering as wounded prey would. This was wrong. He was the Puma. She was the prey.

She ran at him, her crazed-eyes afire, waving the bloodied screwdriver. He grabbed her arm and twisted the damn weapon from her grip. He backhanded her and she went flying across the room, bounced, hit her head on the concrete floor, and lie still.

"Shit!" he said. "Shit! Shit! Shit!

He clasped his hand against his chest to stem the flow of blood pouring from him. Blood from his hands. Blood from his chest. Blood from his shoulder. He could envision *the butcher* laughing. The little boy with so much blood splattered on him.

Chapter 21

I awoke feeling recharged the morning after my little sexual escapade with Steve. And I knew what I had to do about this feeling of doom occupying too much space in my head.

"I have to talk to Edna," I muttered.

Edna is my psychic. The last time I saw her, she said I would stumble upon a murder. Her prediction nearly turned out to be me. In the end I, stumbled across four murders, one of them being my younger brother.

I haven't seen Edna since. Maybe it was the fear of what else might be put in my path. Maybe was the guilt I carried because of Darrin's death. Or maybe it was my depression. I called her and got a ten o'clock appointment.

Angel had started dressing like me about the same time she had her hair dyed blonde, identical to my own color, and it made me nervous. One Billie Bly in this house is enough. I rummaged through my closet for some old gifts Angel presented me with on birthdays and Christmas, which I never wore.

I found a black mini skirt with lace ruffles at the bottom and matched it with a vertical-blue-and-white-striped long-sleeve cotton shirt. I wriggled into a bright blue blazer and pushed the sleeves up enough to reveal the cuffs of my striped blouse.

My reflection in the bathroom mirror indicated I was not hip enough. I smeared on enough calypso red lip rouge to pass for Angelina Jolie and patted a bit of white powder on my face for contrast. I went back to my closet and found a chic black Derby and affixed it on the back of my head with Bobby pins. Dark nylon stockings made my dress appear shorter and my legs longer and stiletto heels added an element of danger.

The stilettos looked nice, but were hard to walk in, so I pulled out a pair of mod faux snakeskin high-heels Angel gave me for Christmas. Perfect, I thought.

I don't know what I hoped to accomplish. Maybe I hoped to shock Angel into her normal fashion disaster self so she would quit copying my look. My dressing up to look like Angel seemed a kind of passive-aggressive statement of sarcasm. If I'd thought ahead, maybe I'd have put some purple highlights in my hair too.

I walked my rebellious self into the main office where Angel sat at her desk in blue jeans, a denim vest, light blue blouse and no makeup. It was like looking at me in the mirror on most days. She tapped at the computer while I paraded around her desk flaunting my new look.

Eventually she looked up from the keyboard. "Oh, you're wearing the dress I got you for your birthday two years ago."

"Yep," I said. "I thought I'd try something different today."

"That's nice," she said and continued typing.

"What? Is that all you can say?"

"What do you want to hear?" She took a puff of her imaginary cigarette. "You look kind of silly all dressed up like some kind of hipster. Not too discreet for going about town on the job. What happens if you run into trouble with those heels on?"

"I'll throw them at you." I let out an exasperated breath and headed toward the door.

"Where are you going?" she said.

"To see Edna. I need some clarity about some things, you not being the least."

"That's a good idea," she said. "You've been acting kind of weird lately. Maybe she can tell you why."

I slammed the door on my way out.

I mounted concrete steps and knocked on the door of Edna's green and yellow English Cottage home on Alpine Terrace about ten blocks west of my Lovejoy Victorian. She opened the door and greeted me with a hug.

"Buna Zia. Why have you not visited Edna for so long?"

Edna is in her seventies, but except for her gray hair, she looks about fifty. She speaks with a Romanian accent and swears in her native language when emotional, which is just about all of the time.

I hugged her. "Good morning to you, my dear friend."

"You be good to see too. Such bright colors you have on today. But underneath I think you wear dark colors, no?"

Edna wore a long yellow granny dress, beige strapped sandals, two or three crystal necklaces around her neck, and unwieldy hair sprawling down her back like a ladder in the Rapunzel story.

"I meant to come earlier," I said, tears dribbling on my cheeks. "I've been having a hard time."

"I understand this," she said. "I read the newspapers. I try to visit you in hospital when you are shot last time, but policemen turn me away. I tell them: *Ma freci la icre / melodie!*"

"What?"

"In my country, it means, *'You pissing me off,'* maybe. Translation in English is, *'You rubbing my fish eggs.'*"

"Oh, I see." I decided not to ask for a translation of the translation.

Edna took my arm and ushered me to a Windsor chair at a round Wilshire pine table in her dining room. Sunlight poured through open tangerine colored drapes, spreading the warm colors across the room. We overlooked downtown Portland, and I could see snow-capped Mt. Hood, fifty miles away.

She rushed into the kitchen and returned a minute later with tea cups, saucers and a pot of steaming brew on a rolling cart. She placed the bone china cranberry-red cups and saucers on the table. A bouquet of summer flowers, against a white background, bloomed from my teacup's bottom even as liquid filled it.

"I think a nice cuppa will raise your spirits," she said. "Then maybe you are able to give better psychic aura, you think?"

"I'll try," I said. "I have some bad energy around me. I need you to help divine it."

"No cacat!" she said. "You aura is very dark. You drink some tea first. Clean away--how Buddhist says--bad karma. I put special herbs in to make strong you karma. Good medicine."

We drank our tea in silence. Edna closed her eyes and chanted to herself between sips of the cleansing liquid. I focused through the picture window on a circular cloud hovering over Mt. Hood like a halo.

"Okay," Edna said. "Give me the catca."

"The what?"

"The shit. Deal me the catca."

I laughed out loud.

"The tea is working already, see. Now you tell me what is bothering you."

I started by telling her of the guilt I still felt at my brother's death. When she said nothing, I told her about my suspicions of a man using Facebook to stalk young women.

She made a serious face, wringing her hands. "This Facebook can be very good. I use it for my business. But it can be very bad in wrong hands. Very bad people out there. No one is safe, not even on Internet."

I took a deep breath and exhaled. She seemed to understand the situation. I told her about the man in the Prius I spotted in Mary Johansen's neighborhood, about John Benson asking me to investigate Mary, and about how Mary's best friend, Janet Domingo, was then kidnapped.

Edna closed her eyes, lowered her head, and took my hands in hers. She hummed and chanted and caressed my palms, never looking up. The light in the room dimmed as a cloud interrupted the sun outside. I felt a chill in the air and the hairs on my neck stood on end.

"You did not come to my home alone," Edna said. "I feel the presence of another when I meet you at the door. I think it was one of the Poliția who turn me away from your hospital room, but I am wrong. This Poliția has a kind heart. He wants me to tell you something."

"Is it Darrin?" I cried. Fear-spiked bile rose in my throat, and I felt my guilt would kill me right then and there. But God in his infinite wisdom kept me alive. "Can you tell him I'm sorry?"

"He say he is with you. He stay with you since his death. First to protect. But after he could not leave because you would not let him."

"I wouldn't let him? Of course not. I want him to be alive. If I could change it so I could die and he would live, I would do that. Tell him."

Edna's eyes remained closed. She hummed a bit. "Yes, I will tell her. . . no, I don't think she knows . . . what do you mean? . . . I see."

I wanted to jump into the conversation Edna seemed to be having with my brother, but I didn't know what to say. Guilt is a great leveler.

"Your brother say you must let him go. It is not your fault he dies. He chooses to save you. It is his destiny. He does good things in his life, but he say you will do great things, therefore he must save you."

Tears trickled from my eyes and my chest heaved as I tried unsuccessfully to keep my emotions stuffed down deep. It sounded just like Darrin. But could it be? Edna had been *spot-on* in some of her predictions in the past, but this talking to a spirit was a new thing, and I didn't know if I believed her. Maybe she was trying to ease my guilt to make me feel better.

"He say, he tells you *before* he is not afraid to die. He say maybe it is not time for you to quit being the private investigator, as you suggest to him."

"Oh my God," I said. "That was a private conversation. He and I are the only ones who knew what was said. It was after I was almost killed. I was afraid of dying. I was going to quit being a P.I."

"I have lost my contact with your Darrin. But he say he will be with you a little while longer. Until you catch this killer. He say you are in danger. He say the killer knows you and thinks he is somehow connect to you. He say the killer is afraid of you."

"What do you mean?" I asked. "You mean we are linked together somehow?"

"Yes, that is the word your Darrin sends to me."

"But how?"

She shrugged and poured another cup of tea. "He does not say. Maybe when you see him, he sees you."

"The man in the Prius?"

"Does he see you?"

I closed my eyes and flashed back to the car drafting behind the UPS truck in front of Sally Brown's house. The guy with the baseball cap pulled down to hide his face. The sideways glance as he tilted his hat and stared at me. The look of disbelief.

"He acted as if he's seen me before," I said. "Like he was afraid of me."

"It is possible," Edna said. "He would be wise to be afraid of you, my Billie. Now I must tell you. There is a darkness surrounding your aura. It tries to break through. You must not let it. It is from an evil source."

"What should I do?' I asked.

"You must meditate daily. Listen to your instincts. They are maybe guided by your brother. Do not allow evil to overtake you. Fight hard and you will achieve greatness."

"I'll try," I said, unconvincingly.

"If you fail, your brother will die for no reason. You must fight this evil with all your power."

Chapter 22

I had just spent an hour meditating, as Edna suggested, and I *did* feel a little lighter in spirit. I strolled into the laundry room where Eric sat glassy-eyed behind his laptop. Stubble dotted his baby face and a cup of coffee nestled in his hands. He looked up at me and yawned, the effect of having spent the entire night at his computer.

"Any luck tracking down our elusive killer?" I asked.

"Yes and no," he said, wearily. "I've been through all of the victims' Facebook pages and correlated similar *friends* between them and came up dry. Only two people seem to have any *friends* in common. But the connection is interesting."

He scrolled down to the bottom of Cynthia Miller's *friends* list and put a cursor on a cute little frog icon.

"Trixie?" I said. "That sounds familiar."

"It should," Eric said. "Trixie has *friended* you too."

"That's right. I remember it appearing on a *friend* request. Angel thought it was a good omen that advertising on Facebook would pay off."

Eric stuck his finger in his coffee and licked it. "I need a refill." He stood up and dumped the cold mud into a sink and refilled his mug from a coffee maker on the washing machine.

I followed behind and filled my Stephanie Plum coffee mug. "So you think this is a correlation because . . .?"

"I'll show you in a minute." He poured the contents of a NutraSweet packet into his coffee and stirred it with a dirty spoon. "My software program scanned forty thousand *friends* and *friends* of *friends* generated from the five victims and came up with nothing, except you and Cynthia."

"How did I get in the mix?"

"It was a complete accident. I was going through the lists and this frog popped up with only one name, *Trixie*. My program is set up to look for abnormalities, so it sent me an alert. I went to Trixie's web page and looked up his *friends,* which to my surprise were viewable. I think maybe he did that so he wouldn't spook potential victims when he invited them to be his *friend.* You were one of his *friends.*"

"That really doesn't prove anything," I said.

"Maybe not," Eric said. "But look at these women. He has a type. He prefers women who are blonde and athletic, with heart-shaped faces, milky white skin, and pouty lips. You fit all the criteria, except the pouty lips. I can't tell what you were going for in your photo, but it isn't flirty.

"Angel caught me by surprise," I protested. But he was right. There were probably a hundred women's pictures and I could have passed for the sister of several of the women. Even Janet Domingo, obviously Spanish had a creamy complexion like mine.

"You can't view his Timeline and no profile information is available," Eric said. "The only thing we're allowed to see is Trixie's *friends'* profiles. Many of them, including you, don't have their privacy features turned on."

"So you think Trixie is our predator, and he used the cute frog icon and a female name to lure women to *friend* him?" I'm a bit slow when it comes to the tech stuff, but even I could see the implications.

"I do. What I don't understand is why he used it with you, since you don't use any privacy features on Facebook to block strangers."

I didn't know either, except it appears he might be playing some kind of mind game with me. After talking with Edna, it's the only thing that made sense. She said a dark force surrounds my aura, and I've felt a dark presence in my life for some time now.

I kept flashing back to the guy in the Prius watching as he sped past me in Mary Johansen's neighborhood. Then to John Benson asking me to investigate his cheating girlfriend who turns out to be Mary Johansen, the best friend of the abducted Janet Domingo. What the hell was going on?

Eric, too, seemed to be tied into this tangled web of coincidences. He and his burglar buddy, Jimmer, casing a house across the street at the same time as me and the guy in the Prius. I watched Eric squinting at his computer screen. Was he destined to be with me on this eerie problem with a serial killer?

I stroked my chin with my thumb and finger. "So we're assuming Trixie is a man?"

Eric frowned. "Of course, it could be a woman, I guess, but . . ."

I paced the floor, kicking up a gritty dust mixed with spilled laundry detergent, wondering how I was fortunate enough to run into this kid.

"No, it's a good assumption. Most serial killers are men." I took the computer mouse from Eric and scrolled through the list of blonde-haired women on Trixie's *friends* list. I noticed one difference between them and me.

"You think he knows you're after him?" Eric asked.

"I'm not sure."

All of the women in the pictures seemed carefree, confident. My picture looked too serious. Nothing ever came easy for me, and I suspect none of these other women had to struggle much, likely getting along with their good looks. I guessed they were successful in every endeavor they pursued. They just had that look of, well, entitlement.

"I think we should find this Trixie," I said. "Can you do that?"

Eric rubbed the sleep from his eyes and yawned. "I've been planning for something like this." He clicked on a browser tab and another Facebook page popped up. "This is Carrie Underhill," he said. She fits the characteristics our Trixie seems to prefer. Shoulder length blonde hair, attractive, confident, blue eyes."

"Where did you find her?"

"I made her up," he said. "From some pictures of a model I found online. She likes hiking, bowling, dancing, and making money."

I tilted my head at the laptop screen. "So this is what?"

"A fake Facebook page that limits what can be seen. It appears Carrie's privacy features are turned on, except for an album page with four provocative pictures designed to get our stalker's attention."

He clicked on her profile album. Carrie in short shorts and a halter top at a bowling alley flirting with whoever took the picture. Carrie in a low-cut blouse holding a bowling ball. Carrie dressed in a scanty outfit and hanging on a stripper pole while some of her friends egg her on. Another photo showed her in front of a slot machine. I noticed this one was her current profile picture.

"Explain," I said, peering over his shoulder.

"We *are* Carrie." Eric's eyes sparkled. "Trixie can only see the pictures I allow him to see. Just enough to whet his appetite. If he wants to see more, he will have to *friend* her."

"And how is he going to find her page out of a million web pages out there?"

"He isn't. Carrie is going to *friend him*."

"Isn't that a little dangerous? He might become suspicious."

"Not to worry. Carrie has already made *friends* with three other women on Trixie's *friend* list. He should notice that when Facebook shows him mutual *friends*."

"I like it." I stood behind him and peered at the laptop monitor. "What's next?"

"Okay, here is the beautiful part of my plan." Eric smiled mischievously and rubbed his hands together. "Once Trixie *friends* Carrie, he will be able to see a lot of provocative postings she's made."

"These go back over a year," I said.

"This is my page, not Facebook's."

"It looks just like Facebook." I squinted at the screen and shook my head.

"This is a phishing page. It has all the right links to take you back to Facebook. But the moment he clicks on my *friend* request two things happen. First, our new *friend* has downloaded a virus that allows me to see the next time he logs in so I can hack his user name and password and check his web surfing history. Second, it clones his page so I can see everything he sees in real time."

"Wow," I said.

He nodded. "Yeah, it's cool. It even has the friends we have in common."

"Will it tell us his location?"

"No, but I have another program I can use when he's online to show us his current and his past login locations using GPS. I could use an Internet Protocol Address tracking virus, but it takes forever and if he's at a remote location, he'd be long gone before we find him."

"The GPS would be faster?"

"Much. But the downside is it will give us a general location within a block, so we will be handicapped a bit."

I high-fived him. "I'll take that in a heartbeat. It's better than what we have now. So, what's next?"

"I'm still not finished with the end product," he said. "When I finish, I'll send Trixie the invitation. At that point we'll have to be patient. It will be Trixie's move. If he doesn't friend us, I'll have to think of something else."

"And we have to hope this Trixie character is the person we're looking for."

He sighed. "Yeah. Otherwise, I've been wasting my time here."

"How ya' doing, Billie?" Brenda was in her brown cop uniform and temporarily off duty at her library gig. "You look tired."

We sat in the Case Study Coffee shop and sipped our brew. The location across from the library conjured up memories of Mr. B-Rude. Wouldn't it be wonderful to stumble into him again now that I wasn't chasing bad guys? I made a mental note to have a friend at the police bureau trace his license plate.

"Not so good," I said. "My psychic says I have an evil aura surrounding me."

"You go to a psychic? What's that like? Does she look into a crystal ball or something?"

"I haven't seen her behind a crystal ball yet. She serves tea and then starts reading my energy. This last time she scared me pretty good. She told me my brother's spirit is with me, and he's afraid the serial killer knows I'm after him."

Brenda stiffened and rolled her eyes. "I don't believe in psychics. I'm surprised you would."

"I'm skeptical about just about anything and anyone I run across on the job." I looked her square in the eye. "But you know, you have to believe in something. Edna knew about a private conversation I had with my brother minutes before he died. There's no way she could know about it, unless she *had* contacted Darrin."

Brenda didn't seem convinced. "So what else did she tell you?"

I shrugged, sensing whatever I said would fall on deaf ears. "Nothing important, I guess. Have you found out if Mary Johansen is cheating on her boyfriend?"

She covered a yawn with her hand. "I've been following her the past couple of days, and she has only been out with one guy. He stops by and they go out sometimes. He stayed overnight at her house last night."

She took a 35 millimeter SLR digital camera out of her camera bag. "I checked this guy out and it *is* her fiancé, John Benson. He hasn't given her much chance to sneak out with another guy. Doesn't he know we're following her?"

She showed me a picture of them eating dinner in a restaurant. I blinked at the scene.

"Something wrong?"

"Can you enlarge it so I can see their faces better?"

She pushed a button a few times. "I can print this out or email them to you. I was up late last night waiting to see if he was going to leave and didn't have time to send them to you before work this morning."

My mind went numb and I think I heard every other word. "Yeah, send them to me."

Brenda squinted at the LCD image on the camera, then at me. "What's wrong?"

"This is not John Benson," I said. "But you said you checked him out."

"Yeah. I paid the cashier twenty bucks in advance to notice his name on his credit card. She said it was Benson."

"It's not the John Benson that hired me. What the hell is going on?"

I fished through my purse and brought out the business card the client gave me. I dialed the number on my cell phone and waited through several rings, expecting it now to go to a voicemail.

"Hello," a voice drawled. It sounded sickly and tired.

"Is this John Benson?" I tilted my phone so Brenda could listen in.

"Billie! I've been waiting for your call. Have you learned anything?" The voice sounded a little stronger now.

"I'm a little puzzled," I said. "Were you out with Mary last night?"

"I'm afraid I've been a little under the weather," he said. "Been in bed the past twenty four hours. Has she been sneaking around with someone?"

"Maybe I should visit you at your home," I said. "It's kind of complicated and not something I can explain over the phone."

"I wish I could accommodate you, but the doctor says I might be contagious. Why don't you try explaining it."

"I was thinking you might do the explaining."

"Oh?"

I thought I heard some snickering. "I stumbled across another John Benson last night."

"Really? Is that what he said? They must have concocted some story to try to confuse you. There is only one John Benson."

Brenda and I exchanged exasperated looks. "I know there is and I met him last night. I also saw his credit card when he paid for dinner with his fiancé."

"Oh dear," the voice on the phone said. "I've been found out."

"Who is this?" I said.

"You know who it is," he said. "I've been waiting for this call."

I didn't know what to say.

"I didn't expect to fool you for long," he said. "I just wanted to meet you. To see if you remembered me."

"You were the guy in the Prius on Foley Street," I said.

"So you did remember me? I'm flattered."

"What have you done with Janet Domingo?" The line went dead for a minute. "Hello?" I thought he might have hung up.

"So you know who I am. I think we've talked enough for now. Don't try to call me again. I'll call you."

"Creepy," Brenda said when the line went dead.

"Worse than creepy," I said in a brittle voice.

Brenda patted me on my back. "Are you okay? Your face is chalk-white."

"Edna is right." I shuddered. "He *is* after me."

"He sounded upset," she said. "I think he's afraid of you."

"I'm damn well afraid of him too," I said. "And I'm afraid for Janet Domingo. When I mentioned her name he said I knew who he was. That means he has her."

"We should trace that number," Brenda said.

She probably was right, but I figured our stalker would likely have bought a throw-away phone with an untraceable number.

I dialed Trixie again. It just rang and rang. There was no invitation to leave a message. I called Steve and got his voicemail. "Steve? I need you to trace a phone number."

Chapter 23

Connie was worried about Brent. She'd tried calling him over a twenty-four hour period and he failed to pick up on his cell or at home. There was no answering machine on either.

She decided to take matters into her own hands and drove over to his home in Southwest Portland. It was early summer and the roses were in full bloom in his neighborhood.

Brent told her his mother was an avid gardener. Now the roses were tall and unwieldy with black spot. Brown grass was littered with dandelions and the spent rhododendron blooms needed deadheading. She could tell by the overgrown varieties of flowers on the property this was once a garden showplace. Surely Brent could afford to hire someone to stay on top of the maintenance. It was as if he didn't care.

She remembered he'd made snide remarks about his mother and her garden friends. The last time they'd made love, Brent told her a horrible story about how his mother often locked him in a storage cabinet in the garage while she tended her garden. His childhood had been terrible, full of abuse and manipulation.

She rang the doorbell and her thoughts drifted to her own adolescent years. She remembered her drunken father coming to her bedroom when she turned twelve. Thoughts of escape overwhelmed her after the first time. Her window was always propped open and ready to help a little girl get away from her drunken father. She often spent those nights sleeping in the family car.

When she told her mother what her father was doing, Barb just denied it. She said Connie was making up stories to get attention. She was fifteen when her father turned his devotion to her younger sister, Julie. She saw it starting to happen in his eyes one night when he patted his lap and encouraged her to sit with him.

She knew she could not allow this to happen again. Not to Julie. Before he could carry through with his plan to destroy another person, she'd stopped it. The fire department said her father had fallen asleep with a cigarette in his hand. The cigarette landed in alcohol from a drink he had spilled and set the bed on fire.

Connie made sure her father had all the booze he needed that night. She poured a bottle of 151-rum onto the floor at the side of his bed and tucked a portion of bed sheet into the bottle as he snored. She lit a cigarette and touched off the make-do wick with it after placing it between her passed out father's fingers.

The label on the bottle said it was 76 percent alcohol. The warning label on the bottle gave her the idea. Extremely flammable, it said. Keep away from open flames. The bottle even came with a metal spark arrester, which she pried off ahead of time,

She and Julie were the only ones to survive the fire. She had coaxed her sister to join her in the family car earlier that night and the flames engulfed the bedroom and spread to most of the house before firefighters arrived. Julie was still asleep when she returned to the car so it turned out to be the perfect crime. They spent the rest of their adolescent years with a favorite grandmother on her mother's side.

She absently pushed the doorbell again. Brent had been so forthcoming about his horrible childhood and it puzzled her. How he could he share those terrible memories when she couldn't? She had opened up about some of the things that happened to her as a child, but barely scratched the surface. It was almost like he wanted her to know about his past. It made her feel sorry for him. At times she wanted to hug him and whisper 'poor baby.'

Mad at herself for delving into her past again, she plunged a fist into her purse to find the key she stole from Brent's dresser the last time she was here. Why hadn't he simply offered her one? Why make her steal it? It was labeled *house key,* and she found it in his top drawer with so much other junk and figured he probably wouldn't miss it.

She opened the door and walked into the stately living room with ornate 1940's crown molding and thick grape tinted carpets. She paced through the living room to a formal dining room with a twelve foot long mahogany table and pearl colored high-back chairs.

No sign of activity in the kitchen. The smaller eating table was empty and the dishes were put away, except for a lone pot on the stove with curdled soup. Even the coffee maker was empty. She noticed a door ajar in the mud room off the back and went to it.

What was she doing? By all intents Brent was a private person. Would he be angry for her invading his privacy? She saw a stain caked on the brown linoleum of the mud room. Was it blood? Alarmed, she turned her attention toward the stairs to the basement.

"Brent?" Connie flicked on a light over the stairs. "Are you down there?"

She reluctantly descended the steps and felt something like a knot caught in her throat. A small area below led to two rooms, each with a closed door.

One door was unlocked. She opened it and was met by darkness. She found the light switch and flicked it on. *It was a garage in the basement*? Why? There was a garage on the main floor and the grounds around the house were level with no access to a subterranean garage.

But the black-and-white checkered tile floor led to a garage door. The room seemed very small for a garage and the ceiling topped out at maybe seven feet. She noticed a storage cabinet against one wall with the doors torn off.

A pool of congealed blood stained the floor in front of her. There were also smaller spots and smears of blood. Had Brent been injured somehow? She went to the other room and tugged at the door. It was locked and she had no key to open it. She cocked her ear toward the door at a whimpering sound.

"Brent? Are you in there? Are you okay?"

The cry came again. But it was faint. He might be dying, she thought. *I've got to get to him.* She ran to the garage in search of an ax or some kind of tool to help her get past the locked door, but found nothing.

She returned upstairs to a key rack in the mudroom. She found a brass key and hurried downstairs, inserted the key into the lock, and opened the door.

A noise from above stopped her cold. A hot tingle radiated down her spine. Probably just old wood cracking, she told herself. A whimper emanated from the room she was about to enter.

"Brent? Are you in here?" She stepped into the dim room and waited for her eyes to adjust. She spotted a workbench with tools, a propane welding torch, and a large double sink off a side wall. She noticed a short hose rolled up on a hook next to the sink and a drain in the middle of a damp concrete floor.

"Oh my God!" she cried. Against another wall, on a stainless steel gurney, a woman lie strapped tightly, her hands and feet and mouth bound with duct tape. Her face was black and blue and dried blood splotched her cheek.

Connie stood stunned for a moment before inching toward her. Tears flowed across the woman's face and her eyes seemed larger than life. Connie took a deep breath and stripped the tape from the woman's mouth.

"Please," she cried. "He's going to kill me."

The words jerked Connie back to her childhood for a moment. She remembered asking for help. She remembered thinking her father might kill her. Did anyone help her? *Hell no!* She finally realized it was up to her to help herself.

A thumping noise rattled above her. It sounded like footsteps. "What are you doing here?" she demanded of the woman.

191

"He kidnapped me. At a bar. He's going to kill me."

"You picked him up in a bar?" Her shrill, angry voice surprised her.

"No. He abducted me."

Connie tuned her out. The noise from above was growing louder. She followed it down the stairway. Her heart raced and for a minute she was the ten-year-old girl fearing her drunken father. He was coming, and he was angry. Would he beat her? Would he finally kill her?

"I can't help you," she told the woman. "I have to go."

Connie turned toward the door and saw Brent standing in its frame with a puzzled smile on his face. It became eerily silent in the room as even the whimpering of the woman ceased.

"What are you doing down here?" He stood in the doorway, bare-chested, with a large gauze bandage to the right of his heart and his face was pocked with dried blood and punctures.

"I -- I was looking for you. I was worried," Connie said. "You didn't answer your phone. I thought maybe something happened.

"I guess you were right to be worried." He opened his hands, revealing several scabbed over puncture wounds and he gazed down at his bandaged chest. "That bitch did this to me."

"I'm sorry. I didn't know." Her voice brittle now, like a little girl in trouble. The thoughts in her mind were jumbled. Fear, escape, empathy. She felt as if any moment she would literally fall to pieces like a shattered glass window.

"So Connie . . . dear, dear Connie. You have a choice to make."

She looked at Brent's eyes, calm and confident and turned to the woman's scared gaze.

"A choice?"

Chapter 24

"That's so disturbing," Angel said after I told her and Eric about my phone call to the John Benson imposter.

"What are you going to do?" Eric asked.

"I don't know." I paced from Angel's desk to a nearby bookcase and turned back to him. "I've been trying all morning to contact Steve, but all I get is his voicemail and the rat won't return my calls. I'll bet he's holed up with his FBI buddies somewhere on a stakeout eating Voodoo Donuts."

"I sent Trixie a *friend* request this morning, but haven't heard anything from him yet." Eric brushed his thick brown hair out of his eyes. "I changed the pictures I had with some new ones I took of Brenda."

"You got a thing for her, don't you kid?" Angel, still dressed in her Billie Bly blue jeans and denim jacket, chuckled.

Eric flushed. "I asked her if she would help and she said okay. She has more the look that this guy seems to be hunting for."

I sat in a chair across from Angel's desk and rolled my eyes. "But her hair isn't the right color."

"I Photoshopped it. Took out all the browns and that left more of a blonde color. Then I adjusted the highlights until I got a hue closer to Billie's."

"And Angel's," I said.

Angel took a sip from my Stephanie Plum coffee mug. "Hey, I told you it was an accident. Although I'm beginning to believe maybe blondes do have more fun and this butch thing seems to be working too. I've got two men fighting over me since I started dressing up like you."

"All I'm getting is stares." I grabbed my mug from her and took a sip of coffee. I had ditched the derby and teased my hair and now it resembled Mt. St. Helens the day it erupted. I swear if I were to color it gray and white, it would look just like columns of ash exploding from the volcano.

"You're starting to get the knack," Angel said. "Don't give up."

I swallowed my frustration. "Just keep working on the Facebook angle, Eric. We need a way to track this guy down."

Angel got up from her desk and walked over to the kitchen counter with the coffee and some extra cups. She grabbed a mug that said "World's Best Detective" and poured some of the dark brew.

"Don't forget, you have a self-defense demonstration day-after-tomorrow at Chapman Elementary," she said. "We have use of the gym and the school says we can use some of their foam mats."

I winced. "This isn't coming at a very good time. I have a lot on my plate right now."

"All you have to do is show up and walk them through a few old police self-defense tactics. I have them diagrammed for you. Heck, I could probably do it."

There was a rap at my office door and I recognized the shape on the other side of the frosted window. It was Chris.

"Great. Another interruption," I said. "You've got to do something about them, Angel. I can't have any more cage matches here. Make a choice between the two of them."

The door opened and Chris entered in a Navajo blanket style long-sleeve shirt with a Nehru collar and white vintage chinos. He lifted a pair of smoke shades from his nose and winked.

"It's me. What do you think of my new outfit?"

Angel practically swooned. "It's a little loud for my tastes."

Chris and I rolled our eyes in unison.

"This from the woman who typically wears her hair in four colors," I said. "And who can forget the red, white and blue?"

"That was for July Fourth," she said. "I was being patriotic."

"You also wore it at Christmas," Chris said.

"Well, that was the old me. I know you like the Billie Bly look, so I'm experimenting."

"The Billie Bly look?" Chris said.

"You must. You've been hanging around here ever since you met Billie. I know you have a crush on her."

I narrowed my eyes at them.

"And here, all this time, I thought you were trying to drive me away with that dopey blonde hair color and all those jeans outfits," he said.

"It may have started that way," she said. "But it didn't work. You seemed to want me even more. I guess I went with what was working for me."

"So are you trying to get rid of me still, or are you dressing like Billie because you think I like it?"

"No comment," Angel said.

"Chris, she likes you," I said. "She's only dressing like that to make fun of me."

"I think she looks kind of hot for an older chick," Eric said. He had a mischievous grin on his face and I could tell he was having fun.

"You get back to work," I said.

Eric slunk out of the office and I turned my attention to Chris and Angel.

"I'm going out. You two figure out who likes who and I expect Angel to be looking like her old self, instead of me, when I get back."

I went upstairs and changed into some black jeans, a white blouse with embossed roses, and some sensible Nike sneakers. I decided I needed help with the disheveled hair, laughing at me in the bathroom mirror, so I made an appointment at my local beauty parlor and set off to tame my wild side.

After getting my hair done, I pulled Myrtle into a parking spot on Southeast Hawthorne Street and winced at the dent she suffered at the foot of B-Rude the day I chased the Facebook burglars.

"I'll get him for that," I told her, and softy caressed her otherwise shiny metallic red finish.

I stopped outside the *Murder by the Book* bookstore. A sign said they were closing after 30 years. Great, I thought, another independent bookstore gone. I hoped my neighborhood Powell's bookstore wouldn't be next. Both stores had nifty police procedurals, but I didn't get over to Hawthorne as often as I haunted the original Powell's.

The store was small, really small. Its books, staged in a long rectangular room, were mostly softcover and smaller paperbacks. Old murderous event flyers decorated the front windows representing the history of famous authors who did signings at the diminutive store.

Mary Johansen stood behind a cashier counter and rang up a sale for a white-haired lady who clutched at a canvas book bag. "Be sure to come back for our clearance sale."

"Have you found Janet?" she asked after the customer left.

"Nothing yet."

"I was hoping. . ." Her demeanor went from hopeful to hapless.

"Sorry to hear the store is closing," I said.

"Yes, it's too bad. The owners are retiring and no one seems to be interested in running independent bookstores anymore. The world is changing." She motioned me toward the back of the store and set up two rickety folding chairs. "We can talk here without too many interruptions."

"Have you seen this man before?" I showed her a picture Brenda emailed me after we met for coffee.

"Of course. That's my fiancé, John. How did you get his picture? He's so camera shy, I can't even get him to take one for me."

I patted my newly coiffed hair to make sure it hadn't reverted back the Mt. St. Helens eruption style. Every blonde strand rested nicely in place and it had a calming effect on me.

"Mary, I was hired by John Benson to see if you had been cheating on him."

"What? Why would he think I would cheat on him?"

"As it turns out, I guess he doesn't. The man who hired me is not your John."

"I don't understand." She reached over and pushed a book in line with some others on a shelf.

"I don't either. But I think the person who hired me might be the person who abducted Janet." I waited for her to absorb this information, expecting a flurry of questions.

"Then you *do* have a suspect. Is he playing some kind of game?"

I reached inside my utilitarian black purse and retrieved a note pad. "I think so. And if he's doing it with me, chances are he's doing it with all of us. I'll need you to go over everything he said the night you danced with him."

Mary seemed to zone out for a minute in deep thought. When she spoke it was almost in a singsong voice. She leaned toward me from a precarious perch on her flimsy plastic folding chair.

"He was very charming, confident, and he seemed to like to hear himself talk. Told me he didn't have to work. He said something about inheriting money from his mother and father and something about playing the stock market."

"Did he tell you anything about his parents?" I asked. "Where they lived? Where they worked?"

"I think he said his father was a butcher. The music was loud and I only heard snippets at times. I remember now. He said his father was a butcher and his mother was a pacifist.

"A butcher?"

"That's what he said. I told him my parents were florists and he said his mother was the gardener in his family. I don't know why, but I asked him if he liked gardening and he just shook his head. He said his mother's garden is overgrown now that she's passed away.

"It was kind of weird. When he said he didn't like gardening he snickered to himself like it was a joke."

I thought about it for a moment and remembered my conversation with the phony John Benson. "Mary, was this Brent in his early thirties?"

"I think so. He may have been in his late twenties." A customer came into the store and Mary looked to make sure he was greeted by a fellow employee. "It was dark and all, but he was pretty sure of himself, so early thirties might be right."

I scribbled on my notepad. "Was he a fairly well-built man with sandy brown hair, blue eyes and fair skin?"

"Oh no," she said. "Well, he had a nice body, but he appeared very tan. His hair was black, very black. His eyes were brown, almost mocha, and he had a goatee and a mustache."

I remembered the description her friends had given me, but I wanted to test her memory now. "Could the beard and mustache have been false? Don't answer right away. Close your eyes and remember him as you danced together."

The customer left the store and Mary sighed. "I'm sorry. I'm trying, but the goatee and mustache looked real. Of course, the lighting was poor so I could be wrong."

I shook my head and leaned back in my wobbly plastic chair. "It was only a hunch. I thought my phony John Benson and your Brent might be the same person."

"I remember his smile, it seemed playful. Almost . . ."

"Impish?" I asked.

"Yes. But at the same time, it held another quality. "

"A little wary or nervous?"

"Yes," she said. "Like he was having fun, but maybe afraid he might get caught. He reminded me of a little boy with his hands in a cookie jar just before his mother catches him."

I thanked Mary for her help and returned to Hawthorne Street, a bustling area of activity brought on by hip retail shops and eateries. I climbed into Myrtle, rested my hands on the steering wheel and gazed through the windshield, oblivious to traffic, jaywalkers and loud talkers on the sidewalks.

You can disguise your face, your skin, and even your height, but it's hard to hide your mannerisms. The guy representing himself in my office as John Benson displayed the same impish, yet nervous smile as the person who abducted Janet Domingo, according to Mary. They must be the same person.

But why did he come to my office with such an elaborate ruse? Why would he ask me to follow Mary while pretending to be her fiancé?

I thought back to the man in the Prius with the cap pulled over eyes and remembered the astonished look on his face, like he recognized me. How could he recognize me? Could he be some perp I arrested when I was still with the police bureau?

Maybe he didn't know me. Maybe he'd seen my picture. Where could he see my picture? It was in the newspaper when I caught Eric and his cohort.

But the picture in the paper appeared after I'd seen him on Mary's street. He must have seen me before our encounter on Foley, but where?

I smacked my forehead with the palm of my hand. *Of course.* He saw my profile photo on Facebook.

Chapter 25

"The woman in your basement was sent to kill you?" Connie's voice vibrated as it rose from her diaphragm.

"She was sent by that bitch, Billie Bly," Brent said. He paused as Connie removed the bandage from his chest as he lie in his bed.

"This is serious," she said. "You need to see a doctor."

"And how would I explain it? Some crazy woman attacked me in my house with a screwdriver and I had to defend myself? She's already cooked up a crazy story about me abducting her. Who do you think the police will believe?"

"Why does this Billie Bly have it in for you?" Connie had to admit it looked bad for Brent. She wasn't sure, herself, about his story, and *she* wanted to believe in him.

"Supposedly some client wanted me investigated. Some sister went missing. This client suggested I had dated her in the past and I was responsible for her disappearance."

Connie considered this for a moment. "Were you?"

"What?" Brent said.

"Were you responsible for her disappearance?"

"No," he said. "We hadn't dated in over a year, and I haven't seen her since. Yet, somehow Bly latched onto me as her prime suspect. She got the police involved and they had me under investigation for a while."

"Oh dear." Connie felt the fear well up in her again, not that it had subsided very much from the scene in the basement.

"They closed the case on me," he said. "There was absolutely no evidence. They even apologized for the trouble they caused. Said Bly was a crackpot and they should have known, but they were under an obligation to follow up with any lead in the case."

"Then why is this P.I. still pursuing it?" Connie rubbed an antibiotic ointment carefully into Brent's chest and cut a patch of gauze to cover the wound.

"I wish I knew," he said. "She apparently hired this operative, Janet Something, to either kill me or set me up as someone trying to kill her or both. She almost succeeded. She broke into my house through a basement door. I heard a noise and went down to investigate.

"This Janet bitch jumped out of the shadows and started stabbing me. If I hadn't managed to knock her out while trying to defend myself, I might be dead."

Connie managed to push an unobstructed breath from her lungs. "And she would have told police it was self-defense." She stripped a length of medical tape from a roll, cut it and affixed it over the gauze on Brent's chest.

"I guess. She kept coming at me like a wild animal, with me trying to wrestle that damned screwdriver from her. She hit her head on the concrete floor really hard once when I pushed her away, but she bounced back up and came at me again. That's how I got all of these wounds on my hands."

"My poor baby." He held his palms open to her and she counted eight defensive wounds. She held each of his wrists and softly kissed his hands. He smiled and she noticed an impish twist to his lips.

"I knew you would believe me," he said. "I don't know what to do. It's only a matter of time before that damn Billie Bly and the police come sniffing around. I'm sure she's aware something went wrong with her plan. I'm surprised the cops aren't at my door now."

Connie wanted to ask why he had the stainless steel gurney in his basement and why he had two garages, but something told her not to. She was uncertain what to say so she blurted out something that stunned her.

"I think I might know how you feel," she said. "Sometimes events are thrust upon us that we don't foresee. I had a similar experience in my childhood. My father sexually abused me until I became a teenager and then he turned his attention to my younger sister. She was only five. I decided I had to do something drastic to stop him. Sometimes we have to take things into our own hands to make the craziness around us stop."

Brent was scrutinizing her now. He had a puzzled look on his face.

"What did you do?"

"I killed him. And my mother too. It was the only way. He would have taken Julie's innocence like he took mine, and my mother would have let him."

Brent's eyes widened and he seemed to smile a bit. "How?"

She told him how she lured Julie out to the family car and stayed with her until she fell asleep. She recounted to Brent how she set fire to her parent's bed in the middle of the night and rushed back to the car to be with her sister.

"When the firemen came, they thought I was asleep with Julie. I told them we had slept in the car to avoid abuse and no one ever questioned it. I'm telling you this because I want you to know I understand your predicament. Sometimes bad things happen to good people. I've learned that you have to take care of yourself because no one else will."

She waited for a response. Brent was silent for a moment. When he finally spoke it was with sadness.

"Thank you for sharing that with me," he said. "And thank you for understanding. I think you're right. There may be only one way to deal with my situation. It's drastic. But after we're done, we won't have to worry about these crazy people any longer. It will be just you and me. We can live a nice peaceful life together."

"What do you have in mind?" Connie asked.

Chapter 26

"Hello, Billie? It's Mar here. I just wanted to phone you and thank you again for finding my hubby's computer invention. He's been so happy since he got it back and apparently the ideas your little burglar chum had has been of immense help."

Angel brought me breakfast, coffee and a bagel, as Mar labored on telling me how great her life was again. The only deviance in her cadence was an occasional reference to me as a catalyst in her success. It was the only thing that kept me listening. That and Eric's apparent helpful innovations.

"Our sex life is even getting better," she said. "If that's possible."

"Well, thank you so much for the update," I said. "I've got a desk full of work I need to catch up on. Maybe if your husband is appreciative of Eric's work, I could put them in touch after Eric works out his, uh, judicial responsibilities."

"Oh, whatever. I really called to see if I could sneak into your self-defense class tomorrow night."

"Tomorrow? I think you're mistaken. It's Friday night."

"I guess you *have* been working too hard. Today's Thursday. It's tomorrow evening at seven-thirty by my calculations."

I circled the date on my desk calendar. "Shit. I mean, I look forward to it. Let me transfer you back to Angel to get you enrolled. Angel? Line One."

I hadn't even looked at the course outline Angel drew up. I searched through a mass of papers on my desk and found it in my *In Basket*, where she'd left it a week and a half ago. I scrutinized it, but quickly became distracted. It had something to do with line one still blinking and a small furor emanating from the outer office.

"Angel, line one!" I shouted.

"I'm busy," she yelled back.

I got up from my desk, opened my office door and walked into an arm wrestling match.

"Chris and Earl are competing to see who is taking me out to dinner tonight."

I watched, mesmerized by the beefy Earl Monroe, with his huge paws wrapped around Chris's tiny mitts, struggling to whip the wiry guy into submission on a card table set up in the middle of the room. Earl's face glowed beet red while Chris whooshed air from his ballooned cheeks, and Angel sat on the edge of her desk with a smile of satisfaction.

"I told you to choose one of them," I said.

Angel raised her hands, palms up. "I can't make up my mind. But don't worry. They promised me no more rough stuff in the office."

"This isn't professional. What if a client walks in?"

"I'll tell them they're competing to see who meets with you next."

I watched, amazed for about two minutes, fascinated by the veins bulging in their arms like snakes attacking and retreating. A few times one snake or another threatened to burst through the skin of the combatants. I glimpsed Angel, thoroughly enjoying the show, and realized this type of behavior might drag on forever.

"Will you please answer line one?"

"There's nobody on line one," Angel said.

"I got you now. Give up?"

I sighed. "Call Mar back and enroll her in the self-defense class tomorrow night."

"Not yet twerp. I'm just resting a minute."

"Really? I never would have thought she was the type," Angel said.

"Not a bad idea. Why don't we both take five?"

"Apparently her life is better than ever since we solved her case and now she's looking for a forum to brag about her sex life."

"Ugh," Angel said.

"Ugh."

"I concur. There's got to be an easier way to decide this."

I rolled my eyes at the Neanderthals. "After you call Mar, clean this mess up."

Angel looked at the two men gasping and grinned. "Yes, Boss."

I walked back to the laundry room hoping for some good news from Eric or at least maybe an intelligent conversation. Instead, I found a star-eyed twenty-year-old in the backyard taking risqué pictures of Brenda in a low-cut swimsuit.

"Are you two insane," I hollered. "Brenda, this is contributing to the delinquency of a minor."

"I'm almost twenty-one," Eric said, grinning from behind Brenda's 35 millimeter camera. "This is cool. I can do more with it than the camera on my iPhone. Better zoom and better focus."

Brenda laughed and reached for a towel on the grass to cover herself. "I'm just helping with the investigation. Eric said he needed more pictures to attract Trixie to his fake Facebook page."

I marched her up the back steps and into the laundry room. "He has enough pictures. Did it ever occur to you he might have a crush on you?"

"Eric? Well, yeah, I guess. But I've already had that talk with him about the age difference and him with a criminal record. I think I've dissuaded him."

"How long have you known men? They don't stop just because you tell them to. If you don't believe me, look at this." I opened the laundry room door and pointed to Earl and Chris arm wrestling on the floor.

"What are they doing?" Brenda asked.

"Trying to figure out which one of them will take Angel out to dinner tonight."

"How cute. But didn't you tell them you didn't want them fighting over her anymore."

"Yeah, and last time she threatened them with a gun. You see what effect that had."

"You're going down."

"Not if I can help it."

Brenda clenched her towel tightly to her chest. "Oh. You think Eric wants to take more pictures of me because . . ."

"And you call yourself a cop?" I laughed and she blushed. "Get dressed and meet me back here."

As Brenda went to the upstairs bathroom to change, Eric entered the laundry room with a sheepish smile.

"I wasn't doing anything wrong. I just thought maybe if we spiced up our profile on Carrie's Facebook page, it would improve our chances of getting a hit from Trixie."

"Have you even checked it lately? I mean with your photography sessions and all?"

"Well, no. Not since yesterday afternoon with you. I've been developing my Internet Protocol Address tracking program. You see, it has a way of detecting spoofing--that's when someone who doesn't want to be found puts out a fake IP address--and I've been updating the program to make it faster."

"But you've had time to set up a photo session with Brenda?"

"Oh, I see what you mean. Well, let's check it. I'm sure nothing has happened yet. This guy could have several Facebook pages out there and . . . Shit! We got him!"

"What?" I pushed him away from the table and stared at the computer screen.

"I said we got him. He *friended* us. Now I can get to work on hacking his page."

I high-fived him and he grinned back at me like a proud daddy at the birth of his first son.

"Now you won't need this." I opened the side of Brenda's camera and removed the flash card.

"Hey, what are you doing? Those pictures are mine."

"Brenda's camera, Brenda's pictures. I'll give them to her. You get back to work."

"Oh, all right." He sulked like a little boy put in a corner.

My cell phone beeped. I received a text message from Mario, the waiter at Huber's Café. It included the phone number of Jeff Jones, Christine Crawford's boyfriend.

As I dialed the number, I recalled the story about him being run over on his bicycle shortly after an argument with a customer paying too much attention to Christine.

"The cops ran me through the wringer," Jeff said. We sat inside Jamison Square, a skyscraper-locked park at the edge of the Pearl District at Northwest Eleventh and Kearney Street. Four layers of fountains in a semi-circle hushed the noises of a sprawling cityscape.

"I was their prime suspect when she disappeared." Jeff stared at the fountains from a park bench we occupied. "They were convinced I was responsible. Then two weeks ago, when they found her body, the whole ordeal started all over again. They brought me in for questioning for thirteen hours without a break."

Tears dribbled down his face. "I loved her. I told them it wasn't me. But they keep coming at me and trying to confuse me, to make me say what they want to hear."

"It's usually the boyfriend or spouse." I handed him a tissue from my purse. "The cops know that and so they concentrate on you until you either prove them wrong or you crack."

"I was at work the day she went missing," he said. "There were witnesses. Why didn't they believe me?"

"The cops probably can't tell when she was killed," I said. "It's been so long that there is no way to pinpoint time of death. She could have been killed before or after you went to work."

I watched as he dabbed the tears from his cheek with the Kleenex. His long wavy brown hair hung precariously above his eyes. Under a thin brown tee-shirt, a sculpted body displayed itself. Jeff, like every young man who lived and worked in the hipster communities, sported a beard, although his was neatly trimmed.

"Mario told me about your confrontation with a man at the restaurant before Christine went missing," I said.

"Yeah." Jeff said. "The guy was a real asswipe. He kept on hitting on her. She came to me all frustrated and said there was something about the guy that scared her."

"So you tried to warn him off." A sparrow flitted across the ground looking for food someone might have left behind. Nearby, pigeons built a wall around scraps from a scone.

"Yeah. I was one of the cooks, so I went to the table and asked if the food was okay. I wanted to see the guy. He asked me for the name of 'that cute blonde waitress' and I told him very politely he should not bother her as she was engaged to me."

"You were engaged to be married?"

"We talked about it."

The sparrow skittered across to the pigeons for a piece of the action.

"What was his reaction?"

Jeff looked over his shoulder. His lip trembled and his nervous demeanor made me wonder if he had post-traumatic stress disorder because of his encounter with the cops.

"He said he just wanted to flirt with her, not marry her. His condescending attitude pissed me off."

"What did you say to that?"

"Nothing. I bit my tongue and let it go." His tone betrayed his anger.

"I heard you got into it with him later."

"He started in on Chrissy again when she took him the check. I told him to get the hell out and not come back."

"You can do that? Banish a person from the restaurant?"

Jeff watched as the sparrow darted in, snapped up a huge piece of scone and flew away before the confused pigeons knew what happened.

"Nah, I was out of line. I swore at him. He called in and complained, saying I'd embarrassed him in front of his friends. My boss gave me a warning and that was the end of it, or so I thought."

"Is that why you quit?"

"Nah, I had a bicycle accident. Hit and run. It took me a couple weeks to recuperate. When I got back to work, the boss said he had to let me go. Didn't say why, but I think it had to do with me being a suspect in Chrissy's murder."

"Tell me about the accident," I said.

"I was on my way home from work about a week after Chrissy's disappearance," he said. "The cops had interviewed me the day before and I was still hung over from the whole ordeal. It was late, about midnight, and I was pedaling over the Morrison Bridge. I took the McLoughlin Street exit ramp and as I was coasting down the dude pulled up alongside me in a Prius."

"A Prius? What color was it?"

"Blue, I think. It was too dark to tell for sure. "Before I could react, he swerved and bounced me off my bike and against the exit ramp wall."

I grimaced. "Were you hurt badly?"

"I suffered bruised ribs, a lacerated spleen, and a lot of road rash."

"And he drove off and left you?"

"No way. The dude stopped at the light at the end of the ramp. He got out and looked back at me. I thought he was going to come back and help until I realized who he was. He laughed, got back in the car, and drove off."

I had my notepad out. "Did you see his license plate?"

"The first thing I thought of. He was about a hundred feet away and the area was well lit. But the car didn't have a license plate."

The sparrow came back and the pigeons regrouped and chased it off. "Did you tell the cops?"

"Yeah. I called the investigating officer, Lt. Hamm, from the hospital and I told him it was the same guy bothering Chrissy at the restaurant."

"What did he say?"

"He came to the hospital and interviewed me. I told him over and over again, it was the same guy, but he didn't seem interested. I thought he was just being a bastard. Then when I mentioned it to the FBI after they found Chrissy, and they told me Lt. Hamm thought I'd staged the whole bike accident to throw suspicion off myself."

I sighed. It was the sign of a lazy investigator. Make up your mind who was responsible and make the facts fit the suspect. I knew a fire investigator in the nearby city of Gresham, once, who did the same thing to a client of mine.

"You're sure this guy was the same person you had a run in with before?" I asked.

"Well, yeah. It was like he was telling me he got in the last laugh."

"Do you think he had something to do with Christine's death?"

Jeff's face grew stern. "I know he killed her. That's what the whole running me off the road was about. He wanted me to know he killed her and there was nothing I could do about it."

"Didn't anyone follow up with this guy? Check his credit card statement to find out who he was?"

"I thought of that," Jeff said. "He paid cash. He knows how to stay in the background."

He certainly does, I thought. The only thing that continued to stand out about him was the blue Prius. But I was beginning to feel confident enough to put a name to him.

Trixie was as good a name as any, and it seemed to fit his mischievous personality.

Chapter 27

Steve walked through the front door just as Angel and I were going over our *To Do* list for the evening's self-defense class. It was three o'clock and he had not returned any of my frantic phone calls regarding my leads on the serial killer.

And to make things worse, although Eric had hacked into Trixie's web page, he had identified only three remote Internet protocol addresses which turned out to be various apartment buildings and a coffee shop.

"Sorry I didn't have time to call you back," Steve said. He wore his tired brown sport jacket instead of his new thousand dollar blue suit. "I traced that phone number you gave me and it was a dead end."

I checked off *whistles* on the list of things to take to the class without looking at him.

"We've been really busy and we're closing in on this guy."

Angel sat in a chair next to me wearing gray sweats and I think a pair of my white tennis shoes. She took an absent puff on the cigarette that wasn't in her hand any longer and blew an imaginary smoke ring.

"Did you hear me?" Steve asked. "We're going to search this guy's house tonight."

"So?" Of course I heard him, but I was pissed.

"I know I haven't returned your calls, but I've been busy."

"Well, go along and arrest your perp," I said. "I hope you got the right guy."

He sighed. "Did you ever stop to think we might be chasing the same person?"

"What do you mean?"

"He has the same general description as this John Benson that met you in your office."

I sat back in my chair and squinted at him. "So you at least listened to my messages."

"It took a while, but I waded through all twelve of them."

"What's his name?"

"Chad Sanford. He lives in a big house up on the West Hills. He's a young bachelor and has been in scrapes with the law before. He was that ex-boyfriend of Cynthia Miller's I told you about. Her sister said Cynthia and Chad had a falling out over her seeing other men. He was extremely jealous and stalked her for a time after their breakup."

I stood and walked over to him. "Do you have a picture?"

He showed me a photo of Chad Sanford. He looked disinterested in his arrest mug shot and sported a beard and mustache. His hair was a light brown and his eyes were blue like the phony Benson I'd met.

"I can't tell you if it's the same man," I said. "There are enough similarities, but he may be using disguises."

"This picture is five years old," Steve said. "He was picked up for a date rape, but the prosecutor dropped the case because the victim changed her mind. The D.A. thinks Sanford paid her off."

"Are you going to arrest him?"

"That depends," Steve said. "We have a search warrant. If he's dirty, we should be able to find something. Maybe even a victim. He's been staying close to home the past couple of days."

"How'd you get the warrant?" I asked.

"We're using the Cynthia Miller murder case as leverage. The perp's past rape accusation combined with a new witness who says he tried it with her a few months back gave us cause. The judge didn't bat an eyelash."

"It's been four days since Janet Domingo disappeared. I don't hold too much hope of finding her alive, but . . ."

"You want to come?"

"On the search? *Yeah, I want to come.*"

Steve grinned. "I cleared it with the task force. We're going to hit Sanford's front door at nineteen hundred hours."

"I have a self-defense class tonight. I can't."

"I'll do it for you," Angel said, returning with a cup of coffee. "I know the course outline and I've taken these classes before."

"Could you?" I said.

"I owe it to you with all the crap that's been going on in the office with my boyfriends. Earl took me out to dinner last night. I'll call Chris and get him to help me tonight."

"Thanks." I hugged her, spilling her coffee.

"I thought she'd be coming too," Steve said. "I have approval from the team for an extra person."

"I'll call Brenda," I said. "She'll be off duty, and she's been helping me on the case. She's a deputy with the Multnomah County Sheriff's Department."

"If it makes you happy, I'm happy. But you'll have to stay outside until the site is secured."

"Understood," I said. "But then can I help with the search?"

"Maybe you'd better not come," he said.

I sneered at him. "Like you could stop me."

Trixie felt better. Today was a big day. Connie seemed one hundred percent on board with his plans and after hearing how she murdered her mother and father, he realized it gave him further control over her. She wouldn't turn him in after confiding her duplicity in a double murder.

Yet, she seemed a bit on edge. He realized the enormity of what he was asking of her. Killing her parents to survive was one thing. Helping him kill someone she didn't have any grudge against, didn't even know, would be difficult for her.

"Brent, a car just went by. I've seen it before." Connie stood in front of the living room picture window and pointed. "It was out there yesterday when I arrived. I noticed it drive by twice this morning and it just passed again."

Trixie jumped up from an overstuffed chair near the fireplace and strode to the window. "What kind of car is it?"

"It's gone now. A black Mercedes sedan."

Trixie smiled a bit. "The Mercedes belongs to a neighbor up the street. He's retired and is always coming and going."

Connie screwed her face at him. "Retired? How old is he?"

"Probably sixty. His hair is graying." Trixie chuckled. "He moved in a couple years ago and we wave to each other, but I just realized I don't even know his name."

"I didn't think he looked that old when I saw him yesterday," she said. "Maybe forty."

Trixie stepped to the window and gazed up the street. He knew Connie was anxious, but she was starting to make him nervous too.

"Let me know if you see him again."

Angel drove her Volkswagen Beetle up a steep hill to Northwest Twenty-Sixth Avenue, which wasn't a street at all. It was a concrete path about eight feet wide that gave access to the back of Chapman Elementary School situated at the edge of a public park. The road was used by school personnel for loading and unloading.

In her rear-view mirror, she watched Chris in his orange rusted pickup, and Earl in his Turquoise BMW, follow behind. She hoped they would behave themselves. Earl had shown up while she and Chris loaded supplies and insisted on coming along to help.

The first thing she noticed about the school was a huge red-bricked, cylinder-shaped chimney towering a hundred-feet above the school buildings. She remembered that during the August evenings, people gathered on the hillside to witness thirty to fifty thousand swifts evade hawks and spiral down the gigantic chimney for refuge at dusk.

"This building is enormous." Earl grabbed a box from Chris's truck and followed Angel into the gymnasium.

"It's not so big," Chris said. He held two boxes of paperwork and various gear for the participants. "The school I went to was twice as big. And it had two of those chimneys."

Angel rolled her eyes and began arranging the signup table. "I need you two to bring those mats over from the wall and lay them out for us to practice on."

When Earl asked to come along she had relented, thinking having both of them to help her set up might be a good idea. She hoped she wouldn't regret it.

"She wants them butted together so no one hits the wooden floor," Chris bellowed.

"I think spreading them out like stations, gives each person their own area to work out," Earl said.

"This isn't calisthenics. They're going to be throwing each other around," Chris said.

"He's right, Earl," Angel said. "Put them together."

A petite thirty-something redheaded woman stepped up to the table. "I'm Georgia Cummings. I registered for the self-defense class. Are you Billie?"

"I'm her assistant, Angel. Billie had to cancel at the last minute, an important development in one of her cases."

"I wasn't sure. I haven't seen her since high school, and you dress like her and have the blonde hair, but your face wasn't familiar. But I'm terrible with faces."

Angel hadn't expected to be mistaken for Billie. She realized she was still dressing in the blue jeans and white blouse apparel her boss wore almost daily and tonight she wore sweats and although her casual dress seemed to spark more interest from Earl and Chris, she wasn't sure she liked being mistaken for her friend.

"She'll try to make it later on if she can," she said curtly.

More women filed into the gym and inked their names on a signup sheet. Chris and Earl arranged the mats the way she wanted them, but Angel grumbled to herself and took a drag from her phantom cigarette.

She had started the class by explaining Billie's absence and begun discussing some basic self-defense moves, when a straggler entered from the back side of the gymnasium.

"I'm sorry I'm late. I took a wrong turn and got lost."

She was tall with strawberry-blonde hair, very attractive, and probably used to getting her own way.

"Everybody who signed up is here," Angel told the woman.

"I didn't sign up. I just noticed it tonight and thought I could make it in time. Is that okay?"

It would have to be. Angel wanted to keep the class moving and this interruption disrupted the flow. She wanted it to be fun as well as educational, and so far it was a snoozer.

"You can sign up at the table over there. One of the boys will assist you, dear."

"My name is Samantha," she said. "Samantha Jones."

"Okay," she said. "I'll need a volunteer for this next move."

"Oh, let me." Mar floated from the crowd of twelve standing women and sauntered up to her.

"Okay, dear, stand in back of me. Now I want you to grab me from behind." Mar approached her carefully and draped her arm around Angel's waist. "No, no, no! Do it like someone who means to hurt you! Wrap your arm around my neck."

"I'll sign her in. You can sign the next one in."

"Oh yeah? Sign this in."

Angel wriggled out of Mar's loose grip and turned in time to see Earl and Chris in a pushing match. At the center of their debate was Samantha, clad in a revealing skin-tight running suit. Angel hated her immediately.

"Okay boys. I need your help over here. Samantha, you too."

Chris and Earl pushed each other again before straggling over behind Samantha to the mat.

"He started it," Chris said.

"Did not," Earl said.

"Earl, honey, I need you to grab me from behind for my demonstration," Angel said.

"You bet," he said. "Like this?"

"Hold me tight. Don't let go."

He laughed. "My pleasure."

"Now, like I showed you earlier, when he grabs you from behind, your first goal should be a secondary target."

Angel lifted her foot and jammed it hard on the top of Earl's foot. The big man winced, hopped up and down, but maintained his hold on her. "Next is the elbow smash into the primary target." She made a fist, covered it with the palm of her other hand and jammed her elbow into Earl's throat.

"Agghh," he croaked, and floundered on the mat.

The sound of a chorus of air being sucked in came from the circle of women students. It was followed shortly by a nervous laughter.

"See how it works?" Angel asked.

"Oh," said Mar. "Can I try it?"

"In a minute," Angel said. "First, I need to demonstrate a frontal attack. Chris? Can you help me?"

"I don't know. That looks kind of dangerous." Chris tried to back away, but the semi-circle of tittering women pushed him forward.

"Well, it can be if you don't know how to take care of yourself, like Earl," Angel said. "But I'm sure you can do a much better job."

"Go ahead," Samantha said. "You can do it."

"I guess I could give it a try." Chris strutted like a peacock, but a nervous smile betrayed his bravado. "You want me to get out of that hold like you did?"

"Not exactly," Angel said. "I want you to come straight at me and grab my throat."

"Then what?"

"You'll know instinctively when it happens."

He grabbed Angel's throat, and she lifted her left arm high over his head and swung it down across his arms, turned away to the right and broke his hold. He tried to reassert his grip, but she swung her elbow back and struck him square in the nose.

A gasp erupted from the class when she followed with a kick to his groin. The normally effervescent Chris keeled over and hit the mat like a sack of rocks.

"Can't believe you did that," he huffed. A mat away, Earl still gasped for breath.

"You two can take your tired act out of here or I'll let the rest of the class practice on you."

"We're going," Earl croaked. "Come on, Chris. I'll buy you a beer."

"Can't move." Chris curled into a ball and groaned. "Save yourself."

Chapter 28

I looked across the expansive front yard at a blue BMW parked in the driveway. Steve told me his suspect didn't own a Prius, blue or otherwise, and I wondered if I had been mistaken about the make of the car I saw drifting behind the UPS truck the day I was in Mary Johansen's neighborhood.

"Is someone in there with him?" I asked.

"Beats me," Brenda said. "I just got here." To avoid municipality conflicts, she had shed her deputy's uniform for slacks and a blouse.

"He's in there with a girlfriend." Sgt. Lewis stared at Brenda's long copper hair. "She arrived yesterday afternoon and stayed the night. Neither of them has been out today."

"I was briefed earlier," Steve said. "You've seen them? Nothing appears to be amiss?"

"Nope," Lewis said. "Saw 'em at lunch through a kitchen window. Then they went back upstairs. Probably going at it like rabbits. That's my guess anyway. We got a bet going."

I thought about the likelihood of Chad Sanford having a woman with him if he had Janet Domingo stashed somewhere on his property, and my mind went wacko and I wondered if the girl the officers spotted might be Janet. A lump formed in my throat and adrenaline surged through my body at the thought she might still be alive.

"Okay, it's go time," Steve said. He raised a massive hand and waved officers into action.

"We got four guys around back in case the rabbits decided to rabbit," Sgt. Lewis said.

Lewis, Steve and two FBI agents ran to the ornate oak door between two colonial columns and knocked. The door opened slowly and the lump in my throat fell into my stomach. A woman, who was not Janet, peered out. She wore a white terrycloth robe with a hotel insignia and not much else. I imagined Sgt. Lewis chuckling to himself.

One of the Feds, a short, plump man in a blue suit, served the warrant to the woman and marched through the front door, almost tearing the robe from her naked body. A group of FBI forensic types followed Steve and his team through the door and a swarm of cops brought up the rear.

"I guess it's our turn." I looked around and we were the only ones still outside.

"I guess so," Brenda said, and we joined the party.

"Is anyone else in the house?" Steve asked.

"Just her and me," Chad said. "What's the idea?" He wore a white terry cloth robe similar to the young lady's.

"It's all explained in the warrant." Steve took the document from the woman and thrust it into his hands. "Not that I don't believe you, but I think we'll look for ourselves."

"I guess you have the right to." He skimmed the search warrant and smirked. "Help yourselves."

Five patrolmen, three detectives and eight FBI agents dispersed in various directions in the gigantic two-story house with probably eight bedrooms. Steve stood and stared at the suspect, who glanced away from the paperwork and winked at me.

Steve glared at Chad. "Who's the girl?"

"My name is . . ."

"Shirley. Her name is Shirley," Chad said.

"But honey."

"You don't need to tell them anything," he said. "The search warrant is for the house only, not its occupants."

"Okay." The oversized robe slipped off her shoulder and she grabbed for it. "I should get dressed though."

"You stay right here," he said. "I don't want one of these cops to get you alone and confuse you."

"But I look a mess." She re-tied her belt and patted her tousled blonde hair, trying to comb it with her fingers.

"You look beautiful to me." He wrapped an arm around her.

"So Chad," I said. "If you were to stash an extra woman around here, where would you hide her?"

He turned away from Shirley and laughed at me, inadvertently glancing toward the staircase before his vision veered abruptly to the ceiling. I noticed a flicker in his eyes a millisecond before he jerked his head and realized he'd understood my attempt to trap him.

"There are no other girls here," he said.

"Hmm. Maybe." I walked to the double width staircase and pushed at a panel on the side, which opened into a storage closet. "Might want to get your men to check this out."

"Nice catch," Brenda said.

Steve tossed us each a pair of latex gloves. "You two can take a look in there. I've identified the areas of the house I want our team to search, and I don't want them interrupted."

Brenda followed me into the closet. We were directly under the stairs and I moved a vacuum cleaner and some coats out into the living room. A twenty-five watt light barely illuminated the inside. The area seemed both larger and smaller than I expected. It was smaller because the stairs hindered ceiling space at one end, but the closet went deeper under the stairs than one might imagine.

Darkness enveloped the closet at its distant points and Brenda and I used Flashlight Apps on our cell phones to check all of the nooks and crannies. When I was satisfied there were no hidden areas along the walls, I dropped to my knees and Brenda followed.

"What are we looking for?" Brenda asked.

"Loose planks, any place where he might be able to hide something," I said. A few minutes of fumbling in the darkness revealed a glimmer of hope.

"There's a notch in the wood here," Brenda said. She knocked at the floorboard. "It sounds hollow."

I retrieved a pocket knife from my jeans and fished its blade into the crack Brenda had discovered. The board loosened and we managed to grab it with our fingers and pry it up. The next board came up easier and another followed. The space measured two-feet by five-feet and was deep enough to fit a petite body. But it was empty, except for a few shoeboxes. I shined the light on the boxes.

"Open one," I said.

"Why me?" Brenda asked.

"Because I'm holding the flashlight." I turned it to her face, which lit up a sour look.

"You and I both know that if he stashed something away like this, it won't be pretty," she said.

"That's my guess. You want me to open it?"

"No. I'll do the dirty work this time."

I turned the light back to the shoebox and held my breath as Brenda peeled the lid away. We stared stupidly at the box and then at each other. There were no body parts; these were trophies of another nature.

"Gross," Brenda said. She picked at several pairs of women's panties, turning them over with a pen so we could see the array of colors and styles. "There's another box. You want to do the honors?"

"Yeah, I guess there's still a chance we'll find something creepier." I took the pen from her and used it to lift the lid from the second box. "More panties," I said. "This isn't getting us any closer to finding Janet Domingo."

224

I wanted to personally scour the whole house for Janet, but I knew Steve would toss me if I tried.

"Maybe Janet's are in the box," Brenda said.

"Perhaps." I scanned the hideaway with my flashlight for traces of blood. "Maybe forensics can turn something."

We crawled out of the space and carried the two boxes to a table in the living room. Chad's eyes scanned the room as if looking for an exit. Shirley sat on an overstuffed chair nearby smoking a cigarette, her legs crossed seductively.

"What's in the boxes?" Steve asked.

"Women's underwear." I removed the two lids and Steve wandered over and eyeballed them.

"There's no law about having women's underwear," Chad said.

Shirley got up from her chair and sauntered over to the table. "Is there a pair of purple panties with black hearts? I lost a pair when I was here last week and he claimed he didn't know what happened to them." She puffed a smoke ring over the boxes. "Oh? Here they are."

"Don't touch." Steve grabbed her wrist from behind. "Sorry, it's evidence in a possible murder case."

"Murder? Chad honey, what are they talking about?"

But when we turned back to Chad honey, for an answer to her question, he was gone.

Angel struggled with one of several oversized cardboard boxes filled with all of the supplies she had packed for the class, most of which went unused. She cursed to herself for bringing so much junk— brochures and other class handouts, self-defense CD's and T-shirts she'd hoped to sell, office supplies for just in case, and a bunch of stuff Chris apparently added without her knowledge.

Because he and Earl carried the boxes in, she hadn't noticed the added junk. But now that they were gone, she alone had to tote all of the crap across the playground to her VW. Chris had brought most of the class equipment in his pickup and, as she sized up her Beetle, she didn't know where she would put everything.

"Damn them," she said. "Choose, schmooze, Billie. They can both hit the bricks as far as I'm concerned."

She might have asked some of the other women for help, if that Samantha hadn't bent her ear after class and disappeared so suddenly.

"The bitch," she said. "She steals my boyfriends and leaves me to clean up the mess."

Luckily, there was enough moonlight for her to make her way to her car. She looked at three boxes sitting on the pavement next to her VW. How was she going to fit all of these big boxes in the back seat? She put her load down, ran her hands along her hips, and sighed.

"Need some help?"

She turned, her heart in her throat, and reached for one of the three guns she normally carried with her. Crap, she'd left two of them at home and the other was in her purse, still back in the gym. She squinted toward the raspy voice and realized the dark figure was Samantha.

"Oh, I wondered where you went."

"I had to use the bathroom. Here, let me help you."

"Thanks," Angel said. She began to feel guilty for the thing's she'd said and thought about her.

Samantha turned toward the Beetle and laughed. "Not much room is there? Let me carry those boxes to my car. I parked back here too because I was late and there wasn't any street parking. I can drop them by your office."

"Well, if it isn't too much trouble," Angel said, feeling completely foolish now. It wasn't this poor girl's fault if Earl and Chris were dopes.

Samantha lifted a bulky box and carried it toward a small sedan under a birch tree.

"I've got another box and my purse in the gymnasium," Angel said. "I'll be right back."

"Can you open the car door for me?" Samantha said.

"Sure. Angel hurried to her blue sedan and opened the back door. "Will it fit in there?"

"Probably not," Samantha said. "Can you open the trunk?"

She offered her car keys to Angel, struggling to maintain her grip on the box. Angel took the keys and hit the fob switch for the trunk on the keychain. The trunk opened and Angel leaned forward to see if the boxes would fit.

"Plenty of room in here, but your light is burned out."

A hand covered her mouth and nose with cheesecloth. The smell was both sweet and sickening--chloroform. She flailed and swung an elbow to Samantha's throat. But the blow met a wall of flesh and Angel realized her attacker was a man.

"Watch your feet," Samantha yelled.

Angel tried to stomp on the tender spot of her attacker's foot like she had shown her students, but he moved it. She retaliated with another elbow, this time aimed higher toward a man's throat. It connected, but the force was muted by the effects of the drug. Someone pulled a burlap bag over her head and a rope of some type tightened it over her arms and chest. The bag reeked of chloroform and Angel felt herself losing consciousness in the suffocating bag.

Why was this happening? What did Samantha have to do with it? An awful thought occurred to her.

"Oh shit."

Chris, tired of Earl's soliloquy of sorrow over a beer at a nearby bar, decided he should go back and help Angel. Beg her forgiveness if necessary. He realized he'd been a jerk when that Samantha chick flirted with him and he'd started competing with Earl again.

It was dark and he hoped Angel would still be at the school so he could lend a hand. He drove up the steep hill to the school and a speeding blue sedan swerved toward him just as he reached the top.

"Damn moron," he yelled, steering sharply toward the curb. He found the narrow drive leading to the back of the school and carefully navigated it with his headlights on low beam. Ahead he spotted Angel's Beetle and he pulled up behind it. He noticed a box and papers strewn across the grounds when he got out of his pickup.

"Angel? What the hell?"

He picked up a wet clump of cloth on the ground and sniffed it. A sickly sweet solvent clutched his throat and he felt light-headed. Angel was nowhere to be found, but a lone light burned in the gymnasium so he sprinted toward it. Fear stuck in his throat when he opened the back door and found a lone box on a bleacher seat with Angel's purse.

"Angel? Where are you?"

Chapter 29

Steve spoke into a microphone clipped to his shirt pocket: "Our suspect has flown the coop. I want every available officer down here now."

"Shit, where did he go?" Steve said off air.

"I noticed he held something in his hand when we came out of the closet," Brenda said. "Now that I think of it, it might have been car keys."

Steve ran to the living room window. "His car is still in the drive." Three FBI agents tramped down the stairway and two cops joined us from the basement.

"Why are you after Chad and what the hell is this about a murder?" Shirley was grinning at the commotion her boyfriend created by his sudden departure and stubbed out her cigarette in a glass ashtray.

"You handle her," Steve huffed, and charged out the front door with his troops hot behind him.

"I'd better see if I can help," Brenda said, and ran out after them.

"Shirley," I began.

"My name is Myra Dandridge. I don't know why Chad told you different. Now what's going on?"

"Uh, Myra. Chad is a suspect in several rapes and the possible murder of a former girlfriend."

Myra clutched at the collar of her robe. Her face went pale and her eyes enlarged to the point I might have guessed she was high if I didn't know better.

"Where did you meet him?" I asked.

"At a bar. The White Owl Social Club on Southeast Eighth and Main. He's a friend of a friend and we hooked up. He's treated me all right. Are you sure you've got the right guy?"

Right now I wasn't sure of anything. Myra was the type my serial killer would go for, blonde, attractive, and fit. But he didn't have a blue Prius, and he seemed different from the guy who came to her office and pretended to be Mary Johansen's fiancé. The two were of the same size and build and even had the same quiet confidence.

"Not for sure," I said. "Do you have any idea where he could have gone?"

She shrugged. "He has a car parked on the street side of the house."

"The BWM," I said.

"No, that's mine. He likes to park his Prius on the side street so he can come in the back door during the day. It's quicker with groceries and booze than coming in through the garage and having to lug things up the stairs."

"A Prius?" I stammered. "He has a Prius?"

"Yeah, it's real cute."

"But I was told he had a BMW."

"He does. It's in the garage. But he likes the Prius his mother left him when she died about a year ago. He says it's more energy efficient."

"What color is it?"

"Kind of a Turquoise, I think. A greenish blue. Maybe it's more of a blue with greenish tint."

"Shit." My stomach roiled and my head was spinning. Had I been wrong all along? Did I just let the man who abducted Janet walk away? And where was Janet?

"I need to get dressed and get out of here." Myra started for the stairway and stopped. "Do you think you could come with me? Just in case? I'm a little nervous."

"Sure," I said, my mind racing.

We went upstairs to Chad's master bedroom where I ran into two forensic investigators coming out of the bathroom. "Is it okay for her to use the bedroom and bathroom?" I asked.

A woman with red hair, a blue paper face mask, and some kind of microscopic bifocals on her nose, nodded. "Yeah, we're done here."

"We're heading down to the basement now," Joe Conrad said. "No trace of blood in the bathroom or the bedroom." I knew Joe from my days on the force, and he was nice enough, but a bit nerdy.

A king-sized bed took up most of the room and its sheets and comforter blanketed the floor. The mattress sat half off of its frame where the cops frisked it. A 70-inch flat screen TV screen enveloped the wall south of the bed and an equally hideous sized dresser straddled a side wall. Myra picked up her red-laced panties and bra from the thick beige carpet, scooped up black leggings and a matching skirt and blouse, and carried them into the master bathroom.

The door was open a bit so I ventured a question through the gap. "Do you have any idea where Chad may have gone?"

"Not really," Myra said. "We spent most of our time here."

"How long have you known him?"

"About two weeks?"

"He never took you anywhere else?"

"We went to dinner a few times and to some bars."

"Do you know where his mother's house is?"

"It's over in Northwest Portland somewhere. He has it up for sale, but the market hasn't been good." She stuck her head out of the door and I watched her pulling a legging up. "I think he's asking too much."

"Do you remember her name or the address of the house?" Janet had to be at his mother's house, I thought.

"I wasn't really that interested, and I don't think he ever mentioned her name."

My cell phone chirped and I retrieved it from my purse. I didn't recognize the number on caller ID.

"Billie? It's Chris." His voice cracked when he spoke.

"Is something wrong?"

"I think so. Me and Earl had a fight and Angel threw us out."

"I'm sorry, but I'm kind of busy right now."

"She isn't with you, is she? I was thinking maybe you came and picked her up. Her car is still here."

My intestines knotted. "Her car is still where?"

"I'm here at the school. I came back to help her, but she isn't here. Her car is here, but she isn't here. Her boxes are here, but she isn't here. Her purse is here . . ."

"Did you check inside the school?"

"Yeah. I went through the whole school. Nobody's here but a janitor, and he says he hasn't seen anybody. I even looked in the ladies restroom."

"I don't understand. Where is she?"

"I don't know," Chris said. "The only person I saw was in a car coming down the hill from the school. The guy was a moron. Had his bright lights on and almost blinded me."

The bile rose in my throat, and I wasn't sure I could keep it down much longer.

"What kind of car."

"It was too dark to tell. It was a sedan, maybe one of those hybrid thingies."

"You mean a Prius?"

"Yeah, that's what it was. They use those LED headlights and they're a lot brighter than the old headlights. Maybe that's why I was blinded."

"What color was the Prius, Chris?"

"I don't know. It was too dark to tell. There was a woman and a man in it though. I could see that."

"Could the woman have been Angel?"

"I wasn't watching that closely. I guess it could have been, but she would have seen my pickup and . . ."

"What are you trying to tell me, Chris?"

"I don't want to frighten you."

"Just tell me."

"I found a rag on the ground near her car. It smelled like some kind of paint thinner, only sweet. I think it was that chloroform stuff they used to knock people out in the old movies. I think somebody grabbed her, Billie. What should I do?"

It didn't make sense. How could Chad have kidnapped Angel in the last half hour if he was watching the cops search his house?

Who else would want to kidnap Angel? If this serial killer had a thing for me and was playing some kind of game it made sense. Angel looked more like me these days than I did. And it was dark enough that Trixie could have mistaken her for me.

I played mental ping-pong for a minute. Chad had a green or blue Prius. I saw Trixie in a blue Prius in front of Mary's house that day. A Prius was seen coming out of the school about the same time Angel disappeared

Chad's mother died during the past year and left him a Prius. Brent told Mary at The Outrigger that his mother had recently passed away. But how could they be the same man and be in two places at once? Does he have an accomplice? Maybe we interrupted his plans to kidnap Angel and his accomplice followed through. The more I thought about it, the more my head throbbed.

"Billie?" Chris said. "Are you still there?"

"Stay put. I'll be there in fifteen minutes. See if you can get hold of Earl. Fill him in and tell him to get to the school."

Myra exited the bathroom just in time. I ran in and threw up in the sink.

"This isn't her!" Trixie screamed. "We've got the wrong one."

"I don't understand," Connie said. "This is Billie Bly. Who did you want?"

They were inside Trixie's garage and he had waited until the overhead door closed before switching another light on. He had been triumphant on the ride home, confident he had finally eliminated the meddlesome P.I. as a threat.

But when he opened the hatchback door of the Prius and yanked the burlap sack from his still unconscious prize, the room became a blur. He tried to focus on the woman in the trunk, but no matter how hard he squinted at her, she wasn't the tough blonde troublemaker who stared into his soul that day on Mary Johansen's street.

"This is not Billie Bly." He threw the burlap bag in Connie's face. "This is her mouthy assistant. I don't even remember her name."

Connie took the bag from her face and let it drop on the garage floor. "But she's the one who taught the class." Her lower lip quivered as she avoided his gaze. "I . . . I didn't see any woman assistant. There were two men. I planned to try to distract them after the class but when I flirted with them, she got mad and told them to leave. I thought I did a good job of getting her alone for you."

The time he had been in Billie's office pretending to be John Benson, her assistant's hair was jet black with punk style orange and purple highlights. Not easy to forget. So why did she dye her hair blonde? Trixie grabbed the woman by her offending hair and yanked her limp body from the trunk. He dragged her across the garage's concrete floor caveman style, opened the door to the house, and turned back to Connie.

"Come on." His gruff voice echoed in the garage. He watched her obey him, afraid of what he might do if she didn't. Another time he would have gotten off on that, but now he had other priorities. If he had her assistant, where the hell was Billie Bly? Had he fallen into some kind of trap?

He draped the unconscious woman over his shoulder and made for the stairs at the back end of the house.

Connie followed whimpering like a nervous puppy. Down the stairs they went, and he opened a door and stepped into the replica of the garage upstairs. The blood on the floor was gone now. Connie had cleaned it earlier while Brent repaired the storage cabinet.

"What are you going to do with her?" Connie asked.

"Same as I planned to do with Miss Bly." He opened the cabinet door he had repaired earlier in the afternoon. He propped the woman on a wooden crate, leaned her against the back wall, and searched the pockets in her sweat suit.

"Damn," he said. He held a cell phone in his hand. He turned it on and stared at the screen. "She texted *911* to someone named Earl."

He opened the back of the phone, removed the battery and threw the phone across the room. "This is worse than I imagined." Little Brucie screamed from somewhere inside. He was scared and so was Trixie.

He took a can of paint thinner from the top shelf and poured some onto the woman's head so she would be sure to smell the stifling fumes as he had so many years ago. "Why did you change your hair color?" he asked the woman.

"I got there late." Connie kept looking toward the door, the only way out of this awful room. "If she ever explained why Billie Bly wasn't leading the class, I must have missed it. When I came in late, she seemed upset with me so we didn't talk much."

Trixie ignored her. He ran up the stairs with her in pursuit and marched to each window on the first floor, scanning the yard carefully and then the street. He saw no evidence anyone had followed them or was staking out the house. He went to his police scanner in the living room, turned it on, and scrolled through various channels listening to chatter.

Officer responding to a domestic, officer requesting warrants at a traffic stop, officer request for tow trucks to clear out cars parked in a special no parking zone near bars in Old Town.

Nothing about him. He turned on a security video monitor and checked eight camera angles outside the house. There was nobody to be seen. Was it that simple? Had he just grabbed the wrong person and not a police decoy?

"Are you angry with me?" Connie stood several paces away from him and looked like she might run at any minute.

"It wasn't your fault." Hell yes, he was mad at her, but he couldn't risk her doing something stupid. "I should have gotten you inside earlier. I wanted to make sure it was safe before I let you go in. And the damn assistant got there earlier than we did. I just assumed it was Billie Bly."

And that was the crux of it. He brought Connie in on his scheme and kept her by his side until the last possible minute, afraid she might turn on him. If he hadn't been distracted, he would have been there to see the assistant and not Billy Bly enter the gymnasium.

"I need a drink," he said. "How about you?"

"I could use a glass of wine."

He poured her a glass of Chablis and spiked it with a knockout powder when she went into the bathroom. She took the glass and practically gulped it down.

"I'm going downstairs for a while," he said. "I have some unfinished work to do. You should go to bed and get some rest. Tomorrow we'll have to get rid of the evidence."

She nodded and staggered to her feet. "What are you going to do? Never mind. I don't want to know."

"Just going to make sure they are comfortable," he said.

He watched her struggle to get upstairs and wondered if she'd make it to the bed before passing out. He stopped in the mud room to switch on an alarm system he had developed for just such a contingency and snickered.

"Time to take care of that Domingo bitch."

Chapter 30

The five of us gathered around the hood of Angel's VW Beetle behind the Chapman Elementary School. Eric shined a light on various sections of maps he had cut out back at my house. The full moon glowered over us.

Earl had shown up in a fit after a 911 text from Angel and Chris had briefed him. I had called Brenda and Eric to the school for a renewed search and now the adrenaline coursed through us like an overflowing river after a month of rain in the Willamette Valley.

"These are the five quadrants that I was able to trace Trixie's locations to while he was on Facebook," Eric said. There are other locations, but these are the most utilized areas. We have a day park between two apartment buildings, a coffee shop which is probably closed now, and earlier this evening I found two homes in the Portland's West Hills."

I shined my flashlight on one of the map's sections. "I want one of the residential neighborhoods on the chance it's his home."

"Keep in mind, he could be stealing a neighbor's Wi-Fi," Eric said. He handed me a section of the map and pointed to scribbling: *Home 8814.* "Use the program I installed on your phone to locate Internet Wi-Fi signals. The number of homes that pop up will give you an idea how far the Internet signals carry.

"*Home 8814* marked on the map is the router identification of the target home, but Trixie could be stealing the signal. Since it's up in the west hills, the wireless signals might travel further. You need to check homes in a two-block radius."

"I'm going with you," Brenda said.

My fingers played a rap tune on the hood of the Volkswagen. "You can't. There are five locations and five of us. We each need to take a section of the map and investigate. You can take the other residential home. It's a mile from my location. Earl and Chris will investigate the two apartment buildings over on the Northwest side. Eric, check the coffee shop and if you don't find anything, jet over to help with the apartment searches."

"I should be on the apartments," Eric said. "I can find the source faster. The coffee shop is probably closed and it's a dead-end anyway."

"Eric can go with Chris," Earl said. "I know what I'm doing. And the first thing we should do is look for the blue Prius parked outside. Did you have a license plate?"

"There was no plate on the car the one time I saw it," I said.

Brenda pulled on a light brown windbreaker. "Are we going to get any help from Steve?"

I flicked my flashlight to the map. "He's busy chasing his own suspect, but he put out a BOLO for the Prius and for Angel. Other than that, we're on our own unless we can turn up a lead."

"What the hell are we doing now, if not following up on a lead?" Chris said.

"This is faster. It would take several hours for the police to assemble and brief a team, and that's assuming we could get an okay from whoever's in charge. By morning it could be too late."

Angel awoke in darkness. Her head ached, a thick semi-sweet odor stung her nose, and she sat upright in a wooden box of some kind. She raised her hands, restricted by duct tape, and clawed at the rough wood in front of her. Maneuverability was difficult because her feet were crammed into a small area surrounded by paint cans. Gradually her eyes became used to the darkness and she had a dim view of her jail.

The box was a storage closet or cabinet, she realized. Her fingers touched round cans, possibly paint cans, and rags, and what felt like a paint roller. Where was she and how did she get here? Her temple throbbed and she started to remember.

Samantha offering to help carry the heavy box to the car. A hand over her face, followed by a burlap sack over her head. The sweet suffocating odor inside the bag with her. Then fighting as much as she could with her arms trapped against her sides. Stifling fumes, like a strong current, her senses struggled to swim against. Succumbing to the fumes and wondering what happened to Samantha. Had she attacked Angel or become a victim herself?

Angel's head cleared, despite the confusing juxtaposition of her body, despite the strong smell of paint thinner in her enclosed prison, and the despite the nauseating after-effects of the chloroform. She now knew the identity of her captor and it scared the hell out of her.

Because of the class, she had shed two of the pistols she normally packed and the third lie in her purse somewhere. But she did have a weapon. Not one she could reach earlier, but she felt it tucked in a reverse roll of her sweat pants near her ankle.

She stretched her bound hands toward her right ankle and huffed out a lungful of air when she realized she'd been holding her breath. She maneuvered her duct-taped hands to her ankle and managed to fish out a three-inch pocket knife from its hiding place.

It was pure luck, she thought to bring it. She could have hidden any number of guns in her firearm collection under her sweats, but they were too bulky to carry during her demonstrations in the self-defense class.

Thinking her derringer might fall out of her pants cuff, she had decided to take her pocket knife. It wasn't much, but a woman had to have some protection.

She rotated her hands to get a proper grip on the knife blade, picked at it until the cutting edge opened, and wrestled the knife in an awkward cutting motion, snipping through the multiple layers of duct tape in painstakingly slow increments.

The tedious work eventually paid off, but she felt no glee. Instead, the fear returned in waves. What should she do now? Wait for him to return and stab him in the eye?

She glanced around the interior of the dark box again. How could she get out?

Connie struggled to stay awake as she sat on the foot of Brent's bed. Why was she so sleepy? Maybe it was the stress of the last few days catching up with her. Seeing the woman in the basement turned her world upside down. She had thought Brent was *the one*.

But now her feelings were mixed. She wanted to believe his story because she loved him. It seemed logical. And why did she tell him about killing her father and mother as a teenager? She told herself it was to create a bond between them. To make him believe she loved him.

She had stuffed her feelings all her life, but during the past few days they rose to the surface. She had long felt she wasn't a good person, and she worked at being perfect so no one would find out. She hadn't realized how much fear and guilt she carried around. Guilt over killing her parents and the fear she would be caught. And a new feeling was haunting her now, panic.

She realized she had told Brent about her parents' deaths because she was afraid he would kill *her*. She reasoned the only way out would be to run at the first chance.

But Brent seemed to have some kind of hold over her. She was afraid if she tried to run he would catch her and kill her. The safe thing to do would be to stay with him and make him trust her. So she stayed. But a scared little girl inside her wanted to get the hell out of this mess.

Brent seemed angry with her for not realizing this other blonde woman was not Billie Bly. She couldn't let herself fall asleep until she knew he still trusted her. She made herself get up and walk around the room. She must stay awake. Coffee. She would make coffee.

She thought about the woman, Brent referred to as the Domingo bitch, lying downstairs on the cold stainless steel gurney and shuddered. In Brent's current state of mind, what would he do to Domingo? But a bigger question loomed. What would he do with *her*?

I drove Myrtle carefully around the curves in the West Hills. Most of the Council Crest neighborhood is too mountainous to accommodate many homes in one block, but there are a few places where residences *are* clustered together. I finally found such a section on Talbot Road after getting lost a few times.

The address, Eric provided, consisted of a nice 1980's home with a large yard and ornate oak doors shining in the porch light. It was after midnight and I became conscious that by tramping across people's lawns, I might be mistaken by some alert homeowner for a burglar or some other miscreant.

I parked up the street from the target address and donned a black sweatshirt I carry in my trunk for stakeouts. I also grabbed a coat hanger from the back seat and a block of wood I use to brace the back tire when Myrtle's parking brake doesn't quite do the job. I pulled a small mag light from my purse and took a deep breath.

Bats rustled in the trees above me, emitting high pitched squeals as I walked to the east side of the street under the cover of trees and shrubs. The five houses, with long and deep lots, were crowded closer to each other than I expected for an upscale neighborhood.

I crouched behind a bush and brought up the Wi-Fi app Eric installed on my phone. It showed ten wireless network connections. Ten? Three more popped up with very weak signals. Shit, this would take all night if there were twelve other homes within range.

Trixie might have a Wi-Fi network in his home and still steal a signal from a neighbor, according to Eric. He told me some passwords were as simple as using a network name and that almost anyone might steal a signal.

I moved across the lawn of the target house until *Home 8814* became the strongest signal. Next, I crept across the front yard and moved to the side of the garage. I walked down a sloped path to the back yard. A sliding door revealed access to the basement and I shone my flashlight through a gap in the curtain and into a spacious family room with a billiard table and lots of toys on the floor.

Kids. Not something you'd expect of a serial killer, but it happens. I remembered an FBI report that said often serial killers had families and were gainfully employed in contrast to the intellectual loners portrayed in the movies.

There were no outbuildings or places a serial killer could operate back here. But to be sure I made my way back to the garage.

I jammed a wedge of wood between the top of the garage door and its frame, straightened the coat hanger, except the hook, and inserted the wire through the crack created by the block of wood. I aimed my flashlight through the crack and snagged the garage door release lever, using the hook on the end of the wire. I pulled and the release latch separated the door from the motorized opener. I raised it open halfway and flashed my Maglite on a white Lexus SUV and a silver Mercedes sedan. No blue Prius here.

Easy Peasy. One down, twelve to go.

Chapter 31

Trixie's mind raced as he negotiated the basement stairs. First, he would have a little fun with Janet Domingo to pay her back for what she did to him. He had hoped to take his time with her over several days, but his plans were falling apart.

His feelings for Connie had distracted him to the point of carelessness. He decided he would have to get rid of all three women tonight. After he finished, with Janet, he would make short work of that meddlesome P.I.'s assistant and then deal with Connie. The simplest thing would be to dump her drugged body into a grave, he had dug before that bitch, Janet, stabbed him, and bury her alive. He couldn't torture Connie. They were too much alike.

He could dig the plot a bit deeper and all three women would fit in it comfortably. He entertained the idea of making another try at Miss Bly and decided it was too risky. He would bury Janet, Connie, and the bitch in the closet and go on vacation for a few months until things settled down.

Another thought occurred to him. His Prius might accommodate two bodies, no more. They would have to take Connie's Subaru Outback. Plenty of room if he covered them with blankets. Shit, things were out of control, and he could feel the butterfly effect wreaking havoc on him.

"Hello, Janet dear. Have you been waiting long?" He closed the door behind him and the fear in her eyes both pleased and calmed him. "We're going to play a little game. Do you like games?"

She shook her head and her eyes pleaded with him. She wriggled on the sterile stainless steel table in her bra and panties. Trixie had removed the rest of her clothes earlier in the day to set the tone. She cried and whimpered and he sighed. He knew, and now she knew, that he was her master.

"Here is how my little game works. I'm going to do a little surgical procedure on you, and I regret I have no anesthetic to offer. But if it becomes too much to bear, you only have to tell me. You can do this by saying: 'Oh honey, I'm sorry I locked you in that closet. Won't you please have pity on me?' Do you understand?"

She nodded her head. Her pupils dilated to the size of nickels and beads of perspiration trickled from her forehead.

"I think you do," he said. "Now I may not stop right away because I sometimes get carried away in my work. If I don't respond, keep repeating the phrase. Of course, you will be tempted to use it right away, but if you do, I will simply ignore you. You must be tough about this and hold back as long as you can. The longer you can hold the pain in, the longer I will give you respite when you finally ask me for pity. Got it?"

She nodded slowly, resigned, as if in the dentist chair. He smiled at her and lifted a scalpel he'd bought with other surgical instruments at the garage sale of a deceased surgeon's wife. She tried to cry out through the duct tape over her mouth.

"Oh dear," he said. "I almost forgot to remove your gag. How are you ever going to tell me if the pain becomes too much." He removed the tape in one sadistic motion and she yelped.

"You can scream all you want. No one will hear you. These rooms are soundproof." Trixie knew that wasn't completely true. He had tried to insulate the room, but he was concerned if his playmates screamed loud enough the sound vibration might permeate the walls into the house above. But he was reasonably sure the noise would not carry outside and by now Connie was probably fast asleep.

"Please let me go," Her eyes darted to the door. "I won't tell anybody what happened. I'd just be happy to be free again."

"Oh, I can't do that," Trixie said. "And you know that's a lie."

"Why are you doing this?" she asked, the words coming out wobbly and high-pitched.

"It relaxes me. How about you?"

"Please don't." Her eyes were moist and tears began trailing down her temples. "I'll do anything you want. You want to make love to me? You can and I'll say and do anything you want. Just don't do this."

"That's quite an attractive offer, Janet. And at another time I might consider it, but you tried to kill me with a screwdriver, you bitch, and you have to pay."

She closed her eyes and started whimpering. Trixie nodded to himself and lifted the scalpel to her soft brown stomach.

It stopped Angel cold. The knife blade had jammed behind a metal plate holding the cabinet door in place. But it was the scream, not the wedged knife that paralyzed her. A muffled cry from somewhere near, and it sent a chill from her tailbone to the hair on the nape of her neck.

What is he doing? She decided she didn't want to hang around to find out. She grabbed the knife handle with both hands and twisted it as hard as she could. The metal hinges began to give and slowly she wrenched it away from the wooden surface. She gave her wrists a brief rest, took a deep breath and muscled the knife again. A metallic twang sprung inside her jail and the blade fell into her lap.

"Oh no," she cried. The knife had another blade, but it was about the size of the file on a fingernail clipper. She heard the muffled cry again and began sobbing. "I don't want to die."

Connie decided to disobey Brent and go downstairs to fix coffee. She wanted to know what he was doing with Janet Domingo, but mostly she just wanted to stay awake so she could stay alive. Why couldn't she just walk out the front door? Get in her car and drive away to a police station?

Because something told her she might regret it. What if she was overreacting? What if Brent was telling the truth about Billie Bly? But what if Brent had lied to her? If he killed Janet and that other woman, what would stop him from killing her?

And the biggest question: why was she so damn indecisive? What hold did Brent have over her that made her afraid to leave him?

She paced near the coffee maker in the kitchen, deliberating over these questions, when a noise startled her. She stopped pacing and listened. It came from the basement. She cocked an ear toward the noise and an eerie scream caused her to clap her hands over her ears.

I jimmied two more garage doors before deciding on a different tact. I would drive through the rest of the neighborhood and see if I could locate the Prius parked outside or maybe see a light burning or some other clue to shorten my search.

Part of this switch in tactics was because I was concerned that my activities might have alerted one of the neighbors. But the biggest motivator was sheer panic over Angel's abduction. I had to find her before Trixie hurt her.

So I climbed into Myrtle with my headlights off and cruised down the street in search of the Prius or Trixie poking his head out the front door.

I turned off Talbot Road and circled around a lower loop behind the houses I had already searched, stopping occasionally to scout homes on both sides of the street. I parked at a curb, unsettled by something I'd seen and not sure what bothered me.

The clouds, once cluttering the sky, departed and a full moon exposed me to anyone who might look out a window. I thought about Angel in the grip of a serial killer and pushed through the fear of having a cop tap me on the shoulder because of a nosy neighbor. I drove around the loop again and slowed along the back hillside of three homes I'd already searched.

I stopped and surveyed homes on the other side of the street. The house across from me was larger and older than the rest. Overgrown shrubs, now visible in the moonlight, cluttered the huge front yard. Rosebushes jetted up seven feet high, dandelions sprouted across the dead grass in the moonlight, and ten-foot rhododendrons hugged the sides of the home.

Something about an ugly yard in this pristine neighborhood captured my attention. Mary Johansen said something about an overgrown yard, hadn't she? What was it? I opened my notebook and read by flashlight.

Told him my parents were florists and Brent said his mother was the gardener in his family. Asked him if he liked gardening . . . said no, his mother's garden is overgrown now that she's passed away.

Well, this is worth a look-see, I thought. I noticed a light on behind a closed living room curtain so I started Myrtle and drove half a block away to avoid prying eyes. I dug out my garage invasion tools and backtracked up the street to the edge of the garage.

I jammed my block of wood between the top of the garage door and the frame at the very center of the door. It opened a crack of about a half an inch. I shot a light through and spotted the cord hanging from the lever which would release the overhead door from the door opener.

It took me almost half a minute to catch the lever with my coat hanger and trip it. I pushed up on the door and, as it cleared the halfway mark, a blue Prius entered my vision. Next to it was a green Subaru Outback, but the Prius had my complete attention.

This Prius had an Oregon license plate hanging from the bottom of the hatchback lid, like the temporary dealer plates car salesman use. Quick and easy to remove if you don't want to be identified.

I stepped inside and lowered the garage door, being careful to step over the red safety beam which would trip the overhead light. I squeezed the rear hatch release on the Prius and aimed my flashlight into the cargo area. I scanned it inch by inch and found what I was searching for. A strand of blonde hair.

I almost dropped my phone when I pulled it out of my pocket and texted Brenda, telling her to round up the gang and get to the address I supplied.

Then I did something rather stupid. Instead of waiting for help I entered the house through the door in the garage. I had gotten three steps into the hallway when I met a young woman with strawberry-blonde hair in some kind of running suit.

"Oh my God, you're Billie Bly." She put both hands to her mouth in surprise.

"You know me?" I pointed my gun directly at her face.

"I'm so glad you're here. I didn't know what to do. I'm afraid my boyfriend might do something terrible. I mean he hasn't yet, but I think he's planning something tonight. I'm afraid he might kill me too. Please help me."

Her rambling caught me off guard. "Who are you?

"My name is Connie."

"Who is your boyfriend?"

"His name is Brent Farmer. He lives here. We've been dating for a couple of weeks. I thought I was in love with him, but now I don't know."

"Where is Brent now?"

"He went into the basement. He kidnapped your assistant tonight and he has another girl down there too. I think he's going to kill them."

"How do I get to the basement?"

She pointed toward the living room.

I stepped through an entry way into the front room with my gun raised and looked toward a formal dining room. Connie followed me making a scuffling sound. I wondered why Trixie left her alone if she knew about him. And why didn't she make a run when she had a chance?

I turned back to ask her and spotted a maniacal woman, teeth clenched, eyes blazing hatred, swinging a bronze table lamp. It clipped the side of my head and a sudden despair engulfed me, swarming over my body like an army of black ants, stinging and biting at my head, until I succumbed to blackness.

After Janet passed out, Trixie decided to wrap things up with the other troublemaker. He went into the other room with a Ruger pocket pistol. Bly's assistant rattled the cabinet door and Trixie smirked. He didn't have time to fight a screaming fight-for-your-life maniac like Janet. He raised the Ruger and emptied three shells into the cabinet door and everything quieted.

Everything but the overhead light, which flashed off and on repeatedly. Someone had breached his motion sensors outside. He swore and opened the door to a closet in the basement hallway to reveal a TV monitor sectioned into six video segments. He scanned the segments and saw nothing.

He switched to one large picture of the front yard and studied it. He flicked to the camera on the side yard and then the one in the back yard, but still nothing. Maybe it was an animal. He rewound the video by three minutes and played it back.

He watched as a person entered the yard from an angle for a few seconds and disappeared from view. He clicked on a camera angle from the side of the house pointing toward the street and waited as the video unwound.

It showed the person entering again and this time the silhouette crept up toward the garage. An instant later the shadow disappeared against the front of the garage where none of his cameras pointed. But in that split second, Trixie identified the intruder.

"Billy Fuckin' Bly. How the hell did she find me?" The world closed in on him and he gasped for breath. The panic bubbling inside erupted like an emerging volcano.

"It's time for the showdown," he muttered.

Chapter 32

Brenda felt the stress levels rise after each wrong turn. She wasted precious minutes looking for the address she could not find. Eventually she realized she was on Talbot Terrace, not Talbot Road. But when she tried to find Talbot Road she took another wrong turn and drove through a maze of streets with hard-to-read signs in the darkness.

She made another bad decision by electing to drive up the mountain before notifying Eric and the boys about Billie's message. There were no bars on her cell phone now. She couldn't call them and a text probably wouldn't work either. She stopped at Council Crest Park, got out of her late model candy-apple-red Mustang, and walked along the edge of the park, searching for more bars to indicate she had a signal.

Damn her phone carrier. It was notorious for weak signals and dropped calls. The phone issued to her at work was super reliable, but she'd left her work cell phone at home. She walked into a clearing where she could see part of the city skyline and stopped. One bar finally showed on her phone.

"Hello, Eric? Brenda here. We've found him."

"That's great," Eric's voice crackled. "Where are you?"

"I'm lost, but the address is on Talbot Road, not Talbot Terrace. My GPS is all squirrely up here. My phone isn't working either."

"You're breaking up," Eric said.

Brenda realized she'd paced around nervously and returned to her original spot. "Look, call Steve for me. Tell him what's happening. Billie might be in danger. Then get up here and tell Earl to bring his gun."

"Got it," Eric said. "What's the address?

She gave it to him, hung up and shivered in the night air. "I've got to find fucking Talbot Road."

Voices woke me from the blow inflicted by Connie, and I forced myself to snap out of a groggy stupor.

"You drag her into the garage. I'm going down to get her assistant and Domingo," a man's voice said. Trixie, I thought

It became quiet, so I opened one eye and saw the man I knew as John Benson kissing the he crazy bitch I knew as Connie. Why was that not a surprise? She was in on it with him. A dizzy spell came over me and I fought to stay conscious. The next thing I knew, somebody grabbed my feet and started dragging me.

I half opened my eyes again. It was Connie tugging me down the hallway. They'd bound my hands behind me and duct-taped my mouth and ankles. I figured the next stop was a deep hole in the middle of nowhere.

Connie stopped to open the doorknob to the garage. Still dazed, I concentrated on what I was going to do and hoped my legs would cooperate. The bitch dragged me down a step and my aching head bounced on the concrete. My knuckles scraped against the cold, rough floor, and I swore under my breath, but remained limp so she wouldn't know I was awake.

She pulled me between two cars and finally stopped at the overhead door. She fumbled with my legs and I heard a car hatchback lid pop open. As she let go of her grasp on me, I kicked her as hard as I could with both feet. She bounced against the garage door, striking her head, and I pushed her with both feet again. She weaved above me dazed, so I kicked at her twice more and watched her fall unconscious halfway into the open hatchback trunk.

Using one of my yoga moves, I scrunched my knees up to my chest and inched my taped wrists past my butt and in front of me. I would have jumped triumphantly to my feet, but I still felt a bit woozy, so I crawled on my hands and knees and managed to push myself up. I picked at the tape for a second and realized I needed something sharper than finger nails.

I hopped to the front of the car to a work bench and found a box cutter. After I freed myself, I went back to the Subaru and pushed the lying bitch all the way into the hatchback and closed the lid. I entered the house looking to see if maybe someone left my gun lying around, but Trixie had not been careless.

A minute later, armed with a kitchen knife, I descended a basement stairway. The dim lights foreshadowed my possible fate and heightened my adrenaline. I opened a door to a room on the left and peered in. A light flickered and a young woman lie on a stark stainless steel hospital gurney.

I scanned the room to be sure Trixie wasn't lurking in a corner before I approached the woman. It was Janet Domingo. Her body was marked by several deep cuts and blood congealed on her stomach after dribbling into a small puddle on the gurney. I felt her still warm skin and checked for a pulse on her neck.

"Don't," she cried.

I jumped back. "You're alive."

"Please help me," she said.

"I will. Do you know where he is?"

She shook her head and closed her eyes again.

"Hang in there. Help is on the way." At least I hoped it was.

I went outside to another door and opened it. I blinked at the second garage. Trixie stood in front of a cabinet, pointing a small caliber gun at Angel.

"I don't know how I missed you, but I won't miss again," he said.

He raised the gun and the reality of the situation struck me harder than the lamp Connie wielded earlier. Angel was still alive. I ran, I screamed, I jumped toward him. He turned and quick-fired and I felt a surge of pain in my side. I landed on him, grabbed for his gun and realized I still carried the kitchen knife.

I slashed at the gun with it and blood spurted from his wrist. He dropped his weapon and we wrestled for it on the floor. Angel jumped on his back and tried to choke him. He flung her across the room and she crumpled after bouncing on the concrete.

But Angel's gyrations somehow kicked the gun across the floor and our struggle now centered on the knife I held. I bent it toward him for a second, but he managed to twist it from my hands. He was on top of me with the knife and me trying to push it away from my throat.

Our struggle momentarily produced the ridiculous memory of Earl and Chris arm wrestling in my house, with neither seemingly able to gain an advantage. I knew this would not be a stalemate. I felt my strength waning and knew I only would only have one chance.

"I have to thank you for coming," he said. "I thought I missed my chance at killing you."

It would be so easy for me to give up. The guilt I carried over my brother's death would be gone. My depression would end. Everything would go black and I could rest forever. The knife came closer and Trixie seemed even more motivated. I said a quick prayer to God and closed my eyes.

"Time to die," Trixie said.

"Then die!" I let go of the knife with one hand, formed a chisel fist, and thrust a ball of knuckles into his Adam's apple.

He let go of the knife and clutched his throat. His eyes stared without seeing. He gasped for breath and his face turned white. I pushed him off me, got to my feet, and gazed at the startled victim of his own violence as he tried to force oxygen though a crushed windpipe.

"Go to the hell that spawned you," I said.

He stopped gasping and convulsing and a sudden innocence appeared on his face. Tears welled up in his eyes and the face of a young, fearful boy stared back at me. He struggled to utter words as he convulsed. It sounded like "thank you"--and he closed his eyes and smiled at death.

I went to Angel, stirring on the floor. "Angel?"

"What happened?" She moaned and tried to sit up.

"It's over. He's dead."

"He almost killed me twice." Angel rubbed her head. "You've been shot. We need to get you to the hospital."

I lifted my blouse and saw a shallow gash in the side of my waist. Instinctively, I rolled up the bottom of my shirt and held it against the wound, applying pressure.

"I'll be okay; he only nicked me. We have a few loose ends to clear up here first. There's a semi-comatose woman in the other room who needs medical help and a crazy girlfriend whom needs to be tied up."

We went back to Janet, still unconscious, and Angel stayed with her while I phoned for help. I trudged up the stairs still not believing we had all come through this bizarre adventure alive.

I picked up a phone attached to the kitchen wall and dialed 911. "This is Billie Bly, I'm a private investigator. We need an ambulance and the homicide squad at this address."

I stood at the kitchen sink and looked through a window into the cool black night. The moon played hide-and-seek between two clouds.

"Yes, Ma'am. Where are you?" The 911 operator asked.

I told her. She asked more questions, but I couldn't answer them. Connie stood with my gun pointed at me from the kitchen doorway.

"Where's Brent?"

"Downstairs," I said.

"Is he okay?"

"No, he's a crazy psychopathic killer." I get mouthy when someone points a gun at me.

"You didn't hurt him?"

"He's dead."

"How . . . ?"

"He choked on something. Don't you think you should give me my gun? It's all over now. He won't be able to hurt you or anyone else."

"I don't believe you." Her grip on my gun tightened. "If he finds I let you go, he'll kill me."

I turned away as she squeezed the trigger and I was sure I was dead. Two shots reverberated in the small room. I winced and said a quick prayer.

But there was no pain. No hot piercing bullet thrashing through layers of my skin. I opened an eye and risked a peek over my shoulder. Connie stood motionless, her mouth open, a look of disbelief on her face. She slumped to the floor and uttered an oath under her breath. Behind her stood a familiar figure.

"Got here as soon as I could," Brenda said. "I got lost a couple of times."

"Thanks for not giving up." I ran to Connie, took the gun from her and cradled her head.

"I'm sorry," she said. "I've been so confused. I'm not a good person." Her shallow breathing told me she didn't have long.

"Is he-really dead?" she asked.

I nodded and she smiled.

"I've done some bad things in my life. I didn't think I deserved good things."

"You should rest," I said. Brenda knelt down beside us. "The ambulance will be here any minute."

"I knew Brent wasn't good for me, but I thought he was all I deserved." She coughed up blood.

"See if you can find a pillow to put under her head," I said to Brenda.

"I needed someone to love me," Connie said. "I was afraid of being abandoned, being all alone. So I had to stop you from taking Brent from me."

She smiled ironically. "Now I'm dying and I *am* all alone. My biggest fear is coming true."

"You aren't alone," I said. "I'm here now, and I won't abandon you." Her smile dwindled. I held her hand and tried to soothe her as her life slipped away.

"I'm here too." Brenda slipped a couch pillow under her head. She took Connie's free hand and squeezed it.

Somewhere in the distance, I heard police sirens screaming and wondered about Steve. Had he abandoned me?

"I thought I was dead," Angel told two uniformed policemen taking her statement. She was clearly in shock. "*Twice*, I thought I was dead." Earl and Chris sat on either side of her on a leather sofa in Trixie's living room.

Forensics assigned the front room to non-essential personal while they documented crime scenes in the kitchen and the two rooms in the basement. The place was a bloody mess and the tech teams would be there for a week.

"He only missed me because I was leaning down to the other side of the cabinet to undo the door hinges with my pocket knife," Angel said. Earl and Chris each held one of her hands, and she withdrew them, shuddered and held herself. "The second time he pointed a gun right in my face. If Billie hadn't jumped him, I wouldn't be here now."

"Yes, yes," one of the detectives said. "But how did you get here in the first place?"

I motioned for Brenda to follow me out to the front porch as the investigators continued questioning Angel. Outside, stars dotted a clear black sky and the moon seemed larger now. I stood in silence for a while considering my mortality.

"How do you feel?" Brenda asked.

"Like I'm going to throw up. Other than that, I feel completely alone, like I'm the only one here right now, even with all of the cops and my friends. Something is missing in my life."

As if on cue, an unmarked squad car rolled up behind twenty other vehicles and the first member of the FBI task force arrived. Steve jumped from his car and ran up the front walk.

"Billy, my God, what happened?"

"I'm fine."

"You've been shot."

"It's a flesh wound." He stared at the blood on the side of my blouse. "It just nicked my side. The EMT's bandaged me up." My voice sounded monotone and disinterested.

"You should be at the hospital."

I shook my head. "They just took Janet and I'm too upset. I'll go after I get a chance to talk with Angel. The cops are interviewing her now."

"I'll take you, then."

"We'll see."

"Uh, I'm going inside to see if Angel needs a ride home," Brenda said.

"I'm sorry." Steve grabbed my hands and kissed me on the lips. "I didn't know. I only heard after we finished with Chad downtown. We caught him heading into Washington, and I've been grilling him all night."

"Any luck?" My question still had no emotion behind it.

"He admitted rape before his lawyer showed up. "We couldn't get him to cop to murder."

"That's probably because Cynthia Miller's murderer is in there." I pointed inside the house.

"Did he admit it?"

"He didn't have much to say after I crushed his windpipe."

"What?"

"I killed him. It was him or me and it was almost me."

"I'm so glad you're okay." He leaned in for a soft hug, but somehow I still felt alone. At the time I thought it was shock.

Chapter 33

Angel reported back to work for the first time after taking a week's leave to recuperate from her near death experience. In typical Angel style, she sported a new hair style.

I shielded my eyes with my hands in mock agony. "I'm blind."

"You like it? The color is called Psychedelic Sunset."

"Your hair is orange and so are your eyelids. What's with the glitter on your cheek and chest?"

"It's part of the psychedelic. I had them cut my hair into a Pixie, because I don't want to be mistaken for you again. You know, I think blonde hair attracts trouble. You should try a new color. Not mine. The last thing I need is to be mistaken for you again."

We laughed and I hugged her. We hadn't seen each other since that night she almost died because she said she needed some time to decompress. I poured coffee and we sat at the kitchen table. It was good to get back into a familiar routine and some sense of normalcy.

"How are you doing?" She motioned to my side and grimaced.

"I'm good. The pain pills are working. It's a flesh wound really."

"Good. Have you heard from Janet?"

"She's doing well. I met with her and her friend, Mary, yesterday over coffee. She wanted to thank me. That Janet is one tough cookie. I'm sure she'll have emotional scars for a while, but she says she won't let that psycho have control over her."

Angel patted her psychedelic orange hair. "I've been having nightmares all week and I didn't have near the experience she did."

"Janet's wounds consisted of several slashes around her lower abdomen," I said. "She had stabbed him with a screwdriver earlier and it took him out of commission for a few days or she'd probably be dead by the time we found her."

Angel stared vacantly toward the ceiling for a moment, and I waited for her to come back. I longed to hug her back to life, but knew nothing I could do would heal her psychological wounds.

"How did the thing with Steve turn out?" she asked.

"He wasn't happy, but I told him I didn't think we were a match."

"No shit?" Angel's hand went to her mouth and she took a puff of her ghostly cigarette.

I laughed. "I thought you quit."

"Heck, no. I think I'm up to three packs a day if I was still really smoking. The gap between my fingers is so pronounced people think I'm making a peace sign."

Her eyes narrowed. "So, what did he say?"

"You know, I gave him the old *'it isn't you, it's me'* line and for the first time I think I really understand what it means even if he doesn't."

"I guess I don't know what it means either," Angel said. "I thought it was just a line to get out of a relationship without trashing a guy."

I cradled my mug in both hands and sipped it. "Our relationship was all about sex. We had no intimacy."

Angel nodded.

"I wasn't able to be there for him emotionally. Anytime our relationship looked like it might get intimate I pushed him away. We both isolated. We'd be together for a while and go off into our own corners and busy ourselves with work. I couldn't share my innermost thoughts with him, and he didn't seem to care.

"It was only when Connie talked about being abandoned, I finally understood. I don't let people get close to me for fear *I'll* be abandoned again."

I'd had a week to do some soul searching and try to decipher what my analyst had tried to tell me. I realized my fear of abandonment stemmed from the time my father was killed in the line of duty and because my mom died a few years later of a broken heart. They didn't mean to, but they abandoned a teenager who needed their love to grow up whole. And when my baby brother, the closest person to me in my life, died, I was abandoned all over again."

Angel took a sip of coffee and waited patiently for me to continue.

"I've spent my whole life trying to get love from people who couldn't give it to me," I explained. "I don't know why I pick these types of relationships, but I'm going to find out."

"How?" Angel asked.

"I'm not sure, but I don't want to wind up like Connie."

The front door opened and Eric called out: "Anybody home?"

"In here," I said.

Eric and Brenda strode into the kitchen. Well, Eric appeared to be flying.

"I got probation and community service," he said. "My attorney and I met with the deputy district attorney, and they worked out two years suspended, probation, and two hundred hours of community service. Brenda spoke up on my behalf."

"It's the least I could do. You're quite the hero. Without your help, Angel might not be here today."

"What about your friend, Jimmer?" I asked.

"He went before a judge already and was remanded to a drug and alcohol inpatient program," Eric said. "When he comes out, he'll be in a halfway house and he'll have to meet some requirements. But if he works hard, he could be free in six months."

"That reminds me." Angel got up and planted a big kiss on Eric's cheek. "Thank you for saving my life."

He flushed. "Aw, I kind of got used to having you around."

"Our hero has more big news," Brenda said.

"Oh yeah," he said. "Robert Roy saw the news about me helping catch the serial killer and called me. He offered me a job. He's quit Intel to start his own business, and I'm going to help with his computer design. It's my dream job come true."

"You're still going to come and fix our computers when we need you," Angel said.

"You guys get my free service for life. Any time you need to hack into a web page or maybe deliver a nasty virus to a bad guy, let me know."

"I have a project for you," I said. "Something I used to have when I was a cop."

"You got it," he said.

Brenda kept glancing over her shoulder. "What are you looking for," I asked.

"The cage match guys, Earl and Chris. Don't they have a show today?"

"I had to let one of them go," Angel said. "I couldn't handle all of the drama."

"You made a decision?" I was flabbergasted. "Which one did you choose?"

"Earl helped me make my decision," she said. "He's been very nice and attentive, especially after my ordeal, but in the end he still cheated on me. Call it working undercover if you want, but he was banging the baddie and that doesn't play in my book."

"The baddie?" Eric said.

"The bitch he was supposed to be investigating," Angel said.

"So Earl is out and Chris is in?" I asked.

"I hope you don't think less of me. I know we both thought he was a slime ball when we first met him, but he's a sincere slime ball."

"I get it," I said. "He has a loyalty quality you won't find in many men. Truth be told, I've gotten kind of used to him hanging around here."

"He says he doesn't really like blondes, but he made an exception for me."

I was driving back from having lunch in the Pearl District a few weeks later, and I spotted an elderly man hiding behind the window of a Mercury Grand Marquis as a larger, younger, man banged his fist on the hood of the car.

An oversized red pickup with the license plate B-Rude blocked the Mercury's path under a freeway ramp on a one-lane road at the extreme North end of Northwest Portland's Pearl District.

It was the same guy who bullied me at the library when I was after Eric and Jimmer. I parked Myrtle behind the scared gentleman's car and ran up to Mr. B-Rude.

"Having some trouble here?"

He turned and snarled at me. "Mind your own business."

He still wore his black hair slicked down, a black leather jacket, blue jeans, black boots, and was still ugly as ever.

"Hey, you're that bimbo who pulled the gun on me." He backed away as if I carried the plague.

I'd forgotten my pledge to Myrtle to get even with this crazy guy, but apparently karma intervened.

"I'm unarmed today." I opened my denim vest and revealed my lack of a gun.

"In that case, I have some unfinished business with you too."

"Is this what you do with your life? Go around attacking helpless women and old men?"

He shrugged. "People got to stay out of my way."

The frail white-haired man, dressed in a cardigan sweater, got out of the Grand Marquis. "You leave that woman alone."

"What are you going to do about it, Pops?" He kicked the man's back fender.

"I'll show you." He stepped toward B-Rude and threw a weak punch at his chin.

B-Rude took it without blinking. "That all you got old man?"

"I may not be as strong as I was in World War Two, but I can still handle a whippersnapper like you."

He whipped out a cane, reached inside B-Rude's leg, and hooked the back of his knee. The brute's leg folded and the old man withdrew the cane and smacked him in the face with it. B-Rude collapsed like a worn accordion.

"I'll fix you." He rubbed his jaw and got to his feet.

When he reached for the old man, I grabbed his coat sleeve and tugged him in my direction. He reached for my throat so I grabbed both sleeves, fell back to the ground with my feet in his gut, and pushed him up and over me.

He landed on his back with a thud and, before he could catch his breath, I lifted his leg for leverage and put my boot on his throat. He made a croaking noise and it reminded me of Trixie fighting for breath just before he died.

"I know you," the old man said. "You're Billie Bly, the gal that killed that serial killer."

"You feel that pressure on your throat?" I said.

B-Rude gagged.

"If I push a little harder, you'll sound like a frog the rest of your life. Is that what you want?"

"No-oh."

"Are finished fighting?"

He nodded.

"Here's the deal." I eased the pressure on his throat. "You're going to pay this gentleman for the damage to his car, and you're going to pay me for what you did to Myrtle too."

"Okay."

"You're going to enroll in anger management classes. I'll tell you where."

"He could use that," the old man said.

"I'm going to make sure you complete them, understand?"

"Yes." It sounded more like a croak.

"And you're going to stay out of trouble. No more road rage. If you do it again, I'll know. I have a direct pipeline with the Portland Police Bureau."

"Maybe you should let off a bit more," the old man said. "His face is turning kinda blue."

"One more thing." I lifted my foot from his throat. I have a video-mounted camera in my car installed by a techy friend of mine. It just recorded everything that happened here.

"If you violate any of my terms, I'll post the video on the Internet and it should go viral when people see a World War Two Veteran and a woman kick your butt."

"You wouldn't do that." B-Rude's face color switched from blue to white.

"I really want to, but I won't as long as you stay on your best behavior."

"I'd like a copy of that video," the veteran said. "I could show it at the VFW."

"No," B-Rude said. "Please, don't give it to anybody. I'll pay for all damages. I'll be a safe driver."

"In that case, I'll have to hold onto it." I sent a conspiratorial wink to the elderly gentleman.

"After all, a deal is a deal."